The Cott

Suzanne Snow writes contemporary, romantic and uplifting fiction with a strong sense of setting and community connecting the lives of her characters. Previously, she worked in financial services and was a stay-at-home mum before retraining as a horticulturist and planting re-designed gardens.

Living in Lancashire and appreciating the landscape around her always provides inspiration and when she's not writing or spending time with her family, she can usually be found in a garden or reading.

Also by Suzanne Snow

Welcome to Thorndale

SUZANNE SNOW

The Cottage of New Beginnings

CANELO

First published in the United Kingdom in 2020 by Canelo

This edition published in the United Kingdom in 2021 by

Canelo
Unit 9, 5th Floor
Cargo Works, 1–2 Hatfields
London, SE1 9PG
United Kingdom

A CIP catalogue record for this book is available from the British Library.

Print ISBN 978 1 80032 979 9
Ebook ISBN 978 1 80032 098 7

Look for more great books at www.canelo.co

Printed and bound in Great Britain by Clays Ltd, Elcograf S.p.A.

1

To Stewart and Fin, for everything.

In memory of the late Pat Howard, first reader.

Chapter One

Willow Cottage had been empty for over a year before Annie Armstrong arrived and the reality of it would have exceeded her expectations had she not found her furniture dumped in the front garden. The earlier disappearance of the sun on a glorious July day meant swirling grey clouds had hurled rain over the few possessions from her old life that she wanted in the new one and drenched the lot. Skies now clear of the clouds that had wreaked this havoc, the sun beamed down again and picked out the glint of raindrops still clinging to her plastic-covered furniture as if mocking her late arrival.

It can't be, she thought, bewildered, squinting again as she took in the series of shapes scattered around the garden, and pushed her sunglasses back over her head to get a better look. But it was. Annie gave a moan as she recognised the remains of her furniture in the long grass, looking remarkably like an unfinished art installation. She didn't know whether to ring her so-called removal men or the Tate gallery as she dived into her handbag for her phone. She tried the driver's number three times before realising there was no signal. Crossly, she climbed out of her Mini and marched towards the house, weeds spilling onto the path and soaking her legs as she strode past.

Aside from the new lawn furniture that she'd have to find a way of removing soon, the cottage was much as she remembered, nestled in an uncharacteristically overgrown garden, the old weeping willow in the back sending shadows through the sunshine over the roof and giving the house its name. The unmistakable scent of damp, clean country air hit her senses immediately and she breathed deeply, eyes closed as half-forgotten memories of endless days playing outdoors tumbled into her mind.

Almost unwillingly Annie opened them again, peering at the house as she pushed thoughts of childhood away. She remembered Molly telling her the cottage was built of sandstone, which gave the building a lovely creamy glow that had begun to fade into a muddy grey. It had been winter, two years ago, when she was here last and Annie was surprised to see how worn and unloved the cottage appeared, and not just because of the state of the garden.

She saw a note pinned to the front door and snatched at it, reading it quickly. It was from the men with the van, apologising for leaving in a hurry but no longer able to wait for her to arrive with a key. She sighed; it was hardly their fault she had been held up on the motorway and hadn't been able to connect the call to let them know. She crumpled the note between her fingers, realising that her old life was beginning to seem less chaotic than the new one, and wondered how she would make a home in this place. She was starting to wish she hadn't come to Thorndale at all, but didn't know where else she might be able to mend her spirits.

Staring forlornly at the heavy lifting she'd have to do, Annie decided instead to head to the village first to pick up sustenance before she started. She knew she'd be in desperate need of food – and wine – by the time she was done moving everything into the cottage, and would rather make the trip now to have supplies as motivation for later. Better to take the car as well, even if it was less than half a mile away, rather than carry it all back if she bought more than one bottle, which seemed likely.

As she drove back into the village she had just passed through, Annie couldn't help thinking how everything seemed smaller than she remembered it. Thorndale was busy with visitors now that the rain had died away; parents were half-heartedly trying to keep eyes on children racing around the village green while pensioners climbed slowly onto a noisily rumbling coach hovering awkwardly on the high street.

A brisk, narrow river ran between the green and the high street, and people were sitting on picnic blankets or coats on the damp grass, eating ice cream or leaning back to sunbathe, faces tilted to the sun. Annie saw that the post office still survived but an art gallery had replaced the tiny garage with its single petrol pump, and people were staring through the windows in search of a masterpiece or a bargain. The small tearoom looked much the same, except for extra seating outside and a sign advertising ice cream from a local dairy farm. Beyond the centre of the village Annie spotted a tall, square church tower peering down on everything else and the canopies of the ancient trees surrounding the vicarage she knew was tucked amongst them.

She drove alongside the green, overlooked by pretty terraced cottages and a row of larger Georgian houses facing The Royal Oak, the only pub. Thorndale Farm, set back as if trying to keep a polite distance from everyone else, was sheltered behind craggy oak trees bordering its walls and she spotted a group of teenagers in the shade, heads bent over their phones as their thumbs moved constantly. She glanced curiously at a couple of modern stone bungalows further on, and realised that the village had altered while she hadn't been looking, becoming more than simply the farming community she remembered.

When her godmother had died aged eighty-nine, Annie had been surprised and delighted to discover she had inherited Molly Briggs's house, a small and simple cottage she had adored so much as a child. Now, Annie hoped that here she would find peace again. Nobody in the village knew she was arriving today and she wanted it this way, still unprepared to voice the devastating circumstances that had brought her here.

With no spaces free in the car park at the far end of the village, she headed back to Thorndale Farm, which had an empty barn whose entrance had often been used as a parking place by locals in the know nipping into the village for a quick visit. Whenever the village was busy with visitors or the farmer wanted the entrance left clear, he would drop a couple of traffic cones in the gap to prevent tourists from taking advantage. Annie crawled along a narrow lane on the other side of the green outside the farm, dodging the group of teenagers who were now on the move with eyes glued to their phones. Outside the barn, cobbles stretching back to the lane were enclosed between grass verges either side of the huge doors and she drove right up to them, not completely blocking the entrance. She thought the barn doors had probably been replaced since she had last bothered to look; they certainly appeared smarter than they used to.

Laughter and voices from the pub drifted over as people lingered outside to enjoy the last of the sun, the river speeding away between uneven rocks as she crossed a humpback bridge onto the high street. She smiled at the children clambering down slippery stone steps to the river, shrieking as they tried not to stumble into the chilly water. It reminded her of the days when she had played the same game, in this same place. As if conjured by her childhood reminiscences, she saw a woman she recognised as Kirstie Blaine standing at the front door of one half of a pair of semi-detached stone cottages further along, and Annie waved to catch her attention.

'Annie! Oh, I can't believe it!'

They met halfway, laughing as they hugged, arms becoming tighter as they clung together for a few moments. When they separated, Annie's eyes ran over Kirstie's face with pleasure, searching for the familiar and finding it despite the years that had passed since they had last seen each other. Kirstie had been Annie's best friend in the village while they were growing up. Her parents were writers, her brother Ross several years older and Kirstie's childhood had been eclectic and unin- hibited. Annie had always envied Kirstie when she'd had to leave the village behind and return to school in Shropshire, her happiness suspended until the next longed-for visit.

Kirstie's thoughtful, distracted brown eyes and lithe figure were unchanged. Her muddy blonde hair was also the same, scooped back in a casual ponytail that left shorter strands drifting loose around her face, meaning she was forever tucking them behind her ears.

'Your hair—'

'You've barely—'

They both laughed again, and then Kirstie spoke. 'You go first. Are you here to see Molly? How is she?'

Annie blinked, her smile becoming smaller as her eyes fell away from Kirstie's curious gaze. Her hand went to her long, dark auburn curls, sweeping them across one shoulder in a casual gesture. It was three months already since she had lost Molly, but it still seemed unreal to say so, especially here in Thorndale, the village they had both loved. 'She died in April, in a nursing home. She had to move in a couple of years before that as her arthritis was getting worse and she was struggling to manage at home. She had a fall just before Easter and then passed on a week later. She would have absolutely hated to linger or be a burden, she was still pottering in the garden every day until she fell.'

'Oh Annie, I'm sorry, I had no idea.' Kirstie's voice lowered and she reached out a hand to squeeze one of Annie's in sympathy. 'I knew she was in the nursing home, of course, Dad mentioned it, but I didn't know you'd lost her. I'm so sorry, I know how close you two were. I bet Dad doesn't know, unless someone from the village has already told him.'

'Thanks, Kirstie. But how are you? You look great, barely any older than the last time I saw you.'

Kirstie's lips pursed together and the expression in her brown eyes altered as Annie deftly changed the subject. Suddenly Annie had an idea of what Kirstie was going to tell her, and wished she'd never asked the question.

'I'm fine. But we lost Mum after Christmas. She'd not been well for a while and after a battery of tests it turned out she had motor neurone disease. The prognosis wasn't great, and she died within three months. It was still a massive shock.'

'Oh Kirstie, you too. I'm so sorry, how awful. How's your dad coping?'

Kirstie glanced away, waving at someone outside the post office before her eyes came back to Annie's and a small smile tugged at her lips. 'I can't decide if he's coping really well or really badly. You know what he's like, Annie. He's gone and taken himself off to a miniscule Hebridean island to discover his spiritual values and live as sustainably as possible. You won't get any argument from me about sustainability, but the values bit? Really?'

Annie was remembering how brilliant and unpredictable Andrew Blaine had been when she and Kirstie were younger. One minute he'd be getting up at five every day to swim outdoors and before they knew it, he'd have changed his mind and taken up yoga, declaring that he'd seen one too many dead sheep in the water and he was never going to swim in the river again. But he'd also been great fun, hugely energetic and had taken both Annie and Kirstie on many an expedition, teaching them about the natural world around them and instilling values in Kirstie that Annie was sure she would never lose.

'It sounds just like him if I'm honest. Is it a permanent move?'

'Not sure, he's planning to stay a year at least. That's why I'm here today.' Kirstie waved a hand towards the building behind her. 'We've had an estate agent round to organise letting the house.'

'Are you still living here? I always imagined you'd have disappeared and gone travelling long ago.' Annie couldn't remember whose turn it had been to email or call last but somehow they'd found it harder to stay in touch once they had left the village to study and travel. Annie wished now that they had made more effort.

'I did, for a few years, and then came back to do a PhD. I'm living in the Dales again now, sharing a cottage with someone from work. A job came up with the National Park after Mum got sick and it meant I could be on hand for her.'

'So what do you do? No, don't tell me, let me guess. It's scientific, of course. Something environmental?'

Kirstie grinned, trying to tuck her loose hair behind her ears. 'You know me too well, Annie Armstrong. I am an environmental scientist, which right now means advising the Park Authority on wildlife. But hey, what about you? Is it even still Armstrong now?'

Annie blinked away her thoughts before replying, forcing a brighter tone into her voice. 'Yep, definitely still an Armstrong. I'm in no hurry to change that.'

'Are you teaching?' They had to shuffle to one side to let a family pass by, the parents trying to persuade two young children to eat their ice creams without squabbling over who had the biggest.

'Yes, key stage two. I did think about high school, but it seemed a bit frantic and I really love my age group. They're so rewarding, mostly.'

'I can imagine,' Kirstie told her with a shudder. 'All those hormones! I go into schools occasionally and it's so much easier to engage primary kids, for a short time at least. But you always were brilliant with the little ones, Annie. Do you remember doing tea parties for my diddy cousins when they came to visit, and Molly would bake her famous scones and bring them fruit she'd picked straight from the garden, bruises and all? I've still never tasted scones as good.'

Annie laughed, marvelling at Kirstie's memory and other recollections spilled into her mind, reminding her again of what she had lost. She wondered for the umpteenth time if coming here really had been wise.

Kirstie pulled a phone from her pocket and glanced at it. 'Annie, I'm so sorry but I've got to go. We've got a group coming later for a guided walk at dusk and I need to be there. Are you staying long enough for us to catch up properly, maybe Friday night at The Courtyard, the old craft centre? They've updated the restaurant and started staying open later at the weekend for pizza and Prosecco. Do you fancy it?'

'I'd love that,' Annie replied honestly. She wasn't planning on having too much social or community involvement just yet. She wanted to spend the summer as quietly as possible, settling into the cottage while she prepared for the coming term at her new school in the next village eight miles away and allowed her shattered heart to ease. But Kirstie was different, and Annie was nodding as she reached for her own phone from her handbag. 'Oh. No signal.'

'Par for the course here, some things don't change much.' Kirstie took a set of keys from the pocket of her walking trousers. 'Why don't we say seven? Give me your number and I'll text you, you'll get the message eventually.'

'Sounds perfect. Thank you.'

Annie reeled off her number and they said goodbye, and Kirstie disappeared into the house. Annie strolled back along the lane and joined the queue at the tea rooms for ice cream; she would do her shopping after this. It was soon her turn and she couldn't decide between salted caramel and apple crumble and greedily decided to have both. She collected her enormous chocolate-topped cone and turned away, closing her eyes in delight as she took her first taste. There was a bench free on the little cobbled terrace outside the shop and she sat down, concentrating on not letting the ice cream run as she fished awkwardly for a tissue in her bag.

'Anyone here drive a white Mini?'

Annie's head snapped up at the words spoken in an abrupt tone that carried easily across the green. A man was striding rapidly over the bridge and she knew at once from the firm set of his wide shoulders that he was angry. Tension radiated from him as he approached the huddle outside the tea rooms, which fell silent as he halted and glared at each of them in turn. Annie had a moment to admire his height and dark good looks before his eyes fell on her at the back of the group. Those eyes, with irises so blue and distinctive she was sure would be remarkable if he weren't so annoyed, seemed to narrow beneath dark brows pulled together in exasperation as they gazed at one another. A swift heat raced across her skin as he dragged his glance back across the group and spoke again, his deep voice only slightly calmer.

'White Mini? Abandoned outside the barn? If the driver doesn't turn up in the next two minutes, we're going to have to tow it out of the way.'

'It's mine.' Annie stood up, already bristling at his curt manner and trying to force an apology into her tone to match her words. 'Sorry. I hadn't realised I wasn't allowed to park there.'

At once the man's gaze swung back to land on hers and he let out a wry laugh as he challenged her. 'Seriously? You just happened to miss the "no parking, access required 24 hours" signs, then?'

His voice had deepened, and her lips tightened at his disbelieving tone. She squeezed past the people sitting nearby, pretending not to listen while they hung on to every word. She came to stand on the edge of the high street, facing him, and felt at once caught by the heat of his eyes on her as everyone else seemed to melt away, her senses flaring into a startling awareness of his physical presence.

His face was tanned, with stubble covering a square jaw, criss-crossed by a scar, below a generous mouth and the suggestion of laughter lines around his eyes. He wore a red top beneath a matching waterproof jacket, a fluorescent stripe running down each arm with a badge below both shoulders, above practical, dark grey trousers and walking boots. His short hair was wet and messy, and mud clung to his boots and trousers.

She suddenly realised her ice cream was melting as it dripped onto her hand and she crossly tipped the whole thing into a nearby bin, her appetite gone. She flashed an angry look at the man, rooting in her bag until she found her car keys. 'I apologise if I've caused a problem. I'll move it now.' Her voice was brisk and low as she fought to diminish her body's surprising reaction to him.

The tension in his shoulders relaxed as his eyes became gentler, and Annie was startled by the sudden warmth and interest in them as he stared at her. She glared back, keen to end the entertainment she had so unwittingly provided, and a long moment passed before he spoke again. A smile broke out on his face, bringing a sudden charm to his expression that Annie found totally disconcerting.

'Right, thanks. It's just that you've parked in front of the Fell Rescue's new headquarters. Thankfully we were heading back from a training exercise and not responding to a real callout.'

Horrified, another blush followed the first and she let her long hair fall forward to disguise her embarrassment as she hurried towards the bridge. 'I'm so sorry, I had no idea. I genuinely hadn't seen the sign, but I suppose I wasn't really looking.'

'Yeah, well, use the car park next time, okay? Sorry if I was a bit sharp.'

She was aware of him passing her on the bridge, his long legs striding ahead as she followed him. Dread spiked in her stomach when she saw an orange and white Land Rover, its roof laden with equipment, parked awkwardly behind her little Mini outside the barn. Two women in the same red waterproofs were unloading bags from the back of the vehicle and they eyed her curiously.

Annie gave the driver an apologetic look as she jumped into her car, aware they were all watching. A quick peek in her rear-view mirror as she started the engine showed the man who had confronted her standing on the running board on the passenger side, unfastening something attached to the roof of the vehicle. She shot forwards, driving quickly around the green and onto the high street, keen to leave the village and the parking debacle behind. When she risked another casual glance towards the barn, the dark-haired man was watching her and she looked away hurriedly. It was only as she turned into the lane leading to Molly's cottage that she suddenly wondered why a member of the local fell rescue team should have an American accent.

Chapter Two

Annie's nerves were still jangling after the encounter with the dark-haired man as she approached Molly's house. Looking at the scattered furniture in the garden, she remembered her original purpose for going into the village had been to pick up food and drink for that evening, and was lost now to the confrontation with the American volunteer. There was still nothing for supper and still no wine, the post office about to close. It would have to wait. She breathed deeply before getting out of the car and walking towards the cottage once again.

She slipped her old key into the lock and opened the front door. The familiar smells she had been half expecting, of fresh baking and flowers collected from the garden, were gone, along with the person who had been most like a grandmother to her, and the cool and musty air horrified her. It seemed dark indoors after the sunshine and Annie headed into the sitting room, not tall enough to have to duck beneath the wooden beams above her.

The house seemed terribly bare, with only a few remaining pieces of old-fashioned furniture, and she knew it was going to take time to turn the cottage into her home without destroying its past. She walked back to the hall and into the little study where Molly had sat every day, and gazed unseeingly out of the dirty window, trying to visualise it as a dining room as well as a place where she could work. Ashes blown in by the wind were scattered on the filthy hearth and threadbare carpet. Annie left the room and closed the door, the gentle click sounding very loud in the silence of the damp cottage.

She walked back through the sitting room into the kitchen, casting her eyes around the unchanged room, almost imagining she could still hear Molly's voice. Above the dirty Belfast sink stood two rows of empty wooden shelves and they, like everything else, including the modern electric Rayburn that had replaced Molly's ancient stove, were covered in a thick layer of dust. Annie blinked tears and sadness away as she headed into the pantry, which stored a twin tub and more empty shelves. From habit she reached onto the top shelf and her fingers found the key to the back door. She slipped it into her pocket.

Upstairs she grimaced at the old-fashioned bath, trying not to think too longingly of the power shower in the Edinburgh flat she'd just sold as she walked out onto the landing again and opened the door to the second bedroom. This pretty, sunny room had been hers and it would now become a guest room. She hoped she could make it as welcoming for others as it had been for her. She made her way into the larger bedroom, which had been Molly's, and knew she would decorate this room first. She crossed to the window, opening it carefully and suddenly her heart was lifted as she stared at the view before her, thrilled that this at least had remained the same.

Willow Cottage was the last house on the lane before the road sloped gently to the upland pastures beyond the village. The hedgerows were still heavy with cow parsley past its best and mingling with wild blackberries spreading along the bank of a narrow stream. A gate just outside her front garden opened onto a low patchwork of fields bordered by ancient and tumbling stone walls, grazed by cattle and sheep and shorn of the long grass safely baled for winter. Beyond clumps of trees the fells rose higher until the meadows gave way to roughened heather-covered moor where the few remaining trees had been bent in the same direction by the force of the wind. Birdsong was louder now, and a twinge of happiness stole through her at the simple and familiar beauty of it all. She pulled the window shut, sighing again as she glimpsed her furniture still in the garden.

The afternoon was gone when Annie went back outside. Some of her new furniture hadn't been delivered yet, so besides a coffee table she had an antique sideboard, two double beds and four packing cases. She was grateful that the men had bothered to cover everything with plastic sheets and underneath these her stuff was pretty much dry. She had returned all the wedding presents and given away the belongings she had collected with Iain. Little remained to remind her, as she'd intended.

She was used to coping with problems on her own but by the time she had breathlessly wrestled a couple of the lighter packing cases into the cottage, she knew she was going to need help with the rest as she finally gave up the struggle. The sideboard was still wedged in the grass and one of the bed frames was now jammed awkwardly between the study and the front door. The pleasure Annie had envisaged in returning to this place was eluding her now that she had managed to bring some of the chaos from the garden into the house and her stomach rumbled hungrily. The day already felt like years, and Edinburgh another life. Her noisy stomach was a reminder of the row with the dark-haired man from the fell rescue and her face flamed again at the recollection. She made her way into the kitchen to see if she still had an emergency chocolate bar in her handbag. The silence in the little house was thunderous and she couldn't ever remember feeling this despondent when she had come to the cottage before.

A sudden rap on the front door made her spring around in startled surprise. She was very tempted to ignore it and hope the unexpected caller would simply go away. But her car was parked all too obviously in the lane, and after the second knock she traipsed past her scattered belongings to answer it. She opened the door, smiling the moment she recognised Elizabeth Howard standing on the step.

'Annie!' Elizabeth reached out to wrap Annie's cool hands between her warm fingers. 'I thought it must be you. Why didn't you let me know you were coming, I would have prepared the cottage for you?'

Robert and Elizabeth Howard had been very good friends and neighbours to Molly, and Annie knew she had much to thank them for. Elizabeth had aged little over the years that Annie had known her. Neat ash-blonde hair seemed a little greyer as her sixtieth birthday approached and there were a few tiny lines around her eyes, but her attractive features and welcoming expression were unchanged. She was tall and slim, and Annie had always thought she was one of the most naturally elegant as well as kindest people that Annie knew, despite her hard-working life on the farm next door.

'That's so kind of you, but there was no need, really. I can sort it out. Please come in if you can.' Annie stepped sideways with a little difficulty and, clutching a wicker basket, Elizabeth carefully followed.

Annie saw her eyes widen as she looked from the jumble of furniture to the scattered packing cases. Her shocked face flew back to Annie's again, clearly stunned by the suddenness of Annie's reappearance along with quite a lot more stuff than just a few days' holiday luggage. 'How long are you planning to stay?'

Looking at the chaos surrounding them, Annie was tempted to say she was in fact just leaving, rubbing one foot against the back of her jeans as she tried to think of an explanation that wouldn't reduce her to tears again. 'I'm starting a new job at the primary school in Calstone.' She met Elizabeth's curious glance, certain her unnaturally cheerful expression said so much more. 'I've always loved Thorndale and Molly so generously leaving the cottage to me has given me a wonderful opportunity to come back.'

Elizabeth looked at her doubtfully. Annie knew she was unconvinced by the brief reply and waited nervously for the next question. 'And Iain?'

Unthinkingly Annie reached out to her ring finger, touching the still unfamiliar emptiness, barely able to meet Elizabeth's concerned gaze. 'We broke up, a few months ago.' The forced brightness in her voice scarcely disguised the sorrow and she tried to smile. 'Anyway, enough of me. I want to hear all about Robert and the family. How is everyone?'

Elizabeth touched Annie's arm gently. 'I'm very sorry,' she said quietly, and Annie nodded her thanks, relieved to change the subject. 'Robert's fine, still happiest at home with the herd but he finds the early mornings more of a struggle now.' They both laughed. 'Mark's taken over the sheep and Jess is down in Dorset, working for a mixed rural practice. It was Mark who saw the car outside, and I thought it must be you. What happened to your furniture?'

Annie's situation seemed funnier now that somebody else was here to share it and she quickly explained why the cottage was in such disarray.

'What a rotten thing to do.' Elizabeth was indignant as she looked around the room before glancing at Annie again, her voice becoming gentler. 'And they knew you were on your own?'

Annie shrugged; it hadn't occurred to her to tell them. 'I suppose so.' She realised that it hadn't taken her very long to pack her life into boxes and cart it somewhere else. Her own furniture in the cottage would emphasise the lack of Molly's presence all the more, saddening Annie again. 'I'm really sorry about the funeral. Molly was absolutely insistent on the woodland burial and not wanting people there. She'd organised everything, as ever, and just didn't see the point in making a fuss, as she called it.'

Elizabeth smiled. 'No need. It's fine, really it is. I know you were following her wishes and, for what it's worth, I think you did the right thing. Those of us who knew her well understood.'

'Thank you.' Annie felt reassured by Elizabeth's words. She had found it so difficult to arrange the funeral without mourners, just herself and one of Molly's oldest friends from her days as an Oxford professor. The friend was almost ninety-five and had had to abandon his walking stick and resort to a mobility scooter to take his place at the short outdoor service.

'Have you chosen the memorial tree yet?'

Annie huffed a laugh. 'Molly did. She wanted a rowan because they're supposed to symbolise protection, something to do with wizards in Celtic mythology. And of course they're brilliant for pollinators and birds, and you know how she felt about wildlife. It'll be planted in the autumn at the burial ground.'

Elizabeth was still smiling as she handed the basket to Annie. 'These are for you, just a few things to get you started. I must go, we've got B&B guests arriving any minute, but I'll send Mark down to move the rest of the furniture. And when you're ready, come to the farm and have supper with us.'

'Thank you very much.' Delighted, Annie peered inside the basket and her mouth began to water as she saw home-made bread, local cheese and perfectly ripe tomatoes nestling amongst half a dozen brown eggs and a carton of creamy milk. She followed Elizabeth to the door. 'I'm fine, honestly. I can manage.'

'But you don't have to.' Elizabeth touched a hand to Annie's arm. 'It's no trouble.'

'Thank you.' Annie shuffled from foot to foot on the stone floor as Elizabeth made her way through the wild garden, calling after her. 'If you don't mind, I think I'll just crash on my own tonight. It's been a long day.'

Elizabeth acknowledged her comment with a quick wave and Annie sighed as she closed the door. She knew her cover was well and truly blown and dreaded the thought of the explanations ahead. Despite her protestations, she was very relieved at the thought of help arriving. A couple of hours later everything was inside, mostly thanks to Mark, Elizabeth and Tom's strapping farmer son who had chatted easily, reminding Annie of her days here as a child, as he helped her to place everything where she wanted it. She made up her bed once he had left and was finally sitting in the kitchen, hungrily eating the cheese and tomatoes with chunks of bread to mop up the juice running through her fingers. Exhausted, she watched the evening slipping into darkness all around her, shivering as she looked away from the window. She plugged in her kettle and cleared up quickly, returning to the sitting room.

She remembered where to find the light switch and pressed it firmly. But the room was still in darkness and she flicked it several more times as her heart began to thump nervously. There was hardly any light from the windows by now, and she headed into the hall and tried that switch instead. This time she wasn't surprised when it failed to produce the light she was beginning to crave and realised despairingly that the electricity must have tripped.

She found the fuse box in the little cupboard in the sitting room and used the torch on her phone to peer at it, draining more precious battery life. Sure enough, the main switch had tripped, and she flicked it back up, realising immediately that it wouldn't stay put. She tried a couple more times with the same result and wondered anxiously where she might find candles or perhaps another torch. The battery on her phone was fading fast and she didn't want to waste it on light if possible. She spent a little while unplugging each appliance and trying the trip switch again but each time the switch refused to stay put.

She knew the sensible thing to do would be to grab a bag, jump in the car and spend the night with the Howards. But she also knew that if she left the cottage now then she might never return, and she wanted that even less than being stuck on her own without power.

She thought there might be a torch in her car and opened the front door, hurrying along the path. After Edinburgh, the silence was deafening, and she could barely see a thing through the shadows. She reached the car and froze in the darkness, wishing for the comfort of bright city street lights as her heart began to pound faster. A gentle breeze and cooling air rustled the trees softly and she shuddered as the branches drifted idly, as though somebody were parting them and peeping through to stare at her. The quick clunk of the central locking freeing the car doors made her jump and she spun around nervously. But there was no one there and when she reached into the glove box and found the torch, Annie almost laughed in frantic relief.

She dashed back to the cottage, incredibly grateful for the narrow beam of light from the torch. The house looked very dark and no longer welcoming, and she shot inside and slammed the door firmly. With no idea where to find a recent bill to call the electricity company for help, and without a wireless signal or the slightest suggestion of 4G, there was absolutely no possibility of searching the internet for clues. In the kitchen she found a few old candles, a box of damp matches and a couple of ancient candlesticks. She wasted several precious matches until two candles were finally lit and carried them carefully upstairs.

She sank down onto the bed, trying not to look at the flickering shapes on the walls as the candles burned. Suddenly she understood that the happy-go-lucky home of her childhood had gone, that she was responsible now for this old building and its care in the future and wished that her heart were soaring instead of sinking. Not only had she lost Molly, but so had the cottage lost its loving guardian. Annie changed into pyjamas and climbed into bed. It was an uneasy sleep when it finally came.

Daylight was streaming through the windows when she woke the next morning, the sun rising early over the fells to the east and shining on the front of the cottage. Annie dressed and flew into action, all too aware there was much to be done before the old building could properly resemble a home. Despite an inauspicious start, she was thankful to be here, at the edge of the village with the cottage as her own little refuge from the world, hiding her away until she was ready to face it once more.

She found an old box of paperwork in the study but there was no suggestion of who Molly might have used as an electrician and Annie knew she would need Wi-Fi and probably a personal recommendation. She was sure The Courtyard would have a decent network and even though she managed to obtain a signal on her mobile by standing on the doddery old bench underneath the kitchen window, it would not be enough, and the battery was virtually flat now.

She stared at the back garden, still soaked in dew until the sun would reach it later in the day. There was a pond somewhere, but Annie couldn't see it for the long grass. She spotted a pile of logs stacked against the old coalhouse underneath a rough shelter, feeling grateful to the unseen person who had left them there. Without power she couldn't even boil the kettle or hope to have a coffee from her beloved Nespresso and so she dressed in jeans and a casual man's shirt and set off for the farm, taking her laptop and phone charger with her, eating her emergency chocolate bar for breakfast en route.

Other than a smart new B&B sign, the Howards' farm seemed unchanged when she reached it and she was glad; at least something of the past appeared to have remained over the years that she had been gone. The big, stone house looked welcoming and homely, the buildings across the cobbled yard were neat and tidy, and she heard the unmistakable sound of cattle somewhere out in the fields. It was the wrong time of day for milking so she wasn't surprised to find the yard deserted, the dogs' kennels empty, and Elizabeth's car gone. Annie sighed as she returned to the lane and carried on to the village. She would have to try local Facebook groups or ask around for an electrician.

She walked along the high street, throwing a casual glance towards the fell rescue's headquarters but wasn't entirely sure if she was relieved or disappointed as she saw that it too appeared deserted. She headed to the far end of the village, past the old bookseller's house at the top of the green and turned into The Courtyard, realising at once that it had changed, as Kirstie had said. Formed around an old farmyard, the tiny cottage had become a museum of local life and, where before just a few artists and craftspeople had occupied one of two barns, now every space was spoken for and each stable or byre converted to house felters to photographers and everything in between, all brought together as The Courtyard. The tiny café in the cottage had gone, replaced by a modern extension with lots of glass and was now a stylish and bright restaurant. Annie found a quiet table and ordered breakfast.

When she had drunk two cups of coffee and eaten the most delicious breakfast she thought she'd ever tasted, of smashed avocado and poached eggs on toast, she had two recommendations from Facebook for electricians. She tried them both and was thankful to make an appointment for that afternoon with the second, who thought he knew what was wrong. Her phone was fully charged now, and she was finally able to answer all the messages from friends she had missed in the last twenty-four hours. There was a voicemail from her parents checking she was okay, and she typed out a cheery reply, knowing they would almost certainly be playing golf and not answering calls. She told everyone she was fine, that the cottage was wonderful, and they must come and stay as soon as she was organised, not entirely believing her own words. She seemed to be the only person sitting alone and she wondered how she would make the village seem like her own once more. Yet again she felt as though she were on the outside, looking in at everyone else's lives.

Shaking off the encroaching despondency, she stood up and gathered her things to leave. Outside in the courtyard she lingered, peering through the window of a small pottery, her eyes darting from piece to piece as she searched for one that she liked.

And then she saw him.

Her heart leaped and a delicious, unfamiliar tingle ignited her skin as she stared at the dark-haired man from the fell rescue. She knew she was blushing as his eyes met hers through the glass, struggling to offer a casual greeting. She saw his expression alter into recognition as they looked at one another, and then he spoke to the man sitting at the wheel and quickly began to make his way towards her. Annie felt a thrill steal though her as he neared the door but then somebody else approached him and he halted impatiently. He glanced in her direction again and although his lips were moving as he tried to get away, she couldn't read what he was saying.

It was enough. Annie wanted no part of this exhilaration, this dangerous sensation scattering her senses whenever she saw him. Even as she heard the clatter of the door, she fled into the village, walking hurriedly and breaking into a run when she reached the top of her lane, not daring to slow down until she was almost at the farm. When she looked back over her shoulder, she was relieved to see he hadn't been mad enough to follow her. She shoved the gate open as she reached her garden and crept breathlessly into the silent house, lifting her hair from the dampness on her neck as she slammed the front door behind her.

Chapter Three

After an early but unsettled night Annie was desperate for a decent breakfast at home. Dressing casually in yesterday's shirt over a vest and a pair of skinny jeans, which flattered the curve of her bottom and slim legs, she scraped her long curls into a clip, grabbed Elizabeth's basket from the kitchen and headed back to the village to bring home a few local supplies. The electrician had turned up yesterday as promised, diagnosed a faulty circuit breaker, and fixed the problem. She had been so pleased and relieved to have power again that she had had to stop herself from hugging him in gratitude. After he'd left, she had scurried around switching on every light in the house to check they were working, at the same time as making a coffee from the Nespresso, especially thankful that the Rayburn had restarted itself.

She barely noticed the early morning activity around the green as she walked into the post office and glanced around. Gone were the rows of everyday biscuits, baked beans and processed meat, replaced by shelves of organic pasta, home-made cakes and chutneys stacked beside jars of jam. One corner was filled with a freezer of ice cream from the local dairy and Annie would've been tempted, even at this hour, if she hadn't been so keen for a square meal that included carbs. The ice cream was another reminder of the dark-haired man from Tuesday and her face became warm as she remembered their exchange and the expression in his eyes as he had looked at her.

The newspapers had been relegated to a pile on the floor to make room for books and maps and she spotted a paperback by Andrew Blaine, Kirstie's father. Annie swiftly filled the basket with more than she'd originally intended to buy, but fresh butter from the dairy looked irresistible and she threw in some organic biscuits as well.

She said hello to the teenage girl behind the till, who nodded wordlessly as she stuffed Annie's shopping into recycled carrier bags. Annie noticed the girl's eyes flicking to the door every time the bell jangled and she smiled in silent sympathy. It was the beginning of the school holidays and wherever the girl wanted to be, it obviously wasn't stuck in a shop. Annie heard the bell again and suddenly the girl's expression was transformed as delight darted across her face, a flash so brief that Annie thought she might've imagined it. She glanced over her shoulder to see who was responsible.

A tall, thin boy had appeared, and Annie saw his eyes flit around until he spotted the girl at the till and he deliberately looked away, bending to pick up a newspaper. His beautiful skin was smooth, and dark brown eyes were widely set, wary and coolly observant. Crazily ripped jeans hung low on narrow hips above long legs and his T-shirt revealed arms that were more strongly muscled than she would've expected on such a lean frame. His dark, tightly curled hair was very short, and he had a gold ring in each ear and one through his right eyebrow, glittering against his skin. He looked about nineteen and she could see exactly why the girl was entranced by his silent appearance. Annie met his gaze when she turned away from the till and gave him a brief smile as she headed to the door. He nodded quickly and then she was outside.

A woman walking a small dog alongside the green stopped Annie to say hello and Annie remembered her as a good friend of Molly's. It was lovely to catch up and Annie promised to pop round for tea and a proper chat soon. Still clutching the basket, she set off for the cottage but as she reached the

Howards' farm, she turned on impulse into the yard when she saw Elizabeth's car. Out of the corner of one eye she spotted a large goose heading towards her, honking noisily as it flapped its wings, gathering speed all the while. Annie squealed in terror and shot towards the house, running like she hadn't done since she was the hundred metres champion at school, the contents of her basket bouncing wildly.

She reached the porch and hammered on the door, not sure if it was her heart or her fist banging the loudest. She thumped on the door again and nearly fell into the house as it was suddenly opened wide. Annie darted inside, and Elizabeth looked at her in amusement as she closed the door again. Annie's hair had mostly escaped from the clip and she didn't need a mirror to know that her face was scarlet and damp as she righted the basket in her arms.

'Morning, Annie.' Elizabeth ushered her towards the table in the centre of the room. 'Don't worry about the goose, it's all show, she won't do you any harm. Sit down and have a cup of tea.'

'Thanks.' Annie wasn't so sure about the show bit, her breathing slowing now that six inches of closed door separated her from the goose. She put Elizabeth's basket down beside a worn armchair as she glanced around curiously. The kitchen was much as she remembered it, except for walls painted pale blue and elegant rose-patterned curtains at the big window overlooking the garden. But the huge table was the same, laid for breakfast and half hidden by local newspapers, brochures for farming equipment and a pair of matching bowls stuffed with fruit and a set of keys. Three tortoiseshell cats were lounging in a cosy bed underneath and they hardly bothered to raise their heads at the intrusion. Two loaves of freshly baked bread were cooling beside an Aga, and Annie's mouth watered as she smelled bacon cooking.

'Would you like to stay for breakfast? The guests have finished and I'm just making some for Robert before he has to go out.'

Annie remembered the shopping still tucked inside the basket and the intention to cook her own. But the smell was impossible to resist as she looked across to Elizabeth. 'Thank you, that's very kind. If you're sure it's no trouble?'

'Of course not, there's plenty. Sit down, it'll be ready in a minute.'

Annie pulled out a chair and watched, almost drooling as Elizabeth made more tea and sliced one of the loaves. She piled a plate with bacon, mushrooms, tomatoes, and scrambled eggs and placed it in front of Annie. Annie tried to protest, resisting the temptation to stuff the whole lot into her mouth at once.

'Don't be silly.' Elizabeth waved away Annie's objections as she dropped a couple of fat sausages onto the plate as well. 'Help yourself to bread and butter.'

'Thank you,' Annie said hungrily, closing her eyes in delight as she tasted the salty, cured bacon and perfectly cooked farm-produced egg.

'Oh, I forgot to tell you, Annie, I've still got two spare keys for the cottage.' Elizabeth filled a cup with tea and passed it to her. 'Shall I keep one back, in case you need me to pop in sometime, and give you the other? I won't be a minute, I'll go and fetch it from the office.'

Annie nodded her thanks, greedily forking up more bacon as Elizabeth left the room. The door to the porch opened and she spun around in her seat, surprised. Robert Howard erupted noisily into the kitchen, talking animatedly to a companion as he stepped out of a pair of wellies. For the second time in twenty-four hours, Annie was aghast to see the dark-haired man from the fell rescue following Robert into the room. If it hadn't been full of breakfast, her mouth would've dropped open in surprise; instead, an infuriating heat raced across her face when he spied her. She saw astonishment and then something much warmer in his eyes as he looked at her. Hurriedly she turned her flustered gaze back to Robert.

'Now then, lass,' Robert roared, clattering towards her with a big grin and sending the cats flying out of their bed at the sudden din. She stood up quickly, thrusting her hand out before he yanked her into one of his famous bear hugs. 'It's about time.'

It was difficult to smile with a mouthful of breakfast but she gave it her best. Robert pumped her arm vigorously and then hugged her anyway, dragging her against him as she tried to wriggle away. She noticed his unruly hair, for once tamed and tidy, was completely white and his appearance was smartened by a checked shirt and green tie worn with presentable brown cords. Annie didn't need to look at the younger man to know that he was still watching her. She couldn't believe he was only six feet away and she was wearing her crappiest clothes with crazy hair and no make-up, as if it mattered. Before she could muster a reply, Robert shot his friend a quick grin, stuffed a handful of bacon between two slices of bread and disappeared from the room. The door banged shut behind him.

Annie cleared her throat in an attempt to lessen its sudden tightness and sank back onto her seat, pretending not to notice that he had pulled out a chair and sat down opposite her. She felt the heat of his look upon her again as she avoided his eyes, and it was only a moment until he spoke.

'Why did you run away from the pottery yesterday?' he asked, the directness of his question softened by the tone of his voice, so different from the anger of the other day.

Annie neatly arranged the cutlery on her plate, the clatter seeming very loud as he waited for her reply.

'I couldn't stay,' she answered truthfully, remembering her imminent appointment with the electrician. She knew she sounded brusque as she twisted her fingers together, wishing she could leg it again and not have to confront the sudden reality of the man who had been flitting in and out of her thoughts since she had first seen him.

'Are you here on vacation?' He spoke quietly, sounding different now that he was calmer, as well as much closer. As she considered her answer, Annie looked at his big hands resting casually on the table, his long, slim fingers browned by the sun. She noticed a signet ring on the little finger of his left hand and wished she were able to appear so unperturbed, unconsciously shrinking back in her seat and thankful for the broad width of the table between them.

'Something like that,' she replied evasively, thinking of her summer break from school.

'Look, I owe you an apology. I was totally...'

Elizabeth reappeared in the kitchen and they both looked around as she crossed the room. Annie could have hugged her in sheer relief that she was no longer alone with this very direct and attractive man.

'Hello, Jon, ready to go?' Elizabeth asked, smiling first at him and then across to Annie. Elizabeth took the teapot from the table and refilled it from the hot kettle on the Aga. 'I thought I heard your voice. I see you two have met.'

'Actually, we haven't. Not properly.' He turned his gaze from Annie to give Elizabeth his quiet attention.

'Then let me introduce you. Annie is Molly Briggs's goddaughter, Jon – she's just moved into Molly's cottage. Jon runs Thorndale Rural Enterprises in the village, Annie, but I'm not sure you'll remember him. I don't think he was here when you used to come and stay with Molly.'

Elizabeth's introduction sent a faint tremor down Annie's back as she realised that she would almost certainly see Jon again, knowing all the while she could well do without the foolish sensations instigating chaos in her mind and body whenever she laid eyes on him. That thought alone was enough to make her feel as though she wouldn't want to set foot on the fells again in case she were ever in need of rescue.

'You live here?'

'I do, yes. Since the beginning of this week anyway.' She was starting to really wish that she didn't as she heard the astonishment in his voice. She wondered if Elizabeth could recommend a decent estate agent. Annie aimed her glance away from Jon's eyes, trying not to notice the two undone top buttons on his shirt and the sunglasses pushed into casually dishevelled hair. She was relieved when Elizabeth passed her another cup of tea, fixing her eyes on her neighbour instead as Elizabeth began to speak.

'Annie knows the village like the back of her hand, don't you, Annie? She more or less grew up here.' Elizabeth frowned then as she tipped more bacon onto Annie's plate before Annie could stop her. 'That reminds me. Why didn't you come and spend the night with us while the power was out at the cottage? You really didn't have to stay down there all alone.'

Annie tried to shrug it off, but they were both waiting for her answer. 'Oh, I was fine on my own, really.' She waved her hand as if it had never occurred to her to be alarmed by complete darkness in unfamiliar surroundings. 'How did you know about that?' She hadn't expected anyone to have found out so soon about her predicament.

Elizabeth laughed, and Annie saw Jon smile too. She noticed the lines around his eyes, the corners of his mouth and the faded hint of the scar on his jaw, and struggled to tear her glance away. Her mind easily observed every little detail as she wondered distractedly if men were supposed to have such beautifully shaped lips.

'Village grapevine.' Elizabeth pushed a plate in front of Jon, and he thanked her as he started to eat. 'The man who came out asked for directions at the post office as his sat nav was playing up and the rest, as they say, is history. But seriously, Annie, promise me if anything like that happens again you will come to us? I hate to think of you on your own down there in the dark.'

'I will, thank you.' Annie gave Elizabeth a grateful look. She could feel her undigested breakfast churning uneasily in her stomach as she picked up her cup and sipped from it slowly.

Elizabeth finally sat down, pulling her drink towards her with a quick clatter of the saucer. She looked at Jon. 'All sorted for today?'

'Think so, it doesn't start until after lunch. Robert and I are leading a navigations skills course this afternoon, near Hawes.' Jon looked at Annie as he gave the short explanation. She really wished he wouldn't smile at her like that. 'Do you know the town? There's a nice pub nearby with an excellent restaurant and microbrewery.'

'I'm not familiar with it but Molly used to like going there by bus when she was still able to.' His deep voice and rich American accent were already imprinted in her memory, and Annie wanted to know so much more about him, knowing she ought to crush such a dangerous wonder before it took hold.

'Ah.' Elizabeth's smile was still in place as she replaced the lid on the butter dish. 'So that's Robert's plan, Jon. You'll be driving, and he can sample a few more of those local ales he likes so much over an early supper.'

'I should get back. I've got so much to do,' Annie said suddenly, remembering the state of the cottage and her impending schoolwork. She replaced her cup on its saucer and stood up quickly, keen to escape and gather her muddled emotions.

'Are you sure? Don't you want to finish your meal?' Elizabeth asked, surprised. Annie shook her head and Elizabeth pointed to the table. 'Don't forget the key. I've still got the other one, just in case.'

'That's really kind of you. And thank you for breakfast, sorry I'm not very hungry after all.' Annie reached for her purse, her hair falling forward and framing her face. She gathered it together, quickly scooping it back into the clip and taking the key from the table, aware all the while of Jon's silent gaze on her as she finally turned to him, simple good manners winning out. 'I hope you have an interesting day.'

He stood up and stuck out a hand as she neared him and she paused, caught unawares by his impulsive gesture. His fingers closed around her palm and she felt the soft roughness of his skin on hers as she looked at him.

'Thanks, Annie. It was great to meet you properly,' he said gently, that blue gaze never leaving her own. 'I'm sure we'll see one another around the village before long. And I still owe you that apology.'

She nodded, completely aware of his strength as he held her hand and then their arms fell away. She excused herself, practically running into the yard as Elizabeth called goodbye. When Annie spotted the goose scavenging near a barn, she really did have a reason to sprint home and it wasn't just because she was afraid of being bitten by the wretched bird. It was only when she was safely back in the solitude of the cottage, she remembered she had left behind the basket and her longed-for shopping at the farm.

Chapter Four

The following morning her new furniture arrived early and Annie hovered while the delivery men hauled the new fridge-freezer and washing machine, along with two small sofas, into her little house. Elizabeth appeared amid it all, bringing a steak pie and the basket of food from the day before, leaving Annie practically drooling as she thanked her, waving goodbye from the garden when Elizabeth hurried off to go shopping for new guests. Once inside Annie laughed in delight; already the cottage was beginning to look more like a home again.

She wasn't sure what she was going to do about plumbing in the washing machine as she'd forgotten to pre-book it, and after the delivery men had left, taking away all the packaging and the twin tub, she made her way to the outhouse in the hope of finding some tools to help with the job. She reached cautiously along the shelves in the darkened space, spluttering as she disturbed years of dirt and spiders long settled in gloomy corners. At the very back of the shed, long forgotten, she stumbled on Molly's ancient shopping bicycle, its tyres flat and useless and the saddle split. A basket hung limply from one handlebar and in her mind she saw Molly riding the bicycle, sailing off into the village to visit friends or collect shopping, and Annie's eyes filled with tears.

Once she emerged from the outhouse – no tools to be found – she desperately wanted a bath. She had a meeting at school that afternoon and really didn't want to turn up with cobwebs in her hair looking as though she'd been living up a tree protesting about cruelty to bats or something. Back upstairs in the bathroom she was thrilled to find hot water pouring out of the tap and threw in a generous splash of Jo Malone's Blackberry and Bay bath oil to celebrate, anticipating the pleasure of a good soak. She still couldn't open the window and steam was already clouding the mirror, but Annie didn't care as she climbed in the bath and closed her eyes blissfully.

Before long, the water became cool, waking her from her half-asleep state and she reached for the tap and turned it on, lying back in anticipation of the warmth to come. But moments later she realised there was no more hot water and sat up, cool air already draping itself over her warm body. She climbed out and wrapped herself in a huge white towel, wondering crossly what could have gone wrong now. She ran downstairs, dripping water onto the stone floor in the kitchen while she peered at the Rayburn.

Shivering now, she realised it must have run out of oil and looked around the kitchen, trying to remember where she would find the storage tank. She dashed outside into the sunshine, barefoot, her sopping wet hair hanging down her back. The tank was behind the outhouse and the oil monitor confirmed what she already knew: that the tank was empty, and she had nothing left with which to cook, heat the cottage or the water. And it was Friday morning already. The weekend seemed to stretch ahead as though it were months, not merely two days, as she thought about how she would manage without the Rayburn.

'Hello, anyone home? Annie?'

Startled, her heart began to beat faster as she pressed herself against the wall, the rough stone cold against her back. She knew that distinctive voice, hoping he would simply give up and go away if she stayed hidden. After a moment or two she cautiously peered around the side of the outhouse and, aghast, saw Jon emerging into the garden as he called her again, realising she must have forgotten to lock the front door. She clutched the towel tightly, desperate for him not to see her like this. But there was no escape, not unless she hurdled the back hedge and she disliked being amongst loose cattle even more than handsome men she barely knew. As every step he took brought him closer to her hiding place, Annie tried to summon a nonchalant expression and emerged to face him, both arms wrapped around her body to keep the towel firmly in place.

She tried to look as natural as possible, pretending it was quite normal to find her soaking wet and practically naked in her own back garden. She saw his eyes widen in astonishment, and the surprise disappeared as a much more sensual expression darkened the blue depths as he smiled incredulously. She knew her face was undoubtedly scarlet and found it very difficult to cling to the idea that the towel offered much of a barrier to all she was certain he was imagining.

'I'm sorry.' The smile became a distracted grin as he turned his back towards her. 'I didn't mean to disturb you. The door was unlocked, so I guessed you were in.'

'I was just checking the oil,' Annie said hastily, aware that her voice sounded shrill and a pulse was leaping madly in her throat. 'Excuse me, I need to change.'

She hurried past him, relieved he had allowed her enough privacy to dart back into the house and she raced upstairs. A torrent of thoughts flew through her mind as she wondered why he was here, what reason could have brought him to her. She dragged on the first pair of jeans she found and a little yellow top, scooping her hair into a ponytail, and returned to the kitchen more slowly than she had left it. Jon was still in the garden and she knew he was waiting for her to invite him inside.

'Hi,' she said casually, taking a moment to observe him until he spun around. The classic fit jeans — with a pager attached to the belt — suited his long legs and a plum-coloured shirt seemed to highlight the unusual blue of his eyes. His sleeves were carelessly rolled up, revealing muscular arms darkened by softly curling hair.

34

'Hey.' He followed Annie back into the cottage, both of them sidling past the washing machine and fridge pushed casually into place but still managing to clutter up the little kitchen. She hovered beside the table, not quite sure what to say, when Jon broke the silence.

'I just had a look at the oil tank – it's empty.'

Annie nodded. She was finding it hard to meet his eyes; she couldn't forget that she had just been standing in front of him barely dressed, and was already beginning to glow at the memory.

'I can give you a number to call and order more. It's probably too late for delivery today but if you call by mid-afternoon, they should be able to bring it tomorrow morning. You should switch the Rayburn off until the tank's refilled, and it'll probably need bleeding again.'

'Thank you,' she replied, rubbing the back of one leg with a still bare foot. 'I will.'

'Annie, look, I owe you an apology. The other day…'

'No really, let's not go back there. I can't believe I missed the sign.'

'You didn't do it on purpose and I should never have spoken to you like that. I'm really sorry. We'd had a very difficult rescue the night before but that's still no excuse. Do you think you'll be able to forgive me?'

She wasn't about to let him see how much he already affected her, so conscious of his tall body close to hers and the slightly playful tone lowering his voice. She found it hard to think straight when she looked up and saw the frank expression on his face. 'Thank you. It's nice of you to come and say so.' She saw him glance around the room.

'Looks like you've got work to do,' Jon said casually. 'Do you need some help?'

'No, thanks,' she said hastily, refusing his offer. 'I can manage.'

'Sure? It won't take me long to get them working.' He pointed to the shiny new appliances on the other side of the table.

Annie hesitated, common sense telling her to accept his offer as she had no other options to fall back on right now, unsettled by the growing realisation that she didn't really want him to leave just yet. 'Okay, thank you. If you're sure it's no trouble? That would be really kind.'

Jon grinned, the gesture deepening the lines around his mouth, the blue irises a quite different shade to the other day. 'I'll go get some tools and be right back.'

She pressed herself against the dresser as he squeezed past. His arm brushed her shoulder as he headed for the door, and she closed her eyes, breathing in the faint scent of spicy citrus drifting in the air. He was back in less than twenty minutes, with a grey jumper over the plum shirt. Annie hid in the study when he insisted that he could manage on his own. She busied herself taking books from the shelves to dust and wondered about Jon nearby the whole time. Twenty-five minutes later, he stuck his head around the door and grinned when she looked up. She smiled warily as her stomach flipped over.

'Done,' he said briskly, dumping a small toolbox in the hall. 'I've switched them both on.'

She noticed a dark smudge on his face, suddenly imagining reaching up to remove it with her finger. She dismissed the idea at once; such thoughts were madness. 'Thank you very much.' She got to her feet, pushing a pile of books on the floor to one side. 'I really appreciate it.'

'You're welcome, I think it was the least I could do.' Jon was still in the doorway, leaning against the frame. 'Do you want me to text you the number of the oil company we use? They're local.'

'That would be so helpful, I'm still trying to find out everything I need to know about the cottage.'

He stepped aside as she headed into the sitting room, a quick jolt of surprise making her wonder if he was asking for her telephone number on purpose. She tried to squash the flare of excitement as she gave him her number and he quickly stored it in his mobile. He seemed in no hurry to leave and they stood in silence for a moment as Annie considered what to do next. This was the point at which he would go, or, and this was definitely the more exhilarating option, she would offer him coffee. And then she felt ridiculous – were it anybody else she would have made it by now.

'Would you like coffee?' she asked brightly. She knew he would accept even before he nodded yes, and he followed her back to the kitchen. Annie busied herself filling the Nespresso machine with water, realising she was running low on capsules and that meant a trip to town to restock. She didn't imagine the post office would run to selling them just yet. She found a couple of mugs and took a pint of milk from the cool bag where she was currently storing it.

'So how do you like the village?'

'I love it,' she said, her voice pensive as she slid one of the mugs onto the coffee machine, glancing across to him. 'But I haven't spent any time here recently, not since Molly had to move into the nursing home. Everything seems so different without her, especially the cottage. Would you like black or white?'

'Black please. Espresso is perfect.'

Annie waited a few seconds while the machine poured the coffee into the too-large mug and then pushed it across the table to him. 'Sorry. Haven't found the espresso cups yet.' She turned away to make her cappuccino and a few moments later joined him at the table, sitting opposite.

'Did you stay with Molly often?'

She smiled wistfully. 'Most of my school holidays.' Annie glanced around the kitchen, remembering how it used to look, not this altered appearance she was already beginning to create. 'My dad was an engineer before he retired and worked abroad for most of his career. I travelled with my parents until I was eleven, when they moved to Singapore and decided I should go to boarding school. There was some reason I couldn't go out to see them during the holidays and so I came here instead. Molly always made the cottage seem like home and I loved her for it.'

'I guess I would've been at university by then.' Jon cradled the mug between long fingers as he watched Annie steadily. 'You must miss her. I heard she was such a presence in the village in her day, although she didn't get on with everybody. She had her beliefs and stuck to them, whatever people thought of her. My father was very fond of her. Although they disagreed from time to time, they both had the good of the village at heart. I'm sorry I didn't know her that well, she left not long after I came here.'

Annie beamed at his summary of Molly's character. 'That sounds exactly like her. She was often on the warpath with somebody, but she was kind, thoughtful and wonderful to me.' Annie paused, replacing her mug on the table, remembering Elizabeth's words about him. 'Have you worked on the estate for some time?'

Jon didn't respond immediately, and she felt her brow furrow as she tried to understand the expression in his eyes as they looked at one another. Eventually he gave her a wry smile as he quickly shrugged his shoulders. 'Kinda. I was born here but moved to America when I was five.'

I'm sorry, she wanted to say but wasn't sure if she should. He sounded pensive and she understood there was regret in his simple answer. Then he said something that completely floored her.

'And I spent six years working with a Christian mission in Kenya.' He laughed at her amazement. 'That always surprises people,' he said dryly, putting his empty mug on the table as he leant back in his seat to watch her. 'But it's also true.'

'A mission?' Annie wondered if she had misheard him, her shock at his revelation enough to distract her from her surreptitious perusal of his broad shoulders.

His eyes flickered with amusement. 'Yes. I went on a couple of trips to South America when I was at university, and after I graduated the short-term trips just kept getting longer. I came home to Thorndale four years ago.'

Annie took in the information, trying to match it to the man sitting opposite her and knew she wanted to know more; he had awakened her curiosity with just a few words. He glanced at his watch and she wasn't surprised, just a tiny bit disappointed, when he looked at her and she saw the coming goodbye in his eyes.

'I'm sorry, I have to go.'

She was taken aback by the reluctance in his expression as he stood up and pushed his chair underneath the table. She followed him through the sitting room, watching as he ducked to avoid the wooden beams. At the front door Jon spoke first, sounding impulsive.

'I guess cooking tonight is out of the question as you're out of oil. We have a youth centre on the estate and you're very welcome to come over later and join the team to eat, if you're not already busy.'

Annie tried to make her expression unremarkable, knowing that prolonging her time in his company would be decidedly risky. At least she was meeting Kirstie and wouldn't have to make do with cheese and biscuits for supper.

'Thank you.' She switched her glance to the scruffy garden beyond the front door. 'That's very kind of you, Jon, but I've got so much to do, and I already have plans.' And unable to help it, she went fishing as she returned her gaze to his. 'But you must have plans with your family too, you won't want me tagging along.'

Jon shook his head and her eyes somehow became lost in his own as he replied. 'My dad and stepmother are away right now, so no family plans.'

She swallowed, feeling her knees tremble as she heard what he was trying to tell her. She stepped back against the bottom stair, half hoping he would go so she could restore her scattered thoughts. 'Thanks for your help earlier.'

He said goodbye as he turned into the garden, hesitating before lifting his hand in a casual wave and walking rapidly away. Annie closed the door and it was only when he had disappeared that she realised he hadn't really explained the reason for his sudden visit, not entirely sure that an apology for the other day was the whole of it. She pulled her phone from her pocket and shrieked: she had no idea that time had passed so quickly, and raced upstairs to get ready. Fifteen minutes later, changed into a simple shirtdress, her still damp hair twisted into a respectable plait down her shoulders, she leapt into her car.

The meeting at school was interesting and she inspected her new classroom, already stripped bare for next term. She did her best to concentrate as the headteacher showed her around again and introduced her to some of her new colleagues on their final inset day, but she couldn't get Jon out of her thoughts, shocked to have become so easily distracted by him.

The afternoon was already disappearing when she drove back into the village, her phone beeping with messages. She pulled over outside the Howards' farm to read them, surprised when she opened the one from Jon. *Don't forget*, he'd written, followed by the telephone number she needed for the oil company. She called the oil company straight away, relieved to arrange a delivery for the following morning and dithered for nearly five minutes before sending a simple *thank you* to Jon in reply. It would have to do. She returned to the cottage, laden down with piles of stuff to organise into lesson plans and projects for her year, dumping it all in the study for now and heading upstairs to get changed to meet Kirstie.

Chapter Five

'Here, get this Prosecco down you, Annie Armstrong, and tell me why you're back in Thorndale after all these years.'

'Aren't you having one too?'

Kirstie shuddered as she placed a glass of sparkling wine on the table in front of Annie and pulled out her chair to sit opposite. 'I am not! Horrible stuff, makes me feel sick.'

'So what have you got?' Annie looked at the other glass Kirstie had set down. It looked very appealing, all fresh, green, and summery, and she tried to focus on that and not Kirstie's question.

'It's essentially vodka, soda and mint. It's gorgeous, and vegan too. I've ordered for us – the waiters will come around later for more drinks and desserts. This new place is definitely a step up from the old café in the cottage, do you remember it? Worst sandwiches I ever had, those horrible sliced plastic cheese things. Urgh.'

Annie smiled, thinking back to the days when they'd sometimes call in at the café and order a picnic lunch to take away, making do with the least popular crisps and chocolate bars warmed in the sun. She glanced around the restaurant, still stalling for time as she thought about her reply to Kirstie's first comment. There was certainly a different vibe here tonight from the quiet atmosphere when she had eaten breakfast alone the other morning.

Most of the tables were full of people taking advantage of the pizza and Prosecco offer, from families with children to a few locals Annie thought she recognised, to the walkers passing through on the Dales Way and maybe staying the night somewhere nearby. The huge, light, airy space was modern and comfortable, the floor-length windows offering views of the cobbled yard and individual studios to one side and the fells stretching up to the sky on the other. Chefs were busy in the open kitchen behind them and a queue was slowly forming at the entrance as more people arrived in search of a simple supper, tempted by the smell of pizzas cooking in a wood oven.

'So is it just a social visit, then? Or is there something more, something I'm thinking you don't want to tell me?'

Annie sighed, unable to bring any humour to the wry stretching of her lips. 'You know me too well, Kirstie, even after all this time. Not social, not really. I've moved into the cottage. Molly very generously left it to me and so here I am.'

'Seriously? How brilliant for you! But why are you surprised she left it to you? It's exactly what I'd have expected. She knew how much you loved the village and how at home you were here.' Kirstie paused, looking intense. 'What about your job?'

Annie thought about the little primary school eight miles away, trying not to compare it to the lively, diverse city centre school and deputy head position she had just left. 'I've taken a supply role at Calstone for now, and I'll see how it goes. I was in Edinburgh before that.' She took a drink from her glass, waiting for the next question.

'So what's changed?' Kirstie leant back in her chair, a casual gesture that didn't match the determined expression in her eyes as she watched Annie curiously.

'My engagement, that's what. It ended, suddenly. Five days before our wedding, to be precise.' There, she had said it. Out loud, and she hadn't cried. That was an improvement, Annie thought despondently.

'No! But how...? I mean, what happened? Hell, Annie, that's bad. I'm guessing it wasn't your idea?'

'No, not my idea. Iain and I had been engaged for a year, then about a month before the wedding he went home as his dad hadn't been well and there was some doubt whether he would make the wedding.' Annie rolled her eyes, still unable to disguise the hurt clouding her face as she thought back to the spring. 'Ironic, really, when none of us actually made the wedding.'

Kirstie leant forward and squeezed Annie's hand, her eyes gentler now. 'You don't have to tell me if you don't want to.'

'No, it's fine, Kirst, honestly. I've got to be able to tell everyone some day without crying.'

The noise around them was increasing as all the tables seemed to be filled now and Annie waited as their pizzas arrived. Italian vegetarian for her and the vegan version of the same for Kirstie. Annie lowered her voice, not wanting to share their conversation with anyone beyond their table. The waiter finished adding parmesan to Annie's pizza and departed with a smile.

'Anyway, on the Monday before the wedding Iain arrived home and announced he was desperately sorry, but it was over.'

'But what had happened, so suddenly? Why would he have done that to you? He's crazy!'

Annie considered her next words, consciously removing all emotion from them before continuing. 'We'd had our difficulties in the past and I thought it was all behind us. But he was spending every weekend at his dad's to help look after him and he met up with his ex – his first love. I did know about her and that they'd been serious, but it had been over for ages and we'd been together for three years, so I really didn't think anything of it. He went to a family gathering given by a mutual friend and there she was. Apparently, they got talking, saw each other every weekend he was there and decided that it wasn't over at all and they couldn't live without each other.'

'What an absolute shit! I hope you chopped his appendages into smaller bits for him! I'm so sorry, Annie. What a vile thing for him to do.'

Annie blinked as she remembered those days, caught up in the excitement of an imminent wedding and planning a new home together. Until it had all come crashing down around her ears and she had barely recognised her own life any more.

'But at least you knew before you married him.'

'I suppose. At first, I used to wish he'd just gone through with the wedding and then left me. At least I wouldn't have had to cancel everything at the last minute, send back the gifts and try to explain without really saying anything at all. I never, ever want to have to do that again. People meant so well, but the endless sympathy and curiosity nearly drove me mad. What was it about me that made him leave? I could see them thinking it. I wasn't enough.'

'Don't ever put yourself down like that,' Kirstie hissed fiercely, startling a woman at the next table, who looked across to them in alarm, and Annie offered a wan smile in an attempt to show that all was well. 'It couldn't have been your fault that he did what he did, and you can't let yourself think it was. The perfect relationship doesn't exist, and he made a choice, Annie.' Kirstie hesitated, her look becoming gentler. 'He could easily do it to her, too, if he can walk away from three years of commitment with you in a moment.'

Annie's eyes filled with tears and her glance fell to her half-eaten plate of pizza. She toyed with a slice, her appetite fading and pushed the plate away, reaching for her glass. 'Maybe. But then maybe she really is the one. He just didn't love me enough and then he left. I get it. But it hurts like hell.'

'Do you think you still love him?'

'No, not really. I just still sort of love what we had before I lost him. But then I find myself going over our time together and wondering, was it ever real? Did he ever really love me, or was he about to settle? And if I didn't know him at all, how will I ever know anyone?'

'Oh Annie.' Kirstie jumped up and hurried around the table to hug her quickly, tightening her grip as she bent down awkwardly. Annie laughed through the tears still threatening to betray her as they separated, and Kirstie returned to her seat. They were attracting more attention than Annie wanted. She caught the eye of the woman at the next table again, who had obviously heard some of her conversation with Kirstie, and the woman's expression was laced with sympathy.

'She probably thinks we're having a lover's tiff,' Kirstie muttered. 'Bet she thinks you're trying to dump me.'

'I'd have more sense than to do that to you, Kirst. It's so good to see you, even though you make me tell you things I don't want to tell anyone.'

'Well then, call it cheap therapy,' Kirstie said with a grin, finishing off the last of her pizza. She caught the eye of a passing waiter and he came bustling over. 'My friend here would like another large glass of Prosecco. And another of those vodka minty things for me please. Don't worry, Annie, I'm not driving, I'm staying at Dad's tonight.'

Their drinks soon arrived, along with the menus. They decided against dessert and Annie slowly sipped her Prosecco, still feeling the effects of the first glass. 'That really is enough about me and my woes. I want to hear all about your brilliant career and what you've been up to.'

Kirstie grinned. 'I'm not sure it's been that brilliant. Years of study, volunteering in the Galapagos Islands, which was truly amazing. I moved to Canada for a bit, got arrested twice and divorced once.'

'What! Run that by me again! Arrested? Divorced? What have you been up to? You were always determined, Kirstie, but mostly law abiding, from what I remember.'

Kirstie laughed, thanking the waiter for clearing the remains of their meal. 'Just that, really. Did uni at East Anglia then managed to get funding for a master's at Stanford. Met a guy there who was lovely, Canadian, and we got married, which was fine until we were set to travel to South America but he got himself a job with a conservation charity in

Ontario, so that was the end of that. We were too young anyway. So I travelled a bit more, came back, did the PhD and now I'm here for another year or so.'

'You've missed out the arrests!'

'Oh that,' Kirstie said airily, still smiling. 'They were just a couple of Greenpeace marches in Toronto that got a bit lively. It was fine. Just makes travelling to the US and Canada a bit tricky now but I've no immediate plans to go back.'

'So are you single, then? Or is there someone else? I always thought you and Mark Howard had a thing for each other, back in the day. I know he's a year or two younger than us but still. All that time spent trying to annoy you had to mean something.'

'Ah, well, funny you should say that.' Kirstie's eyes twinkled, looking mischievous. 'Turns out we both did like each other then but obviously didn't do anything about it. I've been around the village more since I got this job and with Mum and everything. We bumped into each other and got chatting. We've been dating for about a month or so. I really like him.'

'Kirstie, that's wonderful! He seems so nice. I really hope it all works out for you both. He came down to the cottage and helped me move my furniture in.'

'Thanks, Annie. There's no rush. He's very firmly fixed here and I'm not so much, so we'll see. I wasn't going to tell you, given what you've shared tonight.'

'I'm glad you did.' Annie smiled at her friend, so pleased they had found one another again. 'I'm really happy for you both.'

'Coffee, before they close up?'

'Perfect. So now that you're obviously vegan, how are you managing, dating a farmer?'

'Next question!' Kirstie was merry as she replaced the menu on the table. 'Mark has so many plans for the future and how they can farm more sustainably, adopt practices that will benefit the environment. I was a bit worried when I went for

46

lunch, but you know Elizabeth, nothing fazes her. She cooked the most delicious leek and "cheesy" crumble and we all had the same. Robert didn't even know it was vegan until we'd finished.'

'Oh, I'd have loved to see his face! There's a man who's never going to give up his bacon butty or roast beef and Yorkshire pudding dinner!'

They were still laughing as a waitress came to take their order for coffee and then they fell into a comfortable silence, happy to be in one another's company again. One or two people came up to Kirstie to ask how her dad was, enquire about her plans and when he might be back. Annie only half listened, not paying too much attention until their coffee arrived and they were alone once again.

'How's Ross?' she asked Kirstie idly, remembering her friend's handsome older brother who had set out for university before they had left school. 'I bumped into him once when I was visiting Molly, but I haven't seen him in ages.'

'Settled in London with a lovely wife called Stella and busy being an art director designing book covers for famous authors.' Kirstie gave Annie a sideways look. 'Did you and he…? I always wondered but he would never say, and you just used to look loopy whenever he was around.'

Annie smiled knowingly. She had never forgotten her first serious crush, nor that surprisingly outstanding first kiss when she was fifteen and the few weeks of fooling around that had followed a couple of years later when Kirstie had been travelling around Thailand. Deep brown eyes, thoughtful, clever, funny. She had liked him very much at the time, but they had both been ready to move on when the summer was over.

'I knew it!' A phone in Kirstie's bag was ringing and she ignored it, raising her eyes to Annie. 'You never said!' The phone stopped and then started again a moment later.

'Maybe you should answer it. Someone wants to get hold of you.'

'I suppose I had better check, in case it's anything to do with Dad. Sorry. We can come back to you and Ross some other time.' Kirstie pulled the phone from her bag with a grin, scanning it quickly, and Annie saw her frown as she listened to a voice message.

'Is everything all right?'

'It was Mark. His grandad is in the early stages of dementia and he's wandered off. Mark was just asking if I'd seen anything. If you don't mind, I think I should go and help. He and Robert are out looking.'

'Of course you should.' Annie was already standing and swinging her bag over her shoulder, their coffee abandoned. 'Would you like me to come with you? I could help too if they'd like more people.'

'Oh would you, Annie, that'd be great. You know the area as well as anyone, and more hands and all that. I'll call him now and tell him we'll go straight to the farm.'

They weaved their way through the scattered tables and emerged in the courtyard, darkness already settling on the top of the fells. Lights were on in most of the studios, staying open late and hoping for extra customers from the restaurant. People were slowly wandering around or sitting in the courtyard with drinks and chatting quietly at tables. She and Kirstie crossed into the lane and Kirstie was on the phone until the signal packed up as they rushed through the village, the sound of the river scurrying beside them. Within a few minutes, they had reached the Howards' farm and Annie paused.

'I'll be back in a sec.' She pointed to the flat ballet pumps she was wearing below cropped jeans. 'These are no good for walking.'

Kirstie raised a hand as she turned into the yard and Annie hurried back to the cottage, changed her flats for walking boots, grabbed a waterproof coat and raced back to the farm. When she opened the kitchen door and stepped inside, she was surprised to see both Robert and Mark. One look at their expressions told her they hadn't found Mark's grandad yet. Everyone had fallen silent as they glanced at her with hope, and their faces fell again when they realised who it was.

'I'm still not sure we need to call out t'whole bloomin' fell rescue,' Robert said stubbornly, looking at Elizabeth. 'He's done it before and always come back. And he knows these fells better than any of us ever will.'

'Yes, but he's never gone missing at night before! For heaven's sake, Robert.' Elizabeth practically shouted at her husband as she spun away in frustration. 'I know you don't like to hear it but he's not quite as good as he was. I'm going to ring Jon and ask him what he thinks. And we both know what he'll say.'

'Me and Kirstie will head up to Ellerby.' Mark glanced at Kirstie and she quickly agreed. 'No point sitting around here, it's getting on. He used to like it up there, he could have just gone for a wander and walked too far. We'll take Fan with us – she's quickest of the dogs, and sharp. Probably worth checking along the river again, too.'

'Annie, would you mind waiting while I ring Jon, please? I don't think there's much point in all of us heading out again without a proper plan and I'd rather wait and see what Jon suggests.'

Annie nodded, hovering at the table and Robert looked at her as he rolled his eyes and pulled out a chair. He offered one to Annie too, but she shook her head as the door banged behind Mark and Kirstie and they disappeared. Elizabeth spoke for only a minute or two and then she ended the call and looked at Robert.

'Jon's calling it in now and then he'll come straight here. We need them, Robert. Your dad could be anywhere.'

'Aye, and he could be sound asleep in t'barn for all we know.'

Annie saw the look of concern that flashed across his face, belying his words and he sighed as he stood up, running a hand through his wild, white hair. Elizabeth took the kettle from the Aga to make tea, but they both refused it and then a few minutes later the kitchen door burst open. Annie spun around, her heart bouncing as she saw Jon head into the room, already wearing his bright fell rescue kit, and Elizabeth hurried over to meet him, touching his arm with gratitude.

'They're on their way out,' he said immediately, nodding at Robert and then giving Elizabeth a sympathetic look as she thanked him. 'I'm not going as part of the team, but I'll stay in touch and we can hopefully cover more ground and support them.' He glanced around the room, his eyes falling on Annie standing by the table, and she saw them widen in surprise. A quick smile lifted the corners of his mouth as pleasure briefly lit his expression, and she felt warmed by the simple and intimate gesture. He became brisk once again as he listened to his radio and organised where the family should search, starting with the yard. Elizabeth was to remain at home, in case Robert's father did return.

'What about me?' Annie looked at Jon, a question in her eyes as she slid her waterproof coat on. 'I'm going out too. Where shall I go?'

'What about t'river again,' Robert suggested, looking at Jon for confirmation. 'We didn't go that far but it'd be worth going down to Beck Gill at least. With team out on t'fells I think they'll manage if we stay down here.'

'Fine,' Jon said, nodding and already turning to the door. 'But not alone, Annie. I'm coming with you.'

Elizabeth handed her a torch and Annie started to protest as she followed Jon into the yard, suggesting that he would surely be better use on the fells, but Jon was having none of it. He turned and caught her shoulders, gently but firmly, stilling her breath for a second.

'I'm in charge here,' he told her in an exasperated tone. 'There might be a different team leading out there and you might have once known the village like the back of your hand but if you're going out, then you're going out with me. First rule of rescue, no one goes alone. Got it?'

'Fine.' She didn't try to disguise the huffiness in her tone as his hands fell away from her, only the note of pleasure that they were going out together, reminding herself of the reason for it. They strode through the yard, Annie half running to keep up, and out into the lane, and the pace didn't change as they reached the high street. Lights were flaring into life as people settled down for the evening, unaware of the drama taking place outside their doors.

'Do you think he'll be okay?' Annie looked sideways at Jon, having to tilt her head to meet his eyes when they turned to her. She saw the quick hesitation in his before he replied.

'I hope so. But he's vulnerable and the longer he stays out the more trouble he'll be in.'

'Have you had to search for him before?'

'No. He likes to walk and although he's a bit more rambling, or confused now, he's generally kept himself out of trouble and stayed near the village, according to Robert. I don't think he's too worried, to be honest.'

They passed The Courtyard, closed now, and dropped down onto a bridle path beside the water. Jon turned to face her, raising his voice over the rushing water.

'Stay on this side of the river, Annie, I'm going to cross over. Keep looking for anything he might be using for shelter or a likely place to have fallen in. It's not that deep but he wouldn't last long if he's slipped and knocked himself unconscious. His name's Bill, by the way.' Jon lightened his words with a quick smile. 'Be careful, okay? Don't put yourself at risk.'

Jon set off first, crossing the river at a footbridge just ahead of her. They walked on, not too fast, not too slow, trudging carefully alongside both banks as they hunted through the fading light, their torches flashing through the dusk. Jon had given her the easier path as she saw him pushing his way through low-hanging branches and forging a track of sorts through the weeds. It was dirty, muddy work and Annie skidded over a couple of times, scrambling back to her feet in the wet undergrowth, stinging her hand on a clump of nettles she hadn't spotted and already feeling the scratch of rough stems on her face. They had been searching for a good twenty minutes when he called across the water to stop looking. He picked up his radio, listening carefully, and shouted over to her.

'They've found him. They're bringing him straight down to an ambulance.'

She sighed with relief, raising a hand to show she'd understood, and they began the return journey, the path slightly easier this time, worn down by their stomping. She reached the footbridge first, waiting for Jon, and he joined her a few moments later. She questioned him about Bill immediately, knowing how worried Elizabeth was, and no doubt Robert too underneath his bluster.

'Not sure. He's alive but injured. Could be a broken ankle at least but I don't want to say too much until we know there's nothing even more serious. He'll almost certainly be hypothermic too.'

'Where was he?'

Jon rolled his eyes, looking at her through the gloom. 'Not that far away, just beneath Ellerby Moor, as Mark suggested.' He paused, bending his head to stare more closely. 'Hey, are you okay?' He raised his torch, shining it on her face below her eyes. 'You've been scratched.' He reached out, gently holding her jaw with warm fingers for a few seconds, tilting her head to get a better look at the ugly slash already stinging her face. His torch swept down her body as he let her go and Annie was horribly conscious of the mud clinging to her legs between her boots and her cropped, filthy jeans and the redness creeping over her face. She tugged at the leaves trapped in her hair with muddied and stinging hands. 'Are there any others?'

'Don't think so,' she said casually, shrugging off his concern. 'I'm fine, nothing that hasn't happened before. I'm more worried about how I'm going to get these boots off with the amount of mud that's inside them.' The gentleness in the blue depths of his eyes as he examined her and the distracting touch of his long fingers on her face had moved her more than she wanted to show.

Jon grinned, glancing wryly at his own clothes in a similar state. 'Happy to help.' Her raised eyebrows told him she could manage just fine. 'Keep an eye on that scratch. Come on, let's get back to the farm and clean up and let them know about Bill. For now, at least, it's good news.'

Chapter Six

By Sunday evening Annie was feeling cooped up and surprisingly lonely in the cottage. She still hadn't begun her schoolwork and the peace she had longed for was altering into an unexpected isolation, seeping through every part of the house and driving her cherished memories further away. When she had ventured into the village on Saturday afternoon, so many people had stopped to welcome her that she realised she simply couldn't wander around unnoticed. Outside the pub she'd bumped into Charlie Stewart, the vicar, and knew immediately she was going to like him. He was friendly and younger than she'd expected, in his early thirties, and with unexpectedly marvellous legs revealed by navy blue shorts. She'd heard through Elizabeth that Thorndale was his first parish after curacy, having given up a promising career as a professional rugby player, and Annie had been firmly intrigued.

She was cross with herself for still thinking about Jon, and she had tried to push him from her mind. But it wasn't easy, especially after a lorry had turned up on Saturday morning and carefully deposited its load of fuel into the tank in her garden. Each time Annie closed her eyes she could see his inviting expression when he looked at her, or how his eyes would darken without explanation and leave her afraid of trying to decipher their meaning. After the search party had returned on Friday evening, they'd all congregated in the Howards' kitchen for hot drinks and a debrief. Robert had gone in the ambulance with his dad and Elizabeth had followed later in the car, and the initial news about Bill had been encouraging. Jon had walked back to the cottage with Annie and his 'good night' had been pensive when they had eventually parted.

She had managed to get the Rayburn going again and was eating an early supper, sitting outside on the tatty old bench in the back garden. Despite the lotion she had slathered on, she was certain she was beginning to freckle under the warmth of the evening sun on her pale skin. She had never minded her colouring, inherited from her father, and over the years her hair had gradually changed from dark red to a rich auburn. She thought about the past, remembering the times she had sat in this very spot with Molly on countless summer evenings and a slowly growing pleasure began to emerge at living in this house. Birds were calling in the evening light before dusk arrived to claim their silence, flapping through the hedge at the boundary of the garden.

She heard the church bells ringing for evensong, smiling as the familiar call to worship echoed through the village. Molly had insisted on sending her to Sunday school, even though she didn't often attend the services herself, and Annie wondered why it had become more difficult to go to church once she had left Thorndale, despite the certain belief in God that she always carried with her. She had resented it then, furious to forego her freedom while Kirstie had been able to race off on adventures without her. Annie felt sure that Charlie Stewart's services would be different from those she remembered and decided to go and find out for herself. As she left the house, she knew the village would be quieter now as the day visitors began to return home, the weekend ending all too soon.

On the green beside the high street the teenage girl from the post office was sitting with a friend and Annie offered her a smile when their eyes met. The girl's cropped blonde and black hair framed her face, emphasising its delicate shape, and she gave Annie a fleeting smile in return before turning her glance back to her phone. Annie followed the narrow, shadowy lane towards the church, feeling cooler as the sunlight disappeared behind a canopy of leaves. The old trees and tidy hawthorn hedge surrounding the church disguised stony paths swirling around the building to the graveyard, edged with stout shrubs and vibrant summer plants. A wide lawn separated the church from the village hall next door, and she noticed that the hall had been modernised with new windows and a smart wooden veranda. Annie heard the bells again and looked to the church. The big wooden door had opened, and people were spilling out onto the path between a pair of ancient yew trees, the noise increasing in the evening light. Surprised, she glanced at her watch. She was too late. The service was over and when she saw Charlie appear to bid everyone good night, she decided to go home.

Her stomach disappeared into a spin as Jon emerged, talking animatedly to an older woman alongside him. Memories of his finding her in the garden and of searching for Bill together just a couple of days ago tumbled into her mind and she hastened away beyond the churchyard, hoping to be out of sight before he saw her.

'Annie! Hey, wait!'

Jon's long stride carried him to her in moments and she finally paused as he reached her. She stilled as she looked at him, seeing his expressing becoming more intimate as his eyes met hers, and it was impossible not to notice how dark grey jeans with a navy blazer over a white T-shirt casually emphasised his broad shoulders. His face was shadowy with stubble again and she could all too easily imagine reaching out to trace the roughness with her fingertips. She clenched her hands tightly, trying to send the tantalising thoughts away.

'How are you?' he asked, standing together in the lane. Somebody passed by, calling good night and Jon dragged his eyes away from her long enough to give a quick reply to the greeting.

'Fine, thank you.' She knew her voice was cooler than her face and wished it were the other way around. She cleared her throat in an attempt to sound more casual. 'You?'

'Good, thanks. Were you in church? I didn't see you.'

Her smile was rueful as she began to relax. 'No. I heard the bells and thought the service was just starting, I hadn't realised the time. I met Charlie yesterday. He seems really lovely and I thought it might be nice to see him in action.'

Jon grinned. 'I hope you'll enjoy it. He has lots of strengths and leading worship is just one of them. Have you met Sam, his wife, yet?' A car was approaching so they moved to the side of the lane, drawing closer together until it had passed by and then she sidled away, ridiculously unnerved by the brief feel of his arm.

'No. Charlie mentioned that she would probably come over and say hello. I think we're a similar age.'

'I'm sure you'll like her. She's a breath of fresh air for the communities here, and very sincere underneath all her mischief and fun.' Jon paused. 'May I walk home with you?'

Surprised, Annie nodded before she could come up with a reasonable excuse. They soon reached the high street, skirting the edge of the green. He followed her onto the bridge across the river and they slowly halted, pausing side by side to look down at the water rushing below. She was reminded of their first meeting on the green and saw the same recognition in his eyes, amused now, when she tipped her head sideways to glance at him, the sharp citrus scent of his cologne drifting across to her. She knew she was struggling to disguise the way Jon caused her senses to catapult into chaos whenever she saw him, and that her responses to him were defensive and a little impolite, and tried to relax.

'Have you heard any more news about Bill?' Annie kept her tone deliberately neutral. 'Elizabeth says he's coming home tomorrow.'

'Only that he was very lucky, and the ankle is sprained, not broken. They put him on a drip as he was dehydrated but other than that he was fine once he'd warmed up. But Robert was right: he hadn't gone too far and was on his way home again when he slipped. He was quite clear about where he'd been and what he was doing so that will help them to worry a bit less, I guess. That he hadn't just wandered off and was oblivious to everything.'

'I'm so glad it wasn't worse.'

'Absolutely.' Jon's arms were resting on the bridge as he stared at the river again. 'So did you order more oil for the Rayburn?'

She heard the grin in his voice and her breath caught, wondering if he was remembering, like her, everything that had happened since they met, each moment imprinted in her mind. 'Yes thanks, it came on Saturday. And I just wanted to thank you again for sorting out the other stuff. It was really kind of you to spend the time.' She recalled his comment about working for a mission and was beginning to believe nothing he could tell her would surprise her any more. But when Jon spoke next, she was astonished and speechless all over again.

'Sure.' He turned slowly until he was facing her, one elbow still propped on the bridge. 'If you need anything else, places to park, a bit of plumbing, the occasional rescue, give me a call. I'll make sure I'm available.'

Taken aback by his directness and flirtatious comments, Annie's lips parted, her pulse soaring as he watched her, a slow grin deepening the lines at his eyes and around his mouth.

'Annie,' he began again, becoming more serious as he continued to watch her. He straightened up until he was facing her properly, his eyes holding hers. 'Do you think you—'

'Jon, darling!'

The sudden shriek startled them both and Annie spun around, aware of Jon straightening up. A woman was quickly heading towards them, waving breezily. She seemed familiar and Annie was puzzled by the sense of recollection as she approached the bridge. Jon sighed impatiently. The look the woman gave him was affectionate and something else more inviting. When she glanced across to Annie her beautiful eyes became coolly curious for a moment before she returned her attention to Jon.

'I'm sorry I didn't make evensong, darling,' she murmured, dropping a quick hand on Jon's arm as she sidled past Annie to hover between them. 'Shooting went on much longer than expected, you know what it's like, and I simply couldn't get away in time. I hope you didn't miss me.'

Annie had an abrupt and terrible thought then, that this woman might be his partner or girlfriend and his earlier, flirty comments suddenly seemed wholly inappropriate. It was a bitter reminder of why she was in Thorndale and she gave Jon a scathing look when his eyes sought hers across the woman in between them. The woman turned her head when she saw that Jon's attention had wandered and briefly appraised Annie once again as Annie returned the arctic gaze.

'Evening, Sarah.' Jon's smile was bland now and Annie glanced up at him, surprised. She saw the noncommittal way he greeted the woman, his eyes altered from the intimacy of a few moments ago into casual friendliness. 'Annie, let me introduce you to Sarah Holland. She has recently left London and bought a house in the village. Sarah, this is Annie Armstrong, who's just moved into Willow Cottage. It used to belong to her godmother.'

Annie politely held out her hand and Sarah's fingers felt as cool as her eyes against Annie's warm skin. She tried not to mind about her sun-kissed face and curling hair tumbling down her back as she admired Sarah's stylish silk blouse, worn over skinny white jeans and a pair of wedge sandals that didn't look as though they'd come from Primark. Taller than Annie, Sarah's straight, caramel-blonde hair was as immaculate as her perfectly applied make-up. Elegant, toned arms were the colour of pale conkers, and Annie knew instinctively they weren't going to like one another. Sarah could easily pass for a woman in her late twenties, but up close tiny lines around her eyes and mouth were not completely disguised. Annie felt certain her smooth expression was not entirely natural as Sarah seemed to be trying to defy the reality of her mid-thirties.

'I hope you're going to do something about the state of the garden, Annie.' Sarah's tone was offhand as she glanced at Annie and then deliberately looked beyond her, presumably in search of something more interesting. 'It's letting the entire community down, especially as the judging for Best-Kept Dales Village is about to commence. Don't you think so, Jon? Aren't you on the judging panel? I've just volunteered my services. I thought a few little Instagram shots of cute cottages and quaint gardens would be rather adorable.'

Sarah gave her a quick, frozen smile before she looked at Jon and her eyes became flirty again as Annie tried to glare back. Before she could think up a decent reply, Sarah was batting her long, false eyelashes at him with such vigour that Annie wanted to laugh.

'I am not.' Jon laughed, stuffing his hands in his jeans pocket and regarding Sarah evenly. 'I've got enough to do without getting roped into anything else. But you should definitely do it, Sarah. I'm sure they'd love to have you.'

'Well, we'll see,' she said sweetly. 'I have to be so careful and not be seen to support one thing over another.'

'Anyway, from what I knew of Molly she wasn't into tidy gardens and perfect lawns, isn't that right, Annie? Didn't she prefer a more natural look? I'm sure the committee can overlook a few weeds if they're beneficial to wildlife.'

Annie opened her mouth to reply that formal gardens had indeed never been Molly's style, when, not to be deterred, Sarah crashed on. 'You haven't forgotten about our date on Friday, have you, darling?' She tucked a beautifully manicured hand through Jon's arm, sliding a quick glance in Annie's direction to be sure she caught the implication of intimacy. The gesture seemed to take Jon by surprise and he looked down at Sarah, puzzled. To Annie's delight he dropped Sarah back down to earth again when he answered, his dark brows furrowed in confusion.

'I thought you were having a housewarming party. I don't remember anything else.'

Sarah's hand slipped from his arm as she tried to wave off his reply. 'Just us, darling, and a very few friends from work, and of course my new neighbours,' she said merrily, seemingly unperturbed by his remark. She tossed her head, allowing her gorgeous hair to fall across one eye. 'It's all very last minute and casual.'

Jon nodded, and the brief glance he gave Annie was worth the sharp one which followed from Sarah. 'In that case would you mind if Annie joined us, as she hasn't been in the village very long?' he asked Sarah pleasantly, apparently confident of her agreement. 'It would be a great way for her to meet a few people. I know how you like to encourage community fellowship.'

Annie was dying to laugh as Sarah struggled to keep a look of horror from her face. Despite her determination not to go to the party, Annie thought it would almost be worth turning up just to irritate this silly woman, who clearly felt they were in competition for Jon. Annie had no intention of telling Sarah it wasn't so.

Sarah shrugged, her flirtatious manner finally dissolving as she replied grudgingly. 'I'm not sure.' She glared at Annie, as though daring her to accept the invitation. 'It's rather late to alter the numbers.'

Annie was rapidly growing tired of being made to feel like a very unwelcome third wheel by Sarah and couldn't think of anything worse than having to spend time at her party. The last thing she wanted was to waste an evening quarrelling over a man she had zero plans to get involved with in the first place. As far as she was concerned, Sarah was welcome to Jon. But just the thought of them together left her feeling strangely upset, and she replied more sharply than she intended, 'I'm very busy with work and doubt I'll be able to make it.'

Jon seemed not to notice the frostiness around him as he looked at Annie. 'Oh.' His eyes widened in surprise. 'Couldn't you take an evening off?'

Annie wished she'd taken this evening off as well and had stayed in the now-appealing solitude of her little cottage. She was beginning to feel as though she were stuck in a ridiculous pantomime as they hovered on the bridge debating her work commitments. Sarah managed a relieved smile at Annie as she relaxed, confident once again of Jon's company without Annie's. 'There you are then, all settled,' she said with satisfaction. But Sarah still didn't have Jon's attention as he frowned at Annie and Annie glowered back at him, thoroughly fed up with the absurdity of the entire conversation.

'You really should come,' he said almost pleadingly. In the end, flustered and feeling wrong-footed, she said that perhaps work could wait, and she might be able to make it after all. Her furtive glance at Sarah was rewarded as the older woman gave Jon a filthy look. He missed Sarah's angry stare as he smiled at Annie.

'Seven thirty for eight on Friday, then,' Sarah snapped as she looked Annie up and down. She tossed her head again, sending the caramel hair flying. 'It's only casual, Annie. Please don't feel as though you need to make a special effort to look nice.' Sarah turned and marched away, barely managing to throw out a goodbye and clearly dismayed by the change to her carefully laid plans.

Jon grinned as Annie scowled next to him, still feeling the heat of Sarah's critical glance at her skinny jeans and pretty Zara top. She was astonished he seemed so oblivious of the tensions he had unleashed, but Annie realised he was pleased she had agreed to come. They were alone once more and she blinked, wondering what he'd been about to ask her before Sarah had appeared.

Breaking the sudden silence, a mobile phone began to ring. He dragged it out of his blazer pocket with an irritated frown, flicking a glance of apology towards her as he answered. She waved a hand in a quick farewell as he spoke quietly and began to make her way home, not allowing him the opportunity to say anything further.

With her back towards him, Annie couldn't see him watching her, but she knew that he was all the same. She hadn't thought to leave any lights on, and wished now she would find Molly's welcoming presence and ready cup of cocoa waiting when she reached the cottage so they could chat about what had just happened, instead of gloom filtering through the windows and dragging the coming darkness with it.

Chapter Seven

Annie spent most of Monday cleaning the cottage and famil-
iarising herself with the Rayburn so she would be able to cook
again properly, still irritated by her reluctant acceptance of the
forced invitation to Sarah Holland's party and trying to think
of a good excuse to duck out. But it wasn't only that. She was
perturbed, too, by Jon's comments to her last night and the
suggestion that he would have said even more had they not
been interrupted.

Thinking of Jon, an idea came to her as she worked and
after a bath, she walked down to the post office to collect
some shopping. Outside, distracted by the notice about the
Best-Kept Dales Village' competition and reminded of Sarah
once again, she flinched when someone touched her shoulder.
She spun around and looked into the smiling face of a woman
around her age standing nearby, a striped handbag slung across
her body.

'I'm sorry, I didn't mean to make you jump,' the woman
said cheerfully, pushing sunglasses into her hair to reveal warm
brown eyes crinkled at the corners. 'Just a wild guess, but are
you Annie?'

Surprised, Annie's smile was puzzled as she moved away
from the noticeboard to let a nearby couple get a better look.
'Yes, I am. How did you know?'

The woman grinned, her expression open and warm. 'I
think you've met my husband, Charlie, the vicar. He told me
that you're very pretty with dark red hair and I thought it must
be you. I'm Sam Stewart.'

'That's very kind of him,' Annie replied, absurdly pleased by the compliment. 'I've been looking forward to meeting you.'

'Likewise,' Sam said as she stuck out her arm. They both laughed as they shook hands, the formalities over. Sam seemed so friendly, and Annie realised that Sam shared Charlie's warmth and ease with people and knew at once that she would like her. Sam's short blonde hair was cut into a sharp bob and she was not quite as tall as Annie, an hourglass figure perfectly emphasising her subtle curves. She had several rings in each ear and a stud in her nose, and Annie spotted a tattoo on the inside of one wrist.

'Have you got time for a coffee?' Sam asked, slipping a hand to her back, and rubbing gently as she pulled a face. 'I could really do with a sit down.'

Annie noticed the bump beneath Sam's lavender summer dress for the first time, above a pair of bright red canvas Doc Martens. 'That'd be lovely. You're very welcome to come back to the cottage with me but it's a bit of a mess, I've been cleaning all morning and not quite finished.'

Sam shook her head. 'Another time,' she said merrily. 'Let's go to The Courtyard instead. I know it's horribly busy with the school holidays, but they do fantastic decaf lattes and we won't have to do the washing up.'

Annie agreed. They walked along the high street side by side and, once they reached The Courtyard, quickly managed to find a small table for two, jammed into a corner overlooking the children's playground beyond the window. Parents strolled inside to choose ice cream and enjoy a quiet moment while their children cavorted within sight. Paintings by local artists hung on the wall and Annie spotted some handmade jewellery that she planned to inspect more closely. She and Sam ordered lattes and homemade scones after Sam promised her that the scones were without equal.

'Someone in the village bakes them,' Sam whispered, leaning forwards with a mischievous glint in her eye. 'The recipe has supposedly been handed down over generations and is top secret, locked in a safe somewhere. Charlie reckons they're from Asda. He's had so many cricket teas over the years and thinks he's an expert.'

Annie hurriedly swallowed her mouthful of coffee, trying not to choke as they started to laugh again. They fell silent as the scones arrived and she dropped a dollop of clotted cream on top of thick strawberry jam, closing her eyes as she bit into the luscious sweetness. Sam had been right; the scones were superb.

'When's your baby due?' Annie asked her politely, prizing the words out. Sam was the first person expecting a baby she'd met since the end of her engagement and Annie was trying not to be reminded of the discussions she and Iain had had about starting their own family, the familiar pain squeezing her heart.

'First week in September,' Sam answered, wriggling on her narrow seat until she found a more comfortable position. 'We're so excited, although I'm slightly nervous about the nights as I really love my sleep.' She pulled a face, still smiling. 'My maternity leave has already started as I teach drama at the college in town and we've just broken up for the summer. The baby is due only a few days after I would normally be back at work, and of course, I could be early. Or late.'

'You look wonderful,' Annie told her truthfully, a note of wistfulness in her voice. If it was true about blooming in pregnancy then Sam was a perfect example, with clear skin and glossy hair framing bright and intelligent eyes. Annie blinked away her sudden sadness, refusing to let it spoil their time together.

Clearly pleased, Sam pushed her plate away, only crumbs left amongst a blob of jam. 'Thank you, it's really nice of you to say so. But I'd love to hear about you, Annie. I won't ask how you're settling in because you've probably had that from everyone else. Tell me about your job, I've heard that you're a teacher too?'

Annie marvelled at the invisible way information seemed to travel through the village. Although she was certain that Elizabeth wouldn't gossip about her, she wondered how everybody else seemed to know so much about her so soon. She and Sam nattered easily together as she talked of her new school and the move into the cottage, although Annie didn't explain her reasons for returning to Thorndale. That would come later, she decided, unless the village grapevine got there first. Sam chatted about who was who, in between greeting people cheerfully whenever they stopped at the table to say hello. She introduced Annie to everyone and replied patiently when asked questions about Charlie, the next church service or seemingly endless parish business. Eventually they were alone again, their coffee finished, and Annie noticed how heavy Sam's eyes had become.

'Sorry.' Sam covered a yawn with her fingers. 'I'm getting very lazy and napping most afternoons. If you don't mind, I think I'll go home. Those scones always have a soporific effect on me!' Outside in the warm sunshine she turned to Annie. 'It was so lovely to meet you properly, I really hope we'll be good friends. I'd love to come and see how you're getting on with the cottage – it always seemed so sad, standing empty all that time.'

'I'd really like that too.' Annie's eyes fluttered past Sam to a tall, dark-haired man she had spotted beyond the green, and her heart thumped. But it wasn't Jon and she hurriedly transferred her attention back to Sam, amazed how easily she had been side-tracked by the mere suggestion of him. 'I'm around most days. Come whenever you like.' They said goodbye and Annie returned to the house with her shopping, thrilled by the unexpected encounter with Sam and hopeful that a new friendship had indeed begun.

She searched through Molly's old cookery books until she found the recipe she wanted and assembled the ingredients. Before long, a cake was rising gently in the main oven and she started to mix the frosting together. When the cake was cooled and topped, she went upstairs to change, stepping into a vintage, long green skirt and pale pink cardigan. Anticipation was dancing as she returned to the village, holding her cake tin, and hoping she wasn't about to make a fool of herself. She'd heard through Elizabeth that the fell rescue members met every other Monday evening for training, and she was hoping to catch them at their HQ opposite the green. The barn doors were open when she arrived and she peered inside, hearing noise from the back.

'Hello? May I come in?'

She had absolutely no idea if Jon was there or not, trying not to hope too much that he was and then a man with cropped steel-grey hair approached her, dressed in walking clothes and carrying a pair of ropes attached to a harness.

'How can I help you?' The man offered her a friendly smile and she saw his eyes drop curiously to the tin in her hand.

'Hi, I'm sorry to bother you. There was a bit of confusion the other day when I parked outside the entrance by mistake, so I thought I would bring this to apologise. I didn't mean to cause a problem. It's just a banana cake with cream cheese frosting.' Annie lifted the lid off the tin to show him, smiling as the man's eyes lit up.

'That's very good of you,' he said appreciatively, tossing the harness onto a desk and taking the tin from Annie. 'You're the lass with the white Mini, are you? I heard about that.'

Annie rolled her eyes, feeling foolish, and he laughed.

'Don't worry, you're not the first and I don't suppose you'll be the last. But I think you're the first one who's ever bothered to bring us cake.'

'I thought it was the least I could do,' she replied, glancing casually around the room. Radios were stacked on a shelf and chairs were grouped around a couple of desks. A whiteboard was fixed to a wall, opposite a huge OS map of the area and Annie saw monitors and large backpacks in several different colours lined up on the floor. An A4 poster, stuck casually to a wall, was advertising the association's family fun and open day in a couple of weeks.

'Shame it's only me here tonight, lass. I'm just sorting out equipment, some of the others have gone over to Clapham to train with them. But I'll definitely let them know about you and they can call in for a piece of this if there's anything left. Thank you.' He rattled the tin gently.

'Okay, great thanks.' Annie didn't want her disappointment to show and gave him a bright smile. 'You're very welcome, I hope you enjoy it. I'll pop back sometime to collect the tin.' She turned around and the man followed her outside into the warm summer evening, thanking her again as she set off across the green. She was soon back at the cottage, relief already replacing disappointment that she hadn't bumped into Jon.

She escaped the village on Tuesday for the nearby town, spending time trying to choose wallpaper and staring longingly at modern power showers, thinking of the old-fashioned bath back at the cottage. She hated the idea of stripping away more of Molly's life but knew that it had to be done eventually.

While she was in town, Annie gave into temptation to look through some of the clothes stores in case she stumbled across something fabulous for the party on Friday. She knew it wasn't because of Sarah that she wanted to make the effort. Just for the evening Annie wanted to look amazing. She finally found the dress she'd been subconsciously seeking and, as she paid for it and the new shoes as well, tried to convince herself that Jon probably wouldn't notice, even though she knew she was wrong.

Once her shopping was done, she sat down in a café and logged into the Wi-Fi to enjoy a coffee while she caught up with friends and read her emails. She had quite a few to get through. Kirstie had texted to say she was going away on a course for a few days and would be in touch when she got back. Annie opened WhatsApp and her heart did that silly flip again when she saw Jon's name. She clicked on the message at once and laughed in astonishment, her coffee cup slithering precariously back onto the table.

> Nice try, Armstrong, but you don't get off that easily. I don't like cake

She fired off her reply before she could properly consider her words.

> What's the matter with you? Everyone likes cake

She followed it with a rolling eyes emoji and the reply came back moments later.

> Not me. Is there anything else on offer?

> Such as?

> Surprise me

Heart racing and lips twitching, Annie switched to her emails. This was flirting, absolutely, definitely, and she would be on dangerous ground indeed if she continued with it. But unable to dislodge Jon from her mind, she was still smiling as she made her way home, dreaming up ways to surprise him and wondering if she dared. She was unloading her shopping when she heard a car approaching from the Howards' farm and looked up. She didn't recognise the dark blue Land Rover until Jon jumped out, and her stomach toppled to her knees as she met his eyes, their message exchange flashing through her mind again.

'Let me help you,' he called, banging the car door behind him, and heading towards her. He took the bags from her. 'Where do you want them?'

'Kitchen please,' Annie requested as she grabbed the rest and followed him inside. She hoped he hadn't spotted her new dress carefully folded inside its tissue wrapping or, worse, the peach satin underwear next to it. He dumped the shopping on the table and she added hers to the pile, deftly separating food from everything else.

'Coffee?' She made the request sound completely casual as she pointed to a chair.

'Sure, thanks.' Jon pulled the chair out and Annie switched on the Nespresso as he sat down. 'I saw you coming home as I was leaving the farm. Elizabeth sometimes helps with the cooking at the youth centre and I called to see if she can step in on Thursday.'

'And can she?' Annie raised her voice over the noise of the machine. She'd found the espresso cups now and pushed one across to him, and he thanked her.

'Not this time, they've got friends coming to stay for a long weekend.'

'I see.' The offer to help him was on the tip of her tongue. She loved cooking, and her summer spent au pairing in Italy for an extended family had left her undaunted by large numbers. But spending more time with a man who looked like he did, with those extraordinary blue eyes she was finding difficult to resist, was the opposite of everything she had arrived in Thorndale to do.

'Thought it was worth a try before our administrator calls an agency.'

'I could help, perhaps, if that's any use to you?' Annie joined him at the table with her own coffee, the willingness to help him dashing away the caution as his surprised glance landed on hers. 'You helped me the other day, it's only fair.'

'Really?' Jon didn't bother to disguise his pleasure, his coffee already gone. 'Are you sure? There'll be around a dozen people, maybe more. Are you okay with that?'

'Absolutely. I used to cook for at least ten every day when I was au pairing.'

He grinned at her, and she knew he was pleased. She promised to email him with the safeguarding details he needed, and he arranged to collect her around ten on Thursday morning. He also explained that she would only need to cook the early evening meal for the children and support staff, and they said goodbye. Reality kicked in then and she tried not to feel daunted by the prospect.

She had a proper day off on Wednesday, promising herself she wouldn't think about school, the cottage or Jon. The first two were easy as she wandered around Leeds trying to get acquainted with a new city, but she found the third almost impossible and it frightened her. She knew she had been faltering since the loss of her relationship with Iain, and that her sorrow had become a safety barrier, a reason to hover in the past instead of looking forward, protection against anything threatening to hurt her once again.

She had been utterly unable to forget Iain's final words when he'd tried to explain to her what he still felt for the woman he realised he had always loved and who would be his future, rather than Annie. He'd snatched away the life she thought she had waiting for her, and left her sprawling behind him, lost and uncertain, and desperate not to risk such a thing again.

But as she ate lunch alone in a noisy little sushi restaurant, she knew she had finally met someone who could tilt her carefully laid foundations, which sent thrills of both excitement and terror through her. She was nervous about seeing Jon tomorrow, almost wishing she could change her mind. But she knew she wouldn't change her mind and it was partly because she didn't want to let him down. She resolved instead to be sensible, and promised herself after Sarah's party on Friday she would try to keep her distance from him.

Chapter Eight

Being sensible flew right out of the window when Jon arrived promptly the next day looking as effortlessly handsome as always. Annie was casually dressed in jeans and a pale green shirt, and he waited at the gate while she grabbed her bag and locked the cottage.

'Hi,' he called, and she felt ridiculously absurd as her knees trembled when his eyes found hers. 'How are you?'

'Fine, thank you.' She smiled, hoping it didn't reflect the warmth on her skin whenever he looked at her. It was hard to ignore the frank expression of interest in his eyes or how his height emphasised the implied strength. He held the car door open and slammed it behind her once she was settled in her seat. He was beside her moments later, and she tried not to look at the width of his thighs or his big, capable hands casually rolling the steering wheel as he drove off.

'I really appreciate you helping out, I know you're busy.' He glanced at her and she hummed. She kept her eyes on the road ahead as though she were the one in control of the powerful car. 'I hope you'll like the centre. We have a great team.'

'How long has it been open?' She glanced at Jon long enough to notice the top two buttons of his light blue polo shirt were undone as ever.

'Nearly three years. One of the estate's farms became vacant when a tenant died so we converted the house and outbuildings and another tenant took on the land. We mostly run residential adventure programmes for schools and youth groups, or sometimes churches or specialist care homes, often children with social and behavioural difficulties. All the activities are aimed at positive relationship building and teaching them new skills and responsibilities within groups. We work in partnership with a centre in Wales, and we occasionally take a few corporate groups for leadership training or team building.'

They'd left the village behind and the car was climbing quickly as the ground rose up in front of them. Annie glanced outside, seeing green fields becoming untamed moorland covered in dense clumps of heather and wispy bracken. Her eyes were drawn to him again as he continued.

'We can take up to twelve children, plus teachers or assistants, and we provide three team leaders, one of whom lives on site. We also have a specialist activities coordinator who works alongside school groups at different key stages and provides general support.'

Annie was impressed, sensing the weight of his gaze briefly upon her. He pulled off onto a track leading to a big old farmhouse towering just below the top of the moor. 'This is it. Welcome to Kilnbeck.'

The house was surrounded by a chunky stone wall enclosing a simple garden designed with function rather than beauty in mind. Scattered wooden seats were clustered near a barbeque and a couple of goalposts and swing balls for games were propped against a large round table. Jon parked alongside two other cars and a minibus. Annie was out of the Land Rover by the time he was at her side, and when they reached the front door, he pushed it open.

'Come on in. I'll show you around. Most of the staff are out already with the group, but Gillian, our administrator, will be here.'

They were inside a porch filled with waterproof coats and a couple of rucksacks slung casually onto a wooden settle. Jon led Annie through a door off the wide hallway into a big sitting room. A huge stone fireplace, filled with ashes and stumps of burnt logs, took up almost half of one wall. Three comfy, worn sofas were bunched together and a few beanbags lolled on the floor, most of them grouped around an abandoned board game, its pieces scattered onto the carpet.

'This is the main living room,' he said. She knew he was watching her as she looked around and tried to take everything in. 'There's a smaller room on the other side of the house which is for reading and peace and quiet. We deliberately don't have a television or computer games. Most mobiles don't work up here and they're discouraged from bringing any valuable gadgets, so we can minimise the technical distractions quite easily. There is Wi-Fi but it's fairly limited.'

'Don't the children mind?' Annie asked, amused.

Jon grinned. 'Occasionally but they get used to it pretty quickly. We try to teach them other ways of entertaining themselves, and some of them are so unfit that they often want to crash into bed early after a long day outdoors. There are plenty of books and we encourage games that involve teamwork and problem solving.'

She followed him upstairs and glanced into the identical bedrooms, each with twin beds, simple wooden furniture, and plain cream walls, and then he showed her the dining room with its big table already laid for tea. Annie was surprised by the modern and spacious kitchen and knew at once that she would be able to cook in here. Jon leant against the central island, watching her quietly as she wandered around pretending to be oblivious to him, trying to make herself feel at home. The whole building felt comfortable and lived in and seemed noticeably quiet without the young people, who'd gone trekking to a ruined castle.

'What do you think?' he asked finally. Annie glanced at him, noticing the way his eyes seemed to follow her movements, and was unable to disguise the admiration for what he had achieved in her own expression.

'It's fantastic,' she said honestly, finally pausing beside the big American fridge and freezer. 'The children must really love coming here.' He grinned and she dragged her eyes away from his as somebody entered the room and diverted their attention.

Jon introduced her to Gillian Woods, the administrator, who looked every inch a competent right-hand woman in her straight blue skirt and white blouse. Everything about her was square, from collar-length hair and tidy fringe to her shoulders and the shape of her shoes. Annie knew she was being sized up as Gillian shook her hand quickly with a welcoming expression, and Annie tried to look as though she knew what she was doing as she smiled back.

'Gillian generally plans the menus and arranges the shopping,' Jon said, looking first at Annie and then at the older woman. 'But I'm sure if you want to do something different today, that won't be a problem, will it?'

Annie wasn't quite so sure as Gillian looked a little doubtful, flipping open the iPad she held to glance at the screen. 'Today's menu is mushroom soup, sausage and mash, and fruit crumble with custard or ice cream. We have both ordinary and vegetarian sausages and there are no allergies or vegans amongst our guests this week. Will that be all right for you? If not, then of course we can plan something different. I realise you've been kind enough to step in at short notice.'

'The original menu is fine,' Annie said quickly to Gillian, ignoring Jon's suggestion. She was already running through the process in her mind as she envisaged what she would do first and how long it would take her to prepare the meal. 'Absolutely. I don't want to change anything.'

Gillian excused herself politely as a telephone began to ring in her office beside the kitchen, and Annie was alone once more with Jon.

'I have to go. I'll be back later, about three. Help yourself to whatever you want. And call me if there's anything you need, okay?'

'Of course.' She nodded, disappointed he was leaving so soon and wondering if she had imagined the reluctance in his voice. 'Hopefully I won't have to.'

Jon disappeared and Gillian popped back, making coffee while Annie scrabbled around looking for ingredients. Annie listened as Gillian started to chat, quietly gleaning more information about the centre and its recent history. Gillian also explained that the children weren't allowed to help themselves from the kitchen and Annie should send them away if they tried.

'What does Jon do?' she asked Gillian casually as she prepared the fruit for the crumble, dropping summer berries into a pan and adding a vanilla pod, sugar and a little water.

'He's the managing director of Thorndale Rural Enterprises but he spends as much time as he can here. He volunteered at other centres before he set up Kilnbeck and got his Basic Expedition Leader award to qualify as a team leader. Kilnbeck is his baby – he had quite a lot of opposition from the village when it went to planning because some people thought it was just free holidays for bad kids. He was determined to prove them wrong, to show that it's all about developing skills some young people can't even dream of. Of course we've had a few troublesome ones, and it doesn't get any easier to realise that sometimes your best still isn't enough, that we can't always find a way to reach them. He loves working with them, and he's certainly got a gift for it.'

'Does he live in the village?' Annie peered into the pan to hide her face, giving it a gentle shake as she tried to make her interest seem perfectly natural. She sensed Gillian's eyes on her, nonetheless.

'He lives at Thorndale Hall.' Gillian raised her voice above the noise of the tap as she quickly washed their empty cups and replaced them in the cupboard. 'It's his family home. Sir Vivian Beresford is his father.'

Stunned, Annie wondered why she hadn't made the connection before, realising Elizabeth had never given her Jon's surname when she had introduced them. Emerging from the depths of her mind after Gillian's words were forgotten details about the family who owned the estate and the beautiful Georgian house just beyond the village. She tried to remember what she had learned from Molly all those years ago, vaguely recalling Molly telling her about the young son who had gone away and rarely came home. And now, Annie realised, he was back. She digested the information, questions tumbling through her mind as she measured butter and flour for the crumble mixture.

Gillian took herself off to work in her office and Annie was alone, thoughts of Jon whirling around in her mind as she mulled over what she knew of him. She chopped mushrooms for the soup while olive oil and butter warmed in a pan and threw in garlic and onions. It smelled delicious and her face was getting warm as she stirred the contents gently. She added chicken stock she had found in the fridge and turned down the heat to let it all simmer for a while. She made some sandwiches for lunch and took a plate to Gillian, who thanked her gratefully as she turned back to her computer screen.

Altogether Annie had thirteen to cook for and when she returned to the kitchen, she began to peel a mountain of potatoes for the mash. The afternoon seemed to disappear as she chopped, rinsed, peeled, and cooked, relishing the process of creating a meal from scratch once again. She'd barely had time to glance at her watch and was amazed to realise it was almost four already when she heard the excited roar of the children arriving back from their day out. Soon the whole house was filled with noise as they bellowed at each other and a couple of boys stuck their heads inside the kitchen to stare at her curiously. Annie remembered Gillian's advice and sent them away, promising to bring snacks shortly. She quickly rustled up some hot chocolate and filled a big tray with homemade biscuits she'd found in a tin, jugs of cold juice and steaming mugs, and carried it into the sitting room. The children fell hungrily onto the food as though they had never eaten before, the plates emptied in moments.

She flew back to the kitchen to line up dozens of sausages beneath a huge grill and began to pop broad beans from their pods and toss them into a pan. Her face was glowing from the heat as she tasted the soup and whizzed it with a blender until it was thick and creamy. She jumped when she heard Jon's greeting behind her, spinning around to face him and sending drops of soup flying onto the floor. He was propped against the island once more and the smile he gave her was casual, even as his eyes suggested something more.

'It smells amazing in here. Is everything okay?'

Annie met his gaze and it was impossible to prevent a quiver stealing down her back. 'Yes, it's all fine. It'll be ready about five.'

Jon strolled towards her and found a spoon, helping himself to the soup. 'That's fantastic.' He made to stick the spoon back into the warm pan for more and laughed as she shooed him away. 'There's plenty,' he protested, ducking out of her way as she flicked a cloth at him.

'Not if you eat it all.' Steam scorched her face as she hauled the potatoes to the sink and tipped them into a big colander. 'You're not helping.'

'But I'd like to,' he said immediately, and he took the heavy colander from her and tipped the potatoes back into the pan. Annie turned away, distracted by the spitting sausages browning underneath the grill. 'What can I do?'

'Mash them,' she said promptly, passing him butter and cream from the fridge. She listened while he told her about a meeting he'd had earlier in the day, and they both looked around as the door opened and Gillian reappeared. Jon thanked her for staying on to help as Annie snatched the sausages from the grill before they began to burn. Jon and Gillian began to discuss plans for the coming week, and Annie listened idly, almost ready to serve the meal. As she started to ladle soup into bowls Jon was beside her once more, holding the bowls so that she could fill them. She offered her thanks as he and Gillian carried the first course into the dining room and began to clear up the untidy kitchen while the onion gravy gently simmered. Jon returned, and Annie knew he was hovering.

'I usually eat with the children when I'm here,' he said easily. 'Would you like to join us?'

She looked at him, torn between wanting to say yes and knowing she shouldn't, her promise to herself to avoid him after today fresh in her mind. Despite her aching feet she had really enjoyed the day, disappointed the little bit of borrowed time with him was almost over. 'No thanks,' she replied deftly. 'There's quite a lot to do here. You go ahead.'

'Just leave it. The children always help to clear up later.'

She shook her head and the look he gave her told her he understood she was making excuses. After that, everything seemed a whirl of busyness. The soup bowls came back empty and she piled plates with sausages, creamy mash, and chunky broad beans. She quickly made custard to serve with the hot crumble and poured it into a large jug alongside a tub of ice cream. Once the meal was over the noise grew as the children cleared the table and escaped into the sitting room to play. Jon came back and helped her with some more of the clearing up, filling the industrial dishwasher with yet another load.

Annie stuck her head into the sitting room to say goodbye to the children and couldn't hide her pleasure when they chorused that they'd loved her food, the three young teachers agreeing sleepily. Everybody looked tired and one or two boys were already dozing on the sofas. Annie noticed that all of them had the particular glow that comes from spending the day outside in the fresh air, and she knew it wouldn't be long before they were clamouring for bed. Jon was waiting outside, leaning casually against his car. She took a deep breath as he opened the passenger door for her, trying to make herself appear as relaxed as he looked.

He waited as she sank back into the seat drowsily, almost ready to fall asleep too. They were silent until he pulled up outside the cottage and he turned to her. 'A simple thank you doesn't really seem to cover everything you've done today,' he said quietly, and she shrugged. 'I owe you now.'

She laughed at that, glowing from his compliment. 'I think we're quits, don't you?' She jumped out of the car and bent down to look at him. 'I'm sure today will let me off trying to think of a surprise, as you're the only person I know who doesn't like cake.'

His blue eyes twinkled in amusement. 'Maybe. Shall I pick you up tomorrow evening, for the party?'

Annie had forgotten about the housewarming party in the melee of the day at Kilnbeck. Her heart sank at the thought of spending an evening at Sarah's house as an obviously unwanted guest, even if Jon would be there. He was waiting for her reply and Annie nodded slowly.

'See you then, about seven thirty,' he called. She waved goodbye and headed into the cottage.

The next day she spent quite a while getting ready for the party. It had been ages since she'd had occasion to properly dress up and she was certain Sarah would be pulling out all the stops. Once Annie had done her make-up, she tied her hair at the nape of her neck, leaving most of the curls spilling beyond her shoulders. She sprayed Jimmy Choo Blossom perfume onto her wrists, neck and inside her elbows and slid her new dress on over the satin underwear. The lace-trimmed teal dress, with its scalloped neckline and sitting just off her shoulders, flared out into a dipped hem skirt floating around her knees at the front and beyond at the back. Once her shoes were on, high-heeled silver stiletto sandals which right now she loved more than all her other shoes put together, she stood up and found a little clutch bag.

Downstairs, feeling nervous, Annie fished a bottle of champagne from the fridge, hoping it would do as a suitable house-warming present, and switched on a lamp in the study. She glanced out of the window and her heart seemed to leap into her mouth as she saw Jon heading up the path to the door. She was very tempted to run and hide but instead, when he knocked, she went into the hall and opened the door.

'Hi,' she said self-consciously, feeling suddenly shy as she hovered in front of him, clutching the champagne. She hadn't really wanted to arrive at the party alone, but she was beginning to think it would have been preferable now that he was actually here, certain his gaze was taking in every detail. Annie read the approval and more in his expression before he spoke.

'You look beautiful.' He reached out to take the bottle and her mouth dried up as Jon's eyes slipped slowly down the length of her body until she felt the heat of his look imprinted all over her. He was wearing well-cut, smart black jeans and grey suede Chelsea boots with a flattering white Dover cotton shirt and the ever-present pager on his belt. Annie was finding it very difficult to ignore the suggestion of a broad and muscled chest underneath as she breathed in the citrus scent of his cologne and fought the impulse to reach up and touch his face. His dark hair was barely tidier than usual, and she knew the dishevelment was deliberate.

'Thank you,' she muttered, turning around to lock the door. It was a perfect summer evening, and she tried to subdue the unease twisting her nerves into knots as they walked slowly through the village. Annie wondered if every curtain was twitching ready to make gossip as she imagined curious eyes upon them. It was obvious that something exciting was happening as more and more people trickled into Sarah's beautiful house overlooking the green. A harassed-looking man with a large bald patch and an ill-fitting suit was directing traffic towards the car park just around the corner.

Jon grinned, his eyes following the traffic. 'Hope Sarah's got permission for that.' He waved to somebody across the green, and Annie smiled. 'Jerry Gordon's a stickler for procedure – he'll have the whole lot clamped if she's not careful.'

Through the open front door she saw guests swarming through the house, greeting one another with kisses, hugs, and handshakes. She thought worriedly of Sarah's insistence that the party was only for a few friends and neighbours; there seemed to be lots of people there already and Annie wasn't sure if she was more afraid of Jon leaving her alone or remaining by her side. She saw Sarah laughing as she handed an empty glass to a waiter and felt the reassuring pressure of Jon's body against hers as they walked inside. He looked down and gave her a quick wink, and her stomach leapt.

Chapter Nine

When Sarah spotted them, she wriggled through the people around her and hurriedly came over to greet Jon, sliding her hands onto his shoulders and kissing the corner of his mouth. *Much easier if you're five foot ten in heels*, Annie thought grumpily, knowing she was being ungracious and very possibly just the tiniest bit jealous. Sarah barely looked at Annie until Jon slipped an arm around Annie's shoulders and drew her alongside him. Sarah took the bottle of champagne he offered, making a huge fuss over it until Jon reminded her that it wasn't from him. She nodded blandly at Annie as she handed it to a nearby waiter.

Sarah was wearing the most beautiful dress of the palest blue, strapless and carefully embellished, the slim fit and slightly flared skirt perfectly flattering her height and swept-up blonde hair. Annie admitted privately that Sarah looked ravishing, certain the effect was all intended for Jon; Sarah had barely taken her eyes off him in the minutes since he and Annie had arrived.

They followed Sarah through the house into a huge orangery, already full of chattering people clutching drinks and piling plates with food from the tables outside as they mingled together, the sound of laughter carrying on the night air. Caterers were wilting over hot barbeques in the perfectly landscaped garden, sheltered from the moor above by a row of ancient oak trees and a high stone wall. Annie realised some of the guests were staring at her and Jon curiously, mostly women eyeing Jon with interest and obviously wondering who the tall, handsome man was. She was beginning to feel like a naughty schoolgirl trailing around after the prefects.

'Let me get you a drink,' Sarah shrieked over the noise of the DJ revving up on the terrace, reaching back to take Jon's arm once again. She grabbed two glasses of champagne from a passing waiter, managing to point one at Annie while still gazing at Jon.

'No, thank you,' Annie heard him say, his voice raised. He bent down, one hand momentarily on Sarah's shoulder to emphasise his point. 'I don't drink alcohol.'

Annie added this new information to her growing list of surprising facts concerning Jon Beresford as Sarah was forced to disappear in search of something else for him, and Annie saw the flash of annoyance on her face as she hunted down another waiter. Jon half turned to Annie, briefly placing his hand on the small of her back to draw her closer and bent his head to speak into her ear.

'You smell amazing,' he murmured. The warm touch of his fingers against her dress felt as though he was caressing her bare skin, and a tantalising heat inched up her back and stole along her arms, leaving her distracted and hot.

The moment was lost when a loud voice nearby snatched Jon's attention, and Annie saw him grin as a stern-looking woman with short grey hair came over to say hello. Jon introduced her to Annie as Brenda Chapman, one of his tenants in the village. Even though he was no longer touching her Annie sensed the imprint of his tall frame against her side once more as somebody edged into him and he didn't move away. The back of his hand drifted against her thigh as he steadied himself and he caught her eye, smiling suddenly.

Her attention wandered as Brenda began to bend his ear about the number of teenagers lounging around the village, and then Annie did a double take when she spotted a famous young actor laughing in the garden, the centre of his group. Suddenly it dawned on her why Sarah Holland seemed familiar. Annie was a bit vague on the details but thought she had seen her playing a doctor in some daytime soap or other. When Sarah fought her way back to Jon once again with a glass of something non-alcoholic, she insisted on dragging him immediately away to meet somebody 'very useful to you, darling'. Annie felt an unwelcome coolness beside her as he excused himself politely, trying not to follow him with her eyes and wishing she didn't mind his leaving her so much.

Brenda introduced her to another couple recently arrived in the village. Neil and Angie Dawson had moved up from Surrey and taken over the post office, leaving behind a horrible daily commute to London and most of their furniture. They told Annie they wanted to spend more time together as a family, although their teenage daughter, Cara, didn't really see it quite like that just yet. She was convinced her parents had moved her to a primitive land almost beyond the reach of social media and shopping centres, Neil explained, although she had been a bit more cheerful since she'd started working in the shop. Annie realised then that it had been Cara who had served her the other day, smiling inwardly as she guessed the reason for Cara's cheerfulness had everything to do with the presence of the tall, thin boy.

Brenda left them to go on the prowl in search of a local councillor whom she was certain had escaped into the darkest depths of the garden with someone who wasn't his partner. Annie tried to keep her face straight but failed when she caught Angie's eye, and they both laughed as Brenda marched away, determined to right another wrong. Neil disappeared to bring food and Annie chatted with Angie while he was gone. There was still no sign of Jon, and Annie smiled in welcome relief as she saw Charlie and Sam making their way over, a beam of happiness already lighting up Sam's merry face. Charlie was forced to pause, collared by somebody Annie thought she recognised as Jerry Gordon, the local neighbour-hood watch coordinator or village busybody, as she had heard people call him. Charlie caught her eye and winked, and she tried not to laugh.

'Hi,' Sam called breathlessly, shoving her way past a gaggle of screeching girls knocking back champagne like pop. She seemed to have a natural ability to brighten a room just by being in it. 'What a scrum! Come on, let's find a seat somewhere. I can't stand up all evening, I'm saving my feet for dancing.'

Annie excused herself, allowing a quick backwards glance as they headed into the noisy garden. Her heart plummeted as she spotted Jon with a group of people in the drawing room, Sarah by his side. They made a striking couple and Annie felt completely out of her depth. She turned away, certain that he wouldn't have even noticed her. Sam found them a bench further down the garden, and Annie handed their empty glasses to a waiter and grabbed refills, passing Sam the fruit punch.

Sam made a face as she reached for the glass. 'Thanks. It's lovely but I'd rather be having the same as you.'

Annie laughed and took a big gulp of champagne. The bubbles exploded on her tongue and she spluttered uncomfortably as the fizz threatened to pause her ability to breathe. Sam grinned as she handed Annie a tissue to wipe her eyes.

'I should probably stick to fruit punch too,' Annie said, hoping her waterproof mascara hadn't run. Despite the dozens of citronella candles lit to drive away midges, tiny insects fluttered around them and she was tempted to go and huddle with the smokers at the bottom of the garden.

'I love your dress,' Sam said, raising her voice above the music. 'It's so gorgeous on you. I can't help wondering if I'll wear anything with a waist ever again.'

Hiding a wince, Annie remembered the reason she had bought the dress in the first place and felt wretched suddenly, wondering why she had made the effort when she was so determined to avoid him. She changed the subject, afraid of giving away too much. 'Thank you. How are you? You look fantastic, Sam.'

Sam was wearing a beautiful wrap dress, cut to flatter her curvy figure while casually emphasising her growing bump and another pair of Doc Martens, floral this time. 'Oh, absolutely fine, thanks. I just feel as though I'm spreading in every direction and walking with a wobble.' They both laughed at that, their eyes meeting with the warmth of the friendship growing between them.

'So, who's who?' Annie asked, leaning closer to Sam as she tried not to raise her voice too much. 'I'd heard it was supposed to be just a few friends and neighbours. Did I really just see the utterly gorgeous Jed March? Wasn't he in *Stranger Things*?'

Sam leant back on the bench to peer around the garden and scan the various groups of dazzling showbiz people and the locals scattered around it. 'And I'd heard that you were invited at the particular insistence of another guest.'

Annie's face fell as she sensed Sam's inquisitive and perceptive glance upon her again. 'It wasn't my idea,' Annie said hastily. 'Anyway, I asked first!'

'It was indeed Mr March, and he's causing quite a stir amongst the younger members of our community with his occasional sightings, although most of them haven't been invited tonight. I don't get it myself, super cool boys who spend more time in front of the mirror than I do have never been my type. Anyway, he turned up with some friends and an on/off girlfriend in tow so we can no doubt expect to see it plastered all over Instagram. Sarah's allegedly one of his exes, but she's got a new show to promote and I suppose the only thing worse than bad publicity is no publicity. I think she's only invited us lot just so she can show the ordinary folk of the village how the other, more glamorous, half live.'

Annie giggled, already realising that everything seemed much more irreverent when it came from Sam. But even so, it was a very glamorous party and Sam's company apart, she would still much rather be tucked up at home than stuck here. Especially as Jon had invited her and then promptly deserted her for Sarah and her friends.

'Apparently Sarah thinks that village life is the new London.' Sam waved her arm airily, brushing a clematis trailing down from the wall above them. 'And she's still single and seems to have decided it's time she found a country gent to accessorise the country house. Sorry, I'm being bitchy, and I shouldn't. Let's just say she's got her eye on somebody local. And here he is. Hi, Jon, we were just talking about you.'

Annie's gaze flew up and she saw Jon approaching them. She took another huge slug from her glass as she digested Sam's comment, wondering how much Jon had heard, and her face flamed at the thought of him realising they had been gossiping. He bent down to kiss Sam's cheek and straightened up, turning to look at Annie as he spoke. She noticed, even in the coming darkness, the hint of a smile softening his face amongst the shadows.

'Are you okay?' he asked casually. Annie nodded fiercely, determined not to betray her disappointment that he had not remained with her. She couldn't believe she had almost allowed herself to think that her being here this evening had mattered to him. 'Can I bring either of you a drink or some food?'

'No thank you.' Annie reached down to deposit her glass on the stone paving. She stood up and grabbed Sam's hand. 'We were just about to dance.'

It was the last thing she wanted to do, even though Sam followed her enthusiastically. Annie glanced over her shoulder as they reached the dance floor, but Jon had already disappeared. Irrationally she was angry with him and even more with herself for feeling so crushed. The DJ launched into Scissor Sisters' *I Don't Feel Like Dancin'*, and Annie began to feel better as the music took over. She hoped she didn't look like a geriatric aunt at a wedding as she watched a group of wildly fashionable girls dancing nearby, their endless legs revealed by tiny skirts. She smiled at Sam apologetically as they were repeatedly pushed together, watching a villager throwing some shapes Annie felt he'd need a physio to get him out of, utterly oblivious to the cynical amusement of the younger guests. Annie collapsed into laughter when Sam hissed that it was the missing councillor and his dance partner definitely wasn't his actual partner.

Annie stole a quick peek back towards the house and saw Jon, for once alone, leaning against a wall tucked in the shadow of the orangery. Their eyes met as he stared at her. She couldn't read his expression in the fading light and defiantly looked away, determined to show she was having a good time without him. After three more songs Sam pleaded exhaustion and sank onto a seat as Annie went in search of Charlie to take Sam home. Annie lowered her gaze to avoid catching anybody's eye as she stepped back inside the house. But she did have to stop and speak to Brenda Chapman, who wanted to know what Annie thought of her new school's latest results. Surprised, Annie answered as reliably as possible and excused herself; she still hadn't found Charlie and she knew Sam was tired. She spotted Jon in the hallway talking to a woman beside him and wanted to disappear before he noticed her.

Annie shot through the nearest door and found herself in the empty dining room. The French doors were open, leading to a secluded terrace hidden from the main garden. The din of the party was momentarily quietened, and she was about to creep away when she realised someone was huddled on the terrace, speaking quietly to a companion. Annie paused, startled, as Jon's name was mentioned. She clutched the door in the darkened room, hating herself for eavesdropping and yet unable to leave.

'What's his name?' It was a woman who made the request.

The man's voice carried easily to Annie, still hidden inside. 'Jonathan Beresford. It's pretty obvious that Sarah has set her mind on trying to become the next Lady Beresford.'

'How well do you know him?'

'Not very, our paths have crossed once or twice on business and I've shot on the estate with his father. I doubt if Sarah has seen much beyond his looks, money and position. He'll inherit Vivian's baronetcy eventually. Jon's supposedly been single for quite a while but I'm not sure Sarah's going to be the one to change all of that. He's very driven by his faith and his work here. She's convinced herself he hasn't made a move on her yet because of some rumour to do with his ex, the one who went off and got married.'

'I heard at work that she would've cancelled if he hadn't been able to come tonight so she must be pretty keen. Do you think the party's for him?'

Annie heard laughter and saw the quick flare of a cigarette being lit. 'Probably. But she's in a foul mood. Jon persuaded her to invite somebody else at the last minute, and then he turned up with this girl in tow.'

'Ah, so that's who she is. Very pretty. No wonder Sarah's cross.'

'She shouldn't be. He told Jed he had only invited the girl because she's just arrived in the village and doesn't socialise much. They're not seeing each other. Jed got the distinct impression that Jon's just not interested. He was pretty dismissive about her.'

Appalled and knowing it served her right, Annie crept out before she heard anything else and bumped straight into Charlie as she closed the door. Hurriedly she tried to drag her jumbled thoughts into place. 'I've been looking for you,' she stammered, clutching his arm as he steadied her, determined not to betray what she had just learned. 'Sam's outside, she needs to go home.'

'Are you all right, Annie? You look a bit pink.'

'It's the heat,' she replied breezily, anything to avoid having to confess to what she had just heard. She tugged at his arm, pulling him alongside her. 'Come on.'

Despite the noise all around, Sam was practically asleep when they found her, and Annie watched as Charlie carefully helped her to her feet, his tenderness evident in the way he took care of Sam.

'Would you like to come to the vicarage for supper tomorrow evening?' Sam asked impulsively as she leant on Charlie's arm. 'Charlie's going out. It'll be just us.'

'I'd really like that, thank you.' It was true but all Annie wanted to do at this moment was escape the horrid party and climb into bed.

'I won't promise to spend all day slaving over the stove,' Sam called as they walked away, and Annie heard Charlie laugh. 'But don't bring anything, see you about seven. Good night, thanks for the dance.'

'Night. Sleep well.'

Annie really didn't want to find Sarah and thank her for the party, so she stole through the house and stepped quietly out of the front door. She walked as quickly as her shoes allowed, trying to put distance between herself, the party and most especially Jon. Her head began to pound as she skirted the village green, careful to keep her shoes out of the grass. She was so confused and unhappy she hardly noticed the darkness or that she had passed the top of her lane until she saw the eerie shape of a wooden footbridge straddling the river. She stepped onto it, shivering as she listened to the racing water. The moon was almost full, casting a ghostly light around her and illuminating the silver pools beneath her. She remembered the touch of his hand and the interrupted conversation on Sunday evening, and couldn't believe how foolish and mistaken she had been.

An owl, carrying something in its claws, swooped overhead and she flinched. Tendrils of hair trailed across her face and she impatiently reached up and removed the clip, allowing her curls to spill forward, adding to the darkness around her.

She knew she was afraid of how Jon made her feel and the awful reality of another rejection lurched into her heart, when all she had craved from this new and yet familiar place was peace. She stumbled across the bridge, heading back as quickly as she could, her feet really hurting now in her high heels. She kept her eyes down and tried not to notice the strange, ethereal shapes looming from hedges and gardens with every frightened step she took, fearful of this whole other village that had emerged with the darkness.

Annie was very relieved when her cottage eventually came into view and she saw the faint light from the study trying bravely to brighten the garden. She pushed at the gate with cold and shaking hands, and when it wouldn't yield, she kicked it childishly, muttering as she staggered up the path. She hadn't quite reached the front door when a silent figure, sitting in darkness on the step, moved suddenly and she screamed in terror.

'Annie, it's me.'

She heard Jon's quiet voice through the gloom, astounded to see him waiting outside her little house. Barely silhouetted by the light from the window above, his head was low, his arms resting on his knees. Even though she told herself he was the last person she wanted to see after all she'd just heard, she still had to fight the impulse to run and find comfort in his arms, encircled by his strength, and a rigid tension took possession of her body as her back stiffened.

'I'm sorry. I didn't mean to frighten you.' There was an unexpected gentleness in his voice when he spoke.

'What are you doing here?' She bent down to remove her shoes at last, unable to disguise the weariness in her voice, hardly noticing the cool stone against her sore feet as she walked towards him as fast as several glasses of champagne would allow. She rummaged through her bag to find her keys.

'I just wanted to make sure you got home safely.' He stood up, towering above her and she arched away from him as she opened the door. He picked up her discarded shoes, holding them out to her, and she took them with an ungracious snatch.

'Shouldn't you be with Sarah?' Annie remembered how she had felt when he had first seen her this evening and had held her against him, for just those few moments at the party. She tried to chase the thoughts away, determined not to allow their memory to rekindle the heat on her skin.

'Why would I be with Sarah?' There was a reasonableness in his tone that didn't match the weight of his question as their eyes held.

'It's her party, she wanted you there.'

'I was there and now I'm not. I was worried about you.'

Annie unlocked the door, shoving it open with her bare foot, wincing at the flash of pain in her toes. Handbag followed shoes in a discarded heap on the bottom stair. 'Worried! You abandoned me the first opportunity you had!'

'You're a grown woman,' Jon retorted and Annie was astonished by the sudden change in his manner. 'I didn't think you needed a babysitter, you seemed perfectly fine. I'm sorry if you saw it like that.'

She knew he was right, but she was tired and the comment she'd overhead about his ex-girlfriend was still unsettling her and she couldn't quite reach that level of reasoning just now. Instead, she reacted to his tone and her reply was sharp. 'I only went to the damn party because you asked me.' She closed her eyes the moment the remark slipped out, wishing she could open them again and find it had all been a dreadful dream. But her eyes were still shut as his low voice confirmed the reality all around her.

'Annie…'

'I didn't mean it like that,' she said resentfully. She opened her eyes hastily as she heard him take a step closer.

'Annie,' he said softly. 'Look at me, please?'

She tilted her head back, trying to harden her heart against the tenderness in his expression. It became easier when she remembered how he had dismissed her at the party and she kept her face carefully blank as she faced him, shivering.

Briefly there was silence around them and when he spoke, he sounded less certain than she had ever heard before.

'I tried not to be envious of everyone who spoke to you,' Jon said roughly, his hands clenched against his sides. She watched, incredulous, as a muscle flickered in his cheek. The tautness of his body was reflected in the depths of his eyes as he continued. 'And if I had spent the whole evening by your side, every person there would have known how I feel. I'm not proud of behaving that way. I'm sorry.'

She gaped at him in open-mouthed astonishment until he turned abruptly and strode down the path. He yanked the gate open, wrenching it from its hinges and leaving it sprawled in the long grass. Annie watched until he disappeared, trying to find the words to bring him back and make him explain. But he was gone, and it was a few minutes before she closed the door to the night, stunned by his admission.

She took a mug of coffee upstairs, unable to think of anything other than Jon. By the time she had removed her make-up and slipped into bed she was feeling exhausted, confused and tearful. She tried to summon all the reasons why she wasn't prepared to risk everything all over again, and in her mind, she saw Iain's face as she tossed and turned. She remembered how she had felt when he had told her he was leaving and why, staring into the darkness until finally she fell asleep, terrified at the thought of being so vulnerable ever again.

Chapter Ten

Annie had forgotten how champagne always made her feel as she mooched around the house on Saturday morning, nursing a headache and a horrible churning sensation in her stomach, which she was sure had nothing to do with alcohol. It seemed an age since she had last worked on the cottage; so much had happened in just two days, and Jon was constantly in her thoughts as she cleaned the study, emptying the bookcases little by little and coughing through the dust. Afterwards she made some flapjacks and popped down to the farm to catch up with the Howards, pleased to see that Bill was recovering after the ordeal of his night on the fells last week.

The rest of the day flew past and soon it was time to get ready for supper with Sam. After a lovely hot bath Annie dressed and ran downstairs to collect the pretty bunch of sweet peas she had picked from the garden as well as a lemon drizzle cake she had made earlier. The weather was changing so she grabbed a jacket as she stepped outside. Cool clouds were obliterating the warmth of the sun and she shivered, drawing the jacket tightly around her. As she reached the lane, she saw the gate still lying in the grass where Jon had left it last night and her heart squeezed at the abrupt reminder of him.

The large vicarage nestled amongst tall yew trees casting shadows over the house. Facing the church, its huge bay windows overlooked the curved drive and a central, circular herbaceous border filled with sweet box, hydrangeas, geraniums and lady's mantle. Borders following the curve of the drive were planted with viburnum, holly, pheasant's tail grasses, ferns and more geraniums. Annie crunched along the gravel to the front door, wondering how such planting appeared so natural amongst the shade whereas her own garden just looked tatty. She rang the bell and it was only a minute until Sam opened the door.

'Hi, Annie.' She smiled, standing aside to let Annie into the large, rectangular hallway. 'I'm so pleased you're here, come in.'

Annie closed her eyes for a second in anticipation as the smell of supper wafted towards her. 'Thank you, me too.' She hadn't really bothered eating lunch, and the cereal and toast at breakfast seemed a long time ago. 'These are for you.' Annie handed the flowers and cake tin to Sam, who held the sweet peas up to her face and sniffed them lingeringly. She switched her gaze to the cake tin and lifted the lid off, peering inside hungrily.

'Oh wow, that looks gorgeous! Thank you so much, how kind. Having your company this evening is reward enough but these gifts are lovely. The cake will not last a minute once Charlie spies it. Come through.'

Sam took Annie's jacket and hung it on the newel post at the bottom of a wide staircase and Annie followed her along the hallway and down a corridor. The passage narrowed as they neared the back of the house and emerged into a large kitchen. Annie had been half expecting an old-fashioned room but there was nothing ancient about this space. She looked around with pleasure.

'How beautiful,' she exclaimed, realising immediately it would be a joy to cook in such a light and comfortable kitchen.

'Thank you. We practically live in here really, as it's south facing and lovely to sit in the sunshine on the patio in the evening.'

Pale lemon walls were softened by cream units on two sides with a huge, duck egg blue Aga tucked into a space where once must have been a fireplace. A big oak table with eight cream leather chairs stood in the centre, still with lots of room around it, partly covered by a laptop, parish newsletters and a pile of books scattered at one end. Through a large window Annie could see the garden behind the house. It was almost as overgrown as her own, with plants spilling onto the lawn and shrubs, clearly out of control, disguising the view at the far end.

'Don't look at the garden,' Sam said sheepishly, following Annie's glance. 'My sister-in-law, Flora, planted the front and she's almost finished designing the back too. She's a garden historian and can't wait to get her hands on it. Do you mind if we eat in here?' Sam went over to the Aga and carefully opened one of the oven doors. 'We only really use the dining room if we can't fit everyone at this table and I must confess I couldn't be bothered to set it just for us.'

'Of course not. I hope you haven't gone to too much trouble. Here, let me.' Annie dashed over and lifted a large dish from the Aga and set it on top of the simmering plate. She stood back as Sam came over and peered at it.

'Good, that looks ready.' Sam turned away to the fridge and pulled out a large bowl. 'It's just pesto chicken and penne casserole and salad, hope that's okay?'

Annie was nearly drooling as she looked at the bubbling cheese and breadcrumb topping, itching to grab a spoon and dig in. 'Perfect, thank you. It looks absolutely gorgeous.'

'Chianti or Sauvignon Blanc?'

'Sauvignon would be great, thanks.'

Sam poured the wine for Annie and a tall glass of sparkling water for herself as they sat down to eat, helping themselves and chattering throughout. The meal was wonderful, and Annie told Sam so as she reluctantly pushed her knife and fork together. Sam eyed her with a mischievous smile as she arched her eyebrows questioningly.

'Thank you. But from what I've heard, you're a really talented cook.'

Annie squirmed uncomfortably, swallowing a gulp of wine before replying suspiciously. 'What have you heard?'

Sam reached over to fill Annie's glass again. 'Only that you were a big hit at Kilnbeck, and everybody loved the food. Don't worry, it was Charlie who told me. He's one of the volunteers, when time allows. He said that Jon would've liked to ask you to stay on for a few more days but he thought you wouldn't have time with the move and school, and it wouldn't be fair.'

Annie stared at Sam. 'I had no idea,' she replied quietly, relieved that Jon hadn't put her in a position she would have found difficult to resolve sensibly. 'I'm not really that good. I just love cooking but haven't done much of it for a while.'

'Charlie's out with Jon this evening actually, they and a couple of others have taken a group of young people to the cinema. They take it in turns to drive the minibus.'

'Jon seems very involved with the community here.' Annie stood up casually to clear away their plates, sensing Sam's eyes on her.

'He is, definitely – he sees it very much as part of his calling. He's especially good with young people. They really respond to him.'

Sam served dessert, meringues with summer berries and thick cream from the local dairy. They were silent as they ate, and then Annie finally replaced her spoon in an empty bowl.

'Thank you so much, that was all fantastic,' she said drowsily, the effects of a lovely meal and the wine beginning to weaken her senses. 'I'll clear up.'

'No,' Sam replied firmly, picking up the cream jug from the table and replacing it in the fridge. 'Absolutely not, it'll all go in the dishwasher later.'

Annie noticed Sam was looking tired as she rubbed her back absently. Her bump seemed to be growing by the minute and it really didn't look as though it would be too much longer until the baby arrived.

'Please, Sam, let me.' Annie pointed to a chair. 'Why don't you sit down? It won't take long, and I wouldn't like you to be up late doing it.'

Sam rolled her eyes, but she obediently sat down and gave Annie a grateful look. 'Thank you,' she replied sleepily. 'Just leave whatever's messiest. Charlie will help. I'll make coffee in a minute and we'll have it in the sitting room.'

'Are you sure?' Annie turned to look at Sam doubtfully as she rinsed plates under the tap. 'I should go and let you get to bed.'

Sam gently rested one hand on her bump, the other rising to cover a yawn. 'No, I'm fine, honestly. Don't go yet, please. It's only just after nine.'

Annie darted around quickly loading the dishwasher, wondering if she would ever be able to fit one into her own little kitchen. She switched the kettle on and glanced at Sam, whose eyes were closed as she stroked her bump dreamily. Annie found the coffee and measured spoons into the mugs that Sam had left ready on the dresser and followed her through to the sitting room, carrying the tray of coffee. The room was old fashioned and yet still beautiful, with decorative plaster-work on the ceiling above printed floral paper on the walls. Sam switched on two tall standard lamps and drew heavy plum-coloured curtains. A sudden gust of wind made them jump as the blustery branches on the trees outside smacked against the bay window.

'Always sounds worse from inside the house, I think,' Sam said, wrapping her hands around her mug. 'There are one or two trees in the churchyard that need some attention. I hope they don't come down in this storm. Charlie's got a tree surgeon coming over on Monday to see what has to be done with them.'

'How did you and Charlie meet?' Annie asked curiously, happy to keep the subject of their conversation away from Jon. 'Was it at church?'

Sam shook her head, smiling wistfully as she wriggled the cushion beneath her feet. 'Rugby. I have two older brothers who both played in the academy of a professional club with

Charlie, and I'd usually go to matches to watch. I'd had a bit of a crush on Charlie for a couple of years and when I was seventeen he started to notice me after he came back from a tour of Australia. He'd just been selected for the first team but tore a knee ligament and was out for four months. We spent as much time together as we could while he was recovering.

'I was doing A levels at college and volunteering with a church teaching drama to children, and Charlie started to come along. Unlike me he hadn't grown up in a church family and started to really love everything about it – the people, the enthusiasm, the spirit of serving in communities, and he really felt the pull of ministry.'

'Wow. So, what happened next?'

'I got a place at Lancaster to study drama and theatre, and we married and moved to Cumbria so Charlie could study part-time near me. He worked at an outdoor centre, which he loved. It was tough, with both of us studying, but we felt so blessed to be together.'

Sam's gaze drifted away to the fireplace, watching the flames. Annie knew she was remembering those first days of marriage and couldn't imagine what it must have been like for them, as Sam carried on.

'It was such a special time. Anyway, once he'd qualified and done all the placements, he was offered a curacy in Kendal and I taught in a secondary school nearby until the parish here became available and we moved to Thorndale. So here we are.'

'Does Charlie still play rugby?' Annie asked. The room smelt of hot smoky timber and coffee, and Annie could hear the crackling of the logs inside the grate as they fell apart.

'No. He could usually manage to get to training at a club most weeks, but matches were a bit of a problem, not surprisingly. He plays cricket for the village team now. He still loves competitive sport and likes to keep fit. When I first knew him, I never dreamt he'd give up rugby for the church, he was so good. But he's a wonderful vicar and he absolutely loves parish life, and so do I, in my own way, even though I had never imagined myself as a vicar's wife. He's very aware that his calling has a big impact on me and our relationship. We never take our time alone together for granted and he's tremendously supportive of me and my job.'

'Are you going back to work, after the baby is born?'

'I plan to,' Sam replied with a grin, stroking her bump gently. 'My head says yes but my heart isn't so sure. I'm going to have a year off and then we'll see. Anyway, that's enough about me. I want to hear a lot more about you. Charlie tells me that Jon mentions you quite often and lots of people in the village remember you from years ago.'

Annie groaned. 'Oh, please don't say that! After Edinburgh I'm still not at all used to bumping into people who know me every time I leave the cottage and who like to know what I'm up to. I dread the thought of gossip.'

Sam's smile was sympathetic and understanding. 'It's really not that bad. People do mean well, even though there will always be gossip about something. Just about anybody would help you if you needed it and the village has a lovely community spirit, but I realise it's changed over the years.' Sam's expression altered then, became more mischievous, and her eyes glinted with merriment. 'But Annie, if you've attracted the attention of the delectable Mr Beresford then people are bound to take notice. The entire village is practically holding its breath for a new Mrs Beresford and Sarah seems to think she's in with a shot.'

'Oh?' Annie aimed for casual, not certain she'd achieved it and Sam's beady gaze was still on her.

'She hasn't a hope. She's made no secret of the fact that her career comes first and that's fine, but she's not interested in a family or what really goes on here. She doesn't understand what Kilnbeck means to Jon and I can't imagine him living in that house forever without kids, can you? He'd be a brilliant dad. Sarah won't be at the front of the queue, however many fancy parties she lures him to.'

Annie felt her pleasure in the evening slip away like sand through fingers. She couldn't blame Sam for her directness when she knew little of her past and what had really brought Annie to Thorndale, but Sam's remarks slashed home nonetheless, slicing through Annie's heart as she thought of Jon and his words from last night. How could she let herself think of him, or give voice to the attraction simmering between them, knowing he could be looking to settle down, to start a family? Annie was still trying to piece herself together after her recent heartbreak, it wouldn't be fair of her to begin something with Jon that couldn't go anywhere.

'I'm sorry, I didn't mean to make you uncomfortable.' Sam caught sight of Annie's stricken expression and threw her an apologetic glance. 'Let's change the subject. What did you think of the jewellery designer at The Courtyard? I saw you looking at their stuff.'

The wind was still growling outside, its noisy roar becoming louder with every moment, when the sitting room door burst open before Annie could reply. Charlie erupted into the room, followed, to Annie's horror, by Jon and the tall boy she had seen at the post office. Annie felt an explosion of dismay rush through her body and her heart began to beat a little quicker as her glance raced beyond Charlie to meet Jon's gaze. He seemed taken aback when he noticed her, and surprise flared briefly in his eyes.

'Blimey, it's nasty out there,' Charlie exclaimed. He threw his coat onto the back of a chair and hurried to stand in front of the roaring blaze. 'Hey, you two, I'm glad to see you've lit the fire. Can't believe we're still using it in summer.'

'Charlie,' Sam said with an exasperated grin, shuffling up to make room on the sofa and looking across to the boy. 'For goodness' sake, move away. Nobody else can get warm. Hi, Nathan, how are you?' She pointed to the space she'd made nearby. 'Would you like to sit down?'

'I'm fine,' the boy replied quickly, still hovering by the door. Sam stood up as Charlie tipped more logs into the fire and kicked them back with his boot.

'Come and meet Annie,' Sam said kindly, holding out her hand, and the boy tentatively stepped forward. 'Annie, Nathan. Nathan, Annie. Nathan's here for the summer getting some work experience on the estate, and Annie's just moved here from Edinburgh.'

'Hi, Nathan.' Annie's smile was warm and she saw that up close he seemed even younger than she had realised, wariness evident in his eyes. 'It was you I saw in the shop the other day, wasn't it?'

Nathan nodded, more polite than friendly. He looked at Jon, and Annie knew he was uncomfortable as Jon dropped a reassuring hand on his shoulder.

'I'll put the kettle on.' Sam turned to look at Charlie and Jon as she began to move towards the door. 'Who's for hot drinks?'

Annie was quicker. 'I'll do it.' She stood up and Sam gave her a grateful smile. 'I won't be long.'

'No thanks,' Nathan said abruptly, turning towards the hall. 'I'm going to walk back.'

'Stay,' Sam pleaded, glancing across to Jon as though for support. 'You're very welcome and it's grim outside now.'

Nathan shook his head, throwing Jon a quick apologetic glance and then he was gone. Annie too was glad of an excuse to leave the room, hearing the bang of the front door as Nathan escaped into the blustery night. She was glowing, even though she was no longer beside the fire and her foot-fall sounded very loud as she scurried along the darkened passageway to the kitchen. She made coffee for everybody and by the time she was adding milk to three cups, Charlie had appeared, and he carried the tray back to the sitting room.

Sam was talking quietly with Jon and they both looked up when Annie entered. She found her seat again and thanked

Charlie as she accepted a steaming mug. He put the tray down on a coffee table and sank onto the sofa beside Sam, pulling her gently against his side.

Annie would rather take flight and go home, as Nathan had done, then she could almost pretend that she had not seen Jon this evening. Whenever she closed her eyes, she remembered the fleeting touch of his hand and every recollection left her craving more. Certain he was watching her, she glanced up, meeting his gaze with a cool one of her own. She turned to Charlie as he spoke.

'Don't let me forget to look in on Megan tomorrow.' He looked at Sam, a frown wrinkling his brow as he pushed a hand through his short, dark curls. 'There's a storm forecast late in the day, heavy rain and gale force winds, sounds like it's already started. I'll make up a bed in case she wants to come here. Megan's one of our church wardens,' he explained to Annie. 'She gets a bit panicked when the weather's bad and doesn't like to be on her own.'

Annie's eyes widened in alarm as she tried not to worry about the impending storm. She wondered if the cottage could weather it, forgetting it had already withstood many more over the preceding years. She fretted about the state of the windows and whether the roof was strong enough to repel the rain.

'I hate storms,' she whispered, hardly aware she had said the words out loud. She saw Jon glance at her and she shivered, already dreading the next day and night, envisaging the howl of the trees outside and the battering of rain above her through the darkness. She'd never forgotten that first winter at boarding school when a ferocious storm had raged through the night, threatening to take the roof off the building and she'd lain awake, terrified, knowing her parents were too far away to reach her. As a little girl she'd always crept into their room when she was afraid and such comfort was beyond her then.

'Don't take any notice of Charlie.' Sam shot him a cross look. 'He's probably been listening to the forecast for Iceland or something. It's the middle of summer, it surely won't be as bad as all that.'

Annie had reached her limit for the evening, worrying about the storm while trying to avoid Jon. 'I should go.' She stood up, replacing her empty mug on the tray, and turned to Sam. 'Thank you for a lovely evening,' Annie said truthfully. 'The meal was gorgeous. Next time come to mine and I'll cook if you like?'

'I'd love to.' Sam climbed to her feet and gave Annie a warm hug. 'If you're bothered about the storm tomorrow, come to us. We should be at home in the afternoon, at least until evensong and we'll be back again after that.'

Annie squeezed Sam's hand gratefully. 'Thank you. Good night, everyone.' She gave Charlie a friendly smile, hoping it had remained in place as she flicked her eyes over Jon.

'I'll drive you.'

Annie froze as Jon spoke and her reply was cool. 'There's no need thank you, it's barely ten minutes' walk. Please don't bother.'

He ignored her and stood up, reaching into his jeans pockets for keys. Annie could've kicked Sam when she voiced her cheery agreement.

'Oh, would you, Jon? Thank you. Good night both, sleep tight.'

Charlie followed them to the front door and slipped Annie's jacket across her shoulders. 'Thanks for coming to see Sam, she was really looking forward to it. I hope we'll see you again soon. Night, Jon.'

The wind whipped Annie's hair across her face when she stepped outside, and she impatiently dragged long strands away from her eyes, shivering at the sudden cold. Jon opened the front door of a minibus parked in the drive so she could slide in and he was beside her in moments.

'Sorry about the transport.'

She heard the amusement in his voice as the noisy engine chugged into life. Its lights illuminated the church and silent graveyard next door as he crawled loudly along the drive. 'It's fine,' she assured him, trying to relax as she drew her jacket around her to keep out the cool air.

After a three-minute journey, Jon stopped the minibus next to Annie's car in the lane outside the cottage. 'Thanks for the lift,' she said quickly, undoing the seatbelt and grabbing the door handle ready to escape.

'Annie.' She stiffened when she heard his low voice and the light pressure of his fingers on her arm. 'Can we talk about last night?'

She shook her arm free and unlocked the door. As she climbed out, she gave him a quick glance without managing to meet his eyes in the poor light. 'It doesn't matter,' she said casually. 'I'm sure you didn't mean anything by it.'

She heard his quiet sigh as she slammed the door and hurried up the path to the house, half expecting him to follow. But as she slipped the key into the lock, she heard the engine whine as Jon drove away, and for the second time in twenty-four hours she was confused and unsettled. Wearily she climbed the stairs to bed, the comments she'd overheard at Sarah's party churning uneasily in her mind along with his own from last night and all Sam had unknowingly revealed earlier. She wondered whether she ought to have listened to him this evening, yet was afraid of what he might have said.

On Sunday, Annie tried to forget Charlie's comments about the approaching storm and all day the weather strove to remind her. The sun had completely disappeared and as the day wore on, clouds spun wildly overhead as the sky gradually darkened into angry shades of black and grey. By five thirty she'd dragged some of the wood from the store outside and piled it in the fireplace over some newspapers and the soot that had been blowing onto the hearth all day. She checked and re-checked that all the windows were closed and she locked the doors, leaving her keys on the stairs where she could find them in a hurry if needed.

In her bedroom she changed into pyjamas, determined to sit it out as she listened to the drumming of the rain on the roof above. She prayed that it wouldn't leak but the noise on the slates sounded so deafening she almost expected to discover that her mattress had become a waterbed. She ran down to the kitchen and found candles, matches and her torch and placed them on the coffee table within easy reach. She wasn't remotely hungry, so she made a big mug of strong coffee and curled up on the sofa to read.

At nine o'clock she switched off the lamp in the sitting room and went upstairs. Staring out of her bedroom window, she was afraid to see the trees bending so easily, frightened for her car parked underneath. But there was nothing she could do, and she certainly wasn't going outside to move it. She wondered about Megan and if she had gone to the vicarage for company. She remembered Elizabeth's offer of company down at the farm and half wished she'd thought to go to them earlier in the day, before darkness had fallen.

She got into bed and tried to sleep, but each time she closed her eyes another huge gust of wind hurled itself at the house, branches heaving and tumbling outside. Annie sat up, her heart hammering inside her chest. It seemed pointless to stay in bed, so she pulled on thick socks and a woolly sweater over her pyjamas and went around each room in turn flicking on the lights, feeling better as she forced the darkness away.

She was in the sitting room, brushing soot from the hearth yet again when she heard a terrible crash at the back of the cottage and the unmistakeable sound of splintering glass. Annie screamed in horrified terror, certain that the old willow tree must have blown down and landed in the kitchen. She stood up shakily and forced herself to open the door and find out. The kitchen was intact but when she crept into the pantry, she could only stare in horror at the tree thrusting through a smashed window. Cold air was rushing inside, and the branches were rustling eerily against the back door, blocking it completely.

Annie tried to quell rising panic as she wondered frantically what to do next. She knew she needed to find out the extent of the damage in case the house was unsafe, and turned to find a coat, dreading having to go outside. As she returned to the sitting room, she heard a thumping noise at the front of the cottage and paused, terrified it was another calamity about to strike from the sky. Her pulse began to roar in her ears and as the wind paused for a moment, she heard the hammering noise again. She realised it was somebody banging on her front door, and she was so relieved she didn't care who it was. She ran to the door and opened it thankfully. She was expecting Tom or even Charlie, but her heart leapt as she saw Jon standing on the step, the light from the hall revealing his worried expression. Torrential rain was pelting him furiously, plastering his dark brown hair to his head and streaming from his face onto his sodden coat.

'Are you all right?' he yelled above the ferocious noise, trying to shield his eyes with one hand as he looked at her through the wild darkness. 'Annie, are you okay?'

She barely heard him, but it didn't matter; she reached out and grabbed his arm, pulling him quickly into the warmth and comfort of the cottage. She slammed the door to the night, and there was quietness around them as the wind and rain were momentarily drowned out.

Chapter Eleven

Annie was silent as she stared at him, astonished by his unexpected presence and the sudden stillness as they stood together in the tiny hall. Jon pushed a distracted hand through his drenched hair, slicking it backwards. She noticed how the wetness had disguised the natural colour, turning it inky black, and he spoke again.

'Are you all right?'

She heard the concern in his tone and blinked rapidly as she looked down, watching the rain from his clothes dripping onto the stone beneath his feet.

'Not really.' Sure he would hear the fear in her voice, she clenched her fists tightly, determined to drive it away. 'It's so pathetic but I'm scared of storms.' She tried to laugh it off but relief that he was here sent her emotions lurching again and she gulped, horrified by a tiny sob catching in her throat.

'Of course it isn't,' he said gently. There was little distance between them and just a step nearer would take her into his arms. But she remained still, even though for the briefest moment she thought he was going to draw her to him. Another roar of wind outside distracted them both and she shot into the sitting room, relieved to have broken away. Light blazed from each room in the cottage as he followed her, ducking beneath the beams while starting to shrug out of his wet jacket.

'I think the willow's come down,' Annie said worriedly. 'I haven't had a chance to see how bad it is yet.'

Jon frowned as she finally looked at him. 'I'd better go check.' He zipped his coat up once more as he turned back to the door.

'Be careful,' Annie shouted nervously, afraid for him outside in the storm. She pulled the curtains aside, watching apprehensively as he returned with a torch from his car and disappeared around the side of the house. She hurried into the kitchen and switched on the Nespresso machine, reaching for the tray of capsules.

She peered through the window into the dark garden, spotting the quick flash of Jon's torch as he moved around and wished he would hurry back into the safety of the house. She hoped fervently the damage wasn't as bad as she expected; the willow tree was such a part of the cottage that she dreaded the idea of losing it, even though she wasn't too keen on having so much of it inside the house right now. She found a dustpan under the sink and squeezed into the pantry, carefully brushing up the worst of the broken glass.

Realising she was still in pyjamas, she dashed upstairs and changed back into jeans and the same sweater. She returned to the kitchen and was sliding a capsule into the Nespresso when she heard the bang of the front door. She spun around as Jon appeared once again, the rain dripping onto his face and moulding his clothes to his body.

'It's not too bad.' He sounded tired but optimistic. 'The tree's still upright but a fairly big branch has snapped and taken most of the coalhouse roof with it. The house is okay – I don't think the branch is going anywhere until it can be moved in the morning.'

'Thank you.' Annie was filled with relief that the cottage wasn't about to collapse around her ears any moment. 'I was expecting much worse, it sounded like a whole forest crashing on top of me.' She found mugs, jumping uneasily when she heard the loud howl of the wind outside and the porcelain trembled between her fingers. She glanced nervously at Jon, who was still dripping water onto the stone flags. She blurted out the first thought in her head.

'Give me your coat.' He shrugged out of it again and Annie took it from him. The rain had driven through to his shirt, leaving damp patches on his shoulders and chest, and his dark jeans were soaked. She tried not to stare, even as she heard amusement in his voice.

'Thanks.' Jon reached into his pocket and dumped keys and phone on the table, the pager still on his belt. Their eyes met, and she had already forgotten the mess outside as they looked at one another.

'I'll bring you something to dry with.' Annie draped his coat over a chair and pulled it beside the Rayburn. She hurried upstairs and grabbed a soft cotton towel. When she returned, he was standing by the sink, drying his hands with kitchen roll and smiled as she handed him the towel.

'Thank you for checking on me,' she said casually, sliding a mug into place and pressing a button on the coffee machine to pour the first drink.

'I wouldn't have knocked if the lights hadn't been on. May I?' She nodded, and he pulled out a chair and sat down. Annie managed to suppress a smile as she looked at his flattened hair and liquid blue eyes. 'I was on my way home and thought I'd just drive by, make sure you were okay. I didn't want you to feel afraid.'

She was taken aback by his thoughtfulness towards her and didn't want to contemplate the reason why. She took a deep breath before replying quietly. 'I'm glad you did.' She looked away as she told him the truth, pouring another drink for herself. She took her time, eventually handing him a steaming cup of strong black coffee.

The wind still hadn't eased and she shivered, glancing nervously into the blackness beyond the window. Despite Jon's assurance Annie was nonetheless afraid that another catastrophe would clobber the cottage before the storm was done, and she swallowed a mouthful of her coffee anxiously.

'Annie, I'm staying here until it's over,' he said firmly.

She looked at him, startled. She shook her head, disturbed by the idea of his being with her all through the night and worse, leaving in the morning with half the village watching. 'I'm fine, really.' She was afraid of being on her own with him for so long, having to disguise her confused feelings and the persistent impulse to reach out to him. 'You should go.'

'Only if you really want me to.' Jon lowered his voice as he leant forward to watch her steadily. 'Would you rather be alone?'

Her first thought was to nod and say of course she would, but she wouldn't, not really. It was only midnight, and as she imagined the long hours ahead she knew she didn't want him to leave, and her whispered 'no' was cautious. She hoped the sudden glint of pleasure she saw in his eyes wasn't reflected in her own and stood up hastily.

'I'll light the fire.' She grabbed matches from a shelf and hurried into the sitting room. She rearranged the logs and struck a match from the box, holding it against the newspaper until it caught light. Soon sparks began to flutter into flames, turning the paper into charred crumbs, and she turned away from the growing warmth to settle onto a seat.

She had arranged the two cream sofas on either side of the fireplace with the antique coffee table in between, and despite still wanting to change the curtains and paint the walls, the cottage was beginning to feel more like her home. Jon emerged from the kitchen, holding their mugs and his phone, and she pointed to the coffee table so he could set them down. She curled her legs underneath her, trying to relax as she watched him. He bent down and removed his wet shoes.

'Do you mind?'

She laughed, shaking her head as he propped his shoes not too near the hearth. The sound of the fire grew louder as the logs began to burn. It smelled of damp wood and burning dust, and she wrinkled her nose, remembering that the first task every morning when she was here as a child was re-laying and lighting the fire.

His eyes were waiting patiently when she lifted her head, remembering his comments last Sunday and after the party. She wondered where to begin a conversation, how to keep things simple between them. But she was having the strangest feeling that, already, the two of them had progressed beyond simplicity and she was fearful of what might happen next. Finally she spoke, trying to keep her tone vague.

'What was the village like when you were a child?' she asked, letting him know she hadn't forgotten what they had talked about on that first day here in the cottage. 'It must seem different now.'

Jon smiled wryly, tipping his head sideways to consider her question. 'It's very different and yet somehow the same, if that doesn't sound crazy.'

Annie shook her head; it felt that way to her, too. She waited for him to continue, noticing the wistful expression in his eyes.

'I thought I'd live here forever. Farming was all I ever wanted to do, and I never saw the inside of the house until I was dragged to bed.' He grinned, and she couldn't help smiling again as she thought of what he might have been like as a boy. 'Most of the people we knew worked on the land in some way or another, and it never occurred to me that I'd be any different. It was only when my mom went back to America that everything changed.'

'I'm sorry,' she said quietly, wishing she'd never asked the question. 'I didn't mean to drag up something you'd probably rather forget.'

'Don't apologise,' he said gently, the grin fading away. He moved forward until his elbows were propped on his thighs. Annie's eyes drifted to the length of his legs and unnerving thoughts fluttered through her mind. 'My mother had been used to travelling with her parents – my grandfather worked for the U.S. State Department and they'd lived in Europe for some time. She met my father in London and once they married, my mother discovered she hated being in a small village and couldn't wait to escape. She didn't understand my father's ties to the estate or his determination that his children would be born here. I guess it was inevitable they wouldn't stay together but it was a long time until I could forgive her for taking me away. I'm sorry, I don't mean to be boring.'

'You're not.' Annie was quick to reassure him, wondering when he had last spoken of these things. 'Please, don't stop.' Her eyes returned to his face and Jon looked at her, sighing as he dragged a hand through his damp hair, his shoulders slumped. She saw his face become masked with something darker, more painful, and his voice lowered.

'They both tried for full custody when they split and eventually my dad lost. I wasn't allowed to come home very often because Mom was convinced that Dad would find a way to keep me here, so I didn't see a lot of him when I was growing up. She'd never have admitted it, but I think she used some diplomatic contacts to swing things in her favour. I didn't realise until I was about thirteen that she must have suffered from depression for most of her adult life, and it worsened as she got older until she became an alcoholic. I saw her deteriorate into somebody unrecognisable whenever she drank, and I swore that I would never let it happen to me. I guess I'm still afraid that it could, but my faith helps to keep things in perspective.'

Shocked, Annie stared at him in silence.

'She died last year.' Despite the blunt words and composure in his voice, Annie saw grief in his eyes, and she held herself still as he continued. 'She wasn't always careful with her medication, and one evening she mixed it up and took too much. She wasn't found until the following morning and died two days later.'

'I'm so sorry,' Annie whispered, her heart breaking for the pain he must have felt. 'I had no idea.'

Jon gave her a quick smile as the sorrow disappeared back into its hidden corner. She resisted an urge to place her hand against his face to try and smooth away the anguish.

'I can usually deal with death,' he said quietly, leaning back in his seat. Annie was thankful now that her hand had remained by her side, afraid of where her impulsive gesture might have taken them. 'But I don't know if she did it deliberately or not. She might have lived if she'd been found sooner. And I really hate the thought of her lying there alone and I still wonder if she was waiting for somebody to come and save her.'

Annie's eyes filled with tears for him and this time, instinctively, she moved nearer, inching forward until her fingers breached the space between them and found his hand. It was warm and softer than she'd expected, and when her thumb reached his palm, he turned his hand over, gently entwining his fingers around her own. She was vaguely aware of the heat of the fire close by, but it was a quite different warmth that blazed across her skin and sent her senses soaring. And then, slowly, he released her. She didn't know what to say, if she could ever find the words to console him without seeming banal and was staggered by how much she wanted to. His gaze never left her as she sat back, restoring the physical distance between them as the emotional one began to shrink.

'What did you read at university?' She met his look steadily, telling him with her eyes that what he had shared with her mattered, even as they spoke of other things. Jon paused, and she knew he understood.

'Social and political sciences. I developed an interest in politics when I lived in Washington, but came back to the UK to study at Cambridge.'

'What about the farming?'

He grinned. 'Saved that for when I came home. I went back to college and did a course in land management. Everything had moved on while I was away and I needed to catch up.'

Annie slipped down to the floor and threw some more logs onto the fire. She wriggled back against the sofa, drawing her knees up and resting her chin on them as she wrapped her arms around her legs. The storm seemed less wild now, although she could still hear the drumming of water against the windows. It was only a moment until Jon joined her, pushing the coffee table away as he settled opposite her. She noticed that the warmth of the fire had dried his clothes and his shirt no longer clung to his chest.

'Annie, may I ask you a question?' He stretched out long legs as she nodded, and she felt the touch of his knee against her foot. 'Why did you decide to come back to Thorndale, and not just sell the cottage or let it?'

Everything that had been so important to her about Iain McFarlane before she came here was beginning to seem less so, especially now, and she stared into the fire as she wondered how much to share. Finally she lifted her head to find the startling blue of Jon's gaze waiting for her, drawing her into its depths.

'You've probably heard I was engaged, and it ended.' It wasn't a question and Annie saw Jon nod as she took a deep breath. 'We'd talked about having a family one day but it was never certain I would be able to.' She paused, her mind taking her back to those first days of painful, heavy periods followed later by tests and a diagnosis of endometriosis. Hormone treatment had followed before and after surgery while Iain held her hand and reassured her. 'At first it didn't matter but once I started to feel better, we agreed to try for a family straight after the wedding because my condition could get worse over time and there was no point in waiting. Iain really wanted children and the longer we were together, the more important it was to him.' She hesitated, her voice dropping to a low whisper. 'But he left me for someone else and I heard a couple of months later that she was pregnant.'

She hadn't told Kirstie everything. Such disclosure seemed to belong to a stormy night settled indoors by the fireside while wind and rain thundered through the darkness outside, telling someone who was a stranger and yet seemed able to see into her soul. Jon didn't need words to show her what he was thinking as he switched places to sit next to her and slid an arm around her shoulders. Annie stilled for a moment, feeling the solid warmth of his body against hers as he drew her close, and she relaxed, allowing herself to find peace and comfort in his gesture.

The rise and fall of his breathing soothed her, bringing a quiet strength to her voice. 'There didn't seem much point in staying. My flat was already up for sale as we were supposed to be moving, and I left Edinburgh without really thinking what living here would be like. I still wake up in the mornings and wonder how I got here. But Molly and the cottage are the only real home I can remember, and I loved her for it.'

'And she's done it again,' Jon said, his voice low against the diminishing storm. 'Given you a home to be happy in.' He paused. 'Will you stay?'

She couldn't look at him, couldn't lift her head to find his eyes and wonder at the question hovering in them, suddenly afraid that it was important to both of them, her head against his shoulder. 'I wouldn't know where else to go.'

Gradually she drew away and he lifted his arm, removing it from her shoulders and returned to his former place, opposite her in front of the fire. Annie stared into the blaze, knowing she was tumbling headlong into sheer uncertainty, nervous of him and the way he was making her feel. Quietness surrounded them, the only sounds the crackling of the fire and occasional gust of wind outside, and she was thankful he couldn't hear the racing of her heart.

'Why did you want to become a teacher?'

Annie smiled, beginning to relax again as she thought about Jon's question. 'Molly believed that having an education was the most important and liberating gift. She made teaching seem so essential, so inspiring there was no doubt in my mind that I would do the same. She never took her education or right to vote for granted.'

'That's a wonderful reason. She must have been very proud of you.' He gave her a lazy grin as he lowered his voice. 'What's your secret for making a class behave?'

She could feel warmth blooming on her cheeks at his comment, wishing she didn't notice every little gesture as he rested long fingers on his thigh. 'Clapping,' she said promptly, and he grinned.

Annie knew her tone matched his now, and she thought of what had passed between them this evening. A barrier had been demolished and she was already apprehensive of where they would be tomorrow, once they were no longer surrounded by firelight and shadows dancing through the darkness. She turned her head away, listening for the stillness outside. She knew the storm had disappeared into the night, leaving its chaos strewn all around. And, despite everything she had told herself very firmly, she felt only regret at the thought of him leaving.

'It's gone.' She stood up, feeling the heat of the fire on her back as she headed for the kitchen. 'I'll bring your coat.'

Jon didn't disagree, and when she returned to the sitting room, he was pulling his shoes back on. She felt tense without knowing why as he shrugged the coat on as well and she handed him his mobile and keys. He followed her into the hall and before she opened the front door, she turned to him.

'Thank you for staying.' She didn't quite meet his eyes as he towered above her. 'I do appreciate it.'

There was a moment when she thought he was going to touch her face, until he stepped out into the garden. She was astonished by the calmness around them, despite the rain still drizzling in the darkness, adding its dampness to the torrents that had come before. Annie resisted the impulse to check for villagers who might see him leaving her house in the early hours of the morning, hoping it was far too late for anybody to be nearby.

'Night,' Jon murmured, and she waited as he began to walk to his car. He took only a few paces before he surprised her and turned back to the cottage. With a couple of long strides, he was standing on the doorstep once more, his hair already becoming wet again as the misty rain settled on him. She clutched the door, nervousness forcing her heart to beat faster as she stared at his face illuminated by the light from the hall.

'Annie,' he said casually, shoving his hands into his jeans pockets as he looked at her. 'Will you have dinner with me one evening this week?'

There it was. She felt the blood rushing to her face as he asked the question she had wanted to avoid and yet had known would be inevitable since the first time he had come to her cottage. Every sensible thought screamed no, and every sense shrieked acceptance.

'Yes,' she whispered, so quietly she thought at first he hadn't heard. But his uncertain smile lengthened into a grin that deepened the lines around his eyes until he turned. She watched him climb into the Land Rover and roar away before she finally closed the door, anticipation blending into a happiness she didn't want to dismiss just yet.

Chapter Twelve

Annie woke early on Monday morning, stretching sleepily and trying to remember if everything so clear in her mind had really happened last night. A secret smile of pleasure turned into a laugh as she thought of Jon leaving only a few hours earlier and her easy acceptance of his invitation. But then it struck her. What had she done? Why had she agreed to have dinner with him? Returning to sleep was impossible and so she climbed out of bed and opened the curtains cautiously. The storm damage wasn't as bad as she'd feared, and she was thankful. Her car was still upright, even though a few branches in the lane weren't, and the garden was littered with leaves and limp plants.

Downstairs she peered nervously through the kitchen window. But Jon had been right, the snapped branch hadn't inflicted as much harm as she had expected. She knew that the pantry would survive and began to think about how she was going to sort it all out. As if summoned by her thoughts, she heard a knock at the door and rushed to open it, revealing Jon, looking sharp and fresh in the morning sun.

'You're back!' Annie cringed at her startled greeting, sure her eyes were giving away her thoughts along with her pleasure at seeing him again, and he grinned in response to her surprise.

'Annie, this is Arthur Middleton, our facilities manager for the estate. I've brought him to help clear up the storm damage from last night.'

As Jon moved aside, Annie noticed a middle-aged man with a toolbox in his hand. The older man stepped forward and tipped his head to her in polite greeting. She opened her mouth to refuse but Jon was quicker and held up a hand.

'I know you can manage but that branch probably needs a chainsaw and he's here to help. He'll be done and out of your hair in no time.'

Annie's mouth closed with a snap as she tried to figure out how she felt about being managed so effectively by the man in front of her. Mulling over her options, she ultimately settled on feeling grateful for the assistance, but a quick sigh of exasperation escaped before she turned to Arthur. 'I really appreciate your help, Mr Middleton. Thank you.'

Arthur clearly took that as consent to begin work, and he promptly disappeared towards the back of the cottage. Annie turned back to Jon and was pleased to see he at least looked a little sheepish at his behaviour.

'I would stay and do it myself, but I'm needed back on the estate.' He paused, his eyes searching her face. 'Annie, about last night. I'll understand if you've changed your mind.'

She heard the gentleness in his voice and was glad of the opportunity to be rational. She should explain that of course she couldn't accept his invitation now that the shadows had slunk back into the night, and she was no longer surrounded by fear spinning out of control at the whim of the wind. But meeting his waiting gaze, she found that she couldn't get the words out. 'I haven't changed my mind.'

His face lit up with a smile that became more sensual as he looked at her. 'Are you busy on Thursday evening?'

She barely hesitated as she shook her head.

'Good. I'll pick you up at five o'clock then, okay?'

'Why?' She heard the tease in her voice as she nodded. 'Do you need me to cook again?'

He laughed, his smile slipping away until they were staring at one another. 'I think it's my turn next.' He sighed. 'I suppose I'd better get going. I'll ask Arthur to come back in a couple of days and mow the grass if you like. Should be dry enough by then if this better weather holds.'

'Thank you,' she replied, smiling and shuffling from foot to foot as he turned to leave. 'Wait! Where are we going, on Thursday? Is it smart, casual or something in between?'

Jon gave her a mischievous look. 'First, wait and see, I want to surprise you. Second, in between, I guess. Not too smart.'

She rolled her eyes at the typically male, vague response, and then he was gone, hurtling away in his car. She returned to the kitchen and began clearing away the debris from last night, still sparkling at the thought of seeing him again so soon. Arthur reappeared a bit later on, promising to send a glazier later to replace the glass in the window, and she thanked him gratefully for restoring order after the storm, the fallen tree neatly chopped into logs for the fire. She realised after he'd gone that he had also fixed the gate back on its hinges, reminding her of Jon flinging it to the ground after Sarah's party.

Annie had a mountain of work to prepare for the new school term, including the project on Fountains Abbey that she was planning, but when she sat in the study after lunch and tried to concentrate, all she could think of was Jon. She couldn't decide whether she was excited or terrified about Thursday evening, but knew for certain she wasn't managing to create the more peaceful life she sought away from the dangers of dating.

After catching herself staring out the window for the umpteenth time a row, she called it quits on getting any work done today and popped out for some fresh air and supplies from the post office. As she was leaving the shop, her head already feeling clearer for the short walk, she heard someone calling her name and was delighted to see Sam strolling down the high street.

'How are you?' Sam asked – or that's what Annie assumed she said, because at that moment the roar of an oncoming tractor drowned out her voice. They both waited for it to pass before speaking again and Annie was surprised to see Nathan at the wheel.

'He seems incredibly young to be in charge of such a big vehicle,' Annie murmured, eyes still following the tractor.

'He's eighteen, even though he doesn't really look it. But he's very responsible and Jon trusts him,' Sam informed her. 'He loves driving. Apparently he had a summer job after leaving school and saved up enough money to take lessons as soon as he could.'

'Where's he from?' Annie asked curiously, turning back to Sam.

'Nottingham. He lives with his mum. His dad left when Nathan was about seven. He came to Kilnbeck when he left school as part of the National Citizen Service and then last year he came back for two weeks, when previous students can return as volunteers.'

'And now he's working on the estate?'

Sam drew her brows together, her sympathy evident in the small gesture. 'Yes. He was an athlete, by all accounts a talented middle-distance runner, and then he got mixed up in a gang and gave up running and his place at college. A couple of months ago a boy was robbed and badly beaten up. Nathan was arrested, along with most of the rest of the gang, but no witnesses came forward and the police couldn't bring charges. He swore he didn't have anything to do with it, but his mum was distraught and came to see Jon, pleading with him to have Nathan here for the summer, to give him a chance away from the city. Jon agreed and so Nathan's staying with Arthur Middleton and his family, who've had students at home before. I think Nathan loves being here but tries hard not to show it, and he worships Jon. I suppose you don't make friends where he's from if people think you're weak.'

Annie's heart softened as she thought of Nathan trying to become part of a place he had only glimpsed from the outside, and she wondered how he was coping. Sam laughed, her eyes crinkling with merriment.

'But word has it that he's extremely popular amongst the females of our community, and he certainly seems to spend a lot of money in the shop.'

'Of course, Cara! Are they seeing each other?'

Sam brought her hand up to rest on her expanding bump. 'I don't think so. She's only just turned seventeen and her parents aren't too keen. He probably won't stay, and they won't want her to get hurt.' Sam's gaze became mischievous again as she looked sideways at Annie. 'So come on, tell me, what's going on with you and Jon? I saw the way he was looking at you the other night when we had supper. Are you two dating yet?'

Annie couldn't restrain the anticipation at seeing him, leaving her glowing with something she knew Sam wouldn't miss. 'I'm having dinner with him on Thursday,' Annie admitted, hoping she sounded more casual than she felt. 'Nothing more. I'm really not looking for anyone else right now.'

Sam reached across to squeeze Annie's hand with a grin. 'Doesn't matter. These things often find us when we least expect it. Just enjoy it, Annie, I'm sure you'll have a wonderful time together. He's a lovely man. He really went out of his way to help Charlie and me settle in here. And…' Sam drew out the last word, her eyes becoming merry.

'And what?' Annie couldn't keep the amusement from her voice, already guessing what might be about to follow.

'Surely you don't need me to spell it out for you! I might be married but I'm not blind!'

'Sam!'

They chatted for a while, swapping storm stories before heading their separate ways. As Annie was passing the farm, Robert hailed her from the yard and ambled over, asking if she could help at the agricultural show in the village a week on Saturday. Put on the spot, she agreed without quite realising what she'd done until it was too late.

When Thursday arrived, she was almost expecting a fanfare to herald her awakening on the day of the date. Despite the calming effects of lavender crystals in the bath, tension, or anticipation – she couldn't tell which – twisted her nerves into knots as she got ready. She decided her make-up should be simple and understated and chose a foundation that flattered the tone of her already sun-kissed skin. The rest was easy and familiar, and she stroked a little blusher over her cheeks once she had finished her eyes. She slid lip-gloss across her mouth and dropped the tube into a small handbag, shrieking out loud as she realised it was a quarter to five already.

She knew exactly what she was going to wear and deftly removed the cornflower blue, floral wrap dress from the wardrobe, wondering again if it were too casual and hoping Jon wouldn't turn up in a suit. Annie slipped the dress on and it slid down to rest just above her knees, its fit and flare style with a V neck flattering her cleavage perfectly. She found white pumps and slipped them on, already feeling fantastic and decidedly sexy at the thought of seeing him so soon. She told herself that it was just dinner, but it didn't really feel that way as she remembered sitting with him in the darkness of Sunday evening and the things they had shared.

She was still trying to decide whether to wear her hair up or down when she heard a knock at the front door and quickly ran her fingers through her hair, tousling the curls. She grabbed her bag and a denim jacket from the bed and made her way downstairs, pausing in the hall. Jon knocked again and she took a deep breath as she opened the door. He was facing the garden and spun around sharply, smiling as soon as he saw her. He gazed at her for a long moment and she knew her choice of outfit had been right.

He wasn't wearing a suit and in those few seconds she took in every detail of his appearance. Dark indigo jeans and brown suede desert boots looked incredibly sexy on his tall frame, worn with a sky-blue Oxford shirt that seemed to draw out the distinctive blue of his eyes.

'Hi. You look perfect,' he said softly.

'Thank you.' She hardly recognised the high pitch of her voice, clutching her bag with one hand as she draped the jacket across her arm. 'So do you. I like your shirt.' She knew her response was tame and completely at odds with the glowing sensation awakening every sense.

'Thanks.' He gave her a quick grin, holding out his arm for her to take. 'Are you ready?'

She nodded, very conscious of him as they walked to the gate, knowing he had shortened his long stride to keep pace with her. He unlocked the car and as she lifted one foot inside, she felt his hand on the small of her back. The sudden heat flared every nerve ending into complete awareness of his slightest touch. It was only a moment until he was beside her and started the engine.

'Elvis Presley?' Annie raised her voice in disbelief as the sound of *Suspicious Minds* drifted from the speakers. Her eyes darted across to Jon's and he laughed as he lowered the volume, one hand on the steering wheel while he turned the car onto the high street. The pub was still busy, and the warm evening sun was encouraging the last of the day-trippers to linger before they left this pretty little place to its inhabitants and made their way home.

'Hey, what are you trying to say?' His laugh became a smile as he drove. 'It's my stepfather's fault, I guess. Elvis songs were always playing in the house growing up and somehow it didn't put me off. Actually, it's my speciality.' Jon waved at somebody as they headed out of the village, and Annie resisted the impulse to slide a little lower in her seat to make herself less visible, trying to ignore the thought of gossip and the interest their being seen together would bring.

'Excuse me?'

'Impersonating Elvis. It's my party trick.'

'Seriously?' Annie's voice was incredulous, her eyes still on Jon's. 'No!'

'You don't believe me?'

'No! Well, yes of course but really! Elvis impersonator? Do you do weddings?' Annie was enjoying the look of pleasure on his face as she teased him.

'No. But maybe when you've seen me perform you can decide if I'm good enough for a wedding.'

'White jumpsuit or black leather?'

'I haven't got a jumpsuit, so I guess I'd have to say the black leather.' His smile became lazy and she suppressed a shiver.

'So where are we going tonight?' Annie's eyes surreptitiously took in small details she had missed before, the faded scar more prominent on the left side, the strands of grey visible amongst the brown.

'To a restaurant where the two halves of my heritage meet.' Jon turned his head to grin at her until the demands of driving claimed his attention and he looked back at the road in front of them. 'It's not very big but I hope you'll enjoy it. It's in Whitby, hence the earlier start but if I'm honest I'd like the extra time with you.'

Surprised, her gaze flew back to his and she saw the truth of his remark reflected in his eyes.

'It sounds lovely.'

The conversation became simpler as they talked of the village, the people they remembered and those who had moved on. Jon shared some of his plans for Kilnbeck, and Annie was beginning to understand how passionate he was about the centre and relished the opportunity to teach young people ways to improve their confidence and skills. By the time they parked in Whitby, Annie was feeling wonderfully relaxed and desperate to find out more about the man beside her.

'The restaurant is on the other side of the river. If you're happy to walk round I thought it might be nice to see some of the town.'

'Love to.' Annie was glad she was wearing pumps, not heels, as she collected her bag and got out of the Land Rover, Jon already there to open the door for her. He took her jacket from the backseat and Annie slipped it on. It was a beautiful evening but breezy, the sun sliding into the landscape behind them with the smooth calm of the sea stretching far ahead. Across the river she saw people strolling from the abbey now it had closed for the day. The call of seagulls and that typical briny smell made her smile in delight.

'I can't remember when I last came to a seaside town like this,' she told Jon as they set off. 'It must be nearly twenty years.'

'But the smell of fish and chips never changes, does it?'

At some point during their walk, Annie realised they were holding hands and had no idea who had reached for whom, trying not to love the feel of his fingers folded around hers. She still didn't know what to expect for dinner and when they halted, she looked up and laughed, thrilled with his choice. They were outside a glass-fronted American diner with white lettering on a red background, close to the bridge on the other side of the river. Quirky pubs and seaside attractions stretched across each riverbank, clinging to the hillside rising behind them.

'So I've never been here before, but it's meant to be really good and I loved the idea of bringing you somewhere America meets Yorkshire. It's kinda the two halves of me.'

Annie didn't know what to say; she wasn't sure how to tell him how much she loved his originality.

'Ready?' He was watching her, and she nodded.

'It looks wonderful. I can't wait to try it.'

Pale blue walls surrounded low booths with red and white striped seats. They were shown to a corner seat and Jon slid in opposite her. The walls were covered with American posters and paraphernalia and an American flag was pinned to the ceiling. A huge jukebox stood in a corner on the black and white chequered floor and their eyes met, both starting to laugh as an Elvis track came booming through the speakers. A friendly waitress with a broad Yorkshire accent passed menus across the plain white table and listed the specials. Once she'd gone away again with their drinks order, Annie leaned forwards and shrugged out of her jacket.

'I love it here. I feel as though I've stepped straight into *Grease*.'

'The movie? I've never seen it.'

'No! You must have, everyone's watched it.'

'Not me.' His glance was amused as he looked up from the menu. 'I know, something for the bucket list. Maybe we could do that together.'

Annie shrugged casually, not wanting her body to reflect the acceptance her mind was already clamouring for, turning to the menu, sensing him still looking at her all the same. Within a few minutes the waitress had returned with root beers and took their order.

'Is your family home yet?' Annie asked, lifting her head to find Jon's waiting gaze. The noise was building around them now that every table was taken, and she had to raise her voice.

'Saturday.' He took a sip of his root beer. 'My dad hasn't been well and Emma, my stepmother, took him on a Mediterranean cruise to recuperate.' And then he grinned, mischief in his eyes as he continued. 'He hated the idea of a cruise. I can't really see him trundling around a huge ship with a load of other OAPs getting in his way. He'll probably run them over. Sorry, I should've explained earlier. He's in a wheelchair now after a bad accident a few years ago. He came off a quad bike on the estate and was left paralysed from the waist down.'

'I'm sorry,' she murmured.

Jon nodded his thanks. 'He might not have survived without the fell rescue team. They realised immediately when they found him how serious it was and treated him at the scene before he was flown to hospital.'

'Is that why you volunteer with them now, because of your dad?'

'Partly. I knew I had good experience to offer and I feel it's another way to be useful in the community. It was kinda because of my dad's accident that I ended up coming home. I'd left the mission and was working with a summer camp in France when it happened. I'd planned to look around for something else once Dad was settled but Emma sat me down in the hospital one day and was pretty blunt. She made it clear that Dad needed me here, not just for the business but in the family as well.'

'Do you miss Kenya and the missionary work?' Annie asked, watching him steadily.

'Not any more. At first everything at home was so different to what I was used to, especially the pace of life, even in a quiet village.' He rested his elbows on the table as he leaned towards her. His voice lowered and she unconsciously copied his gesture until the distance between them shrank further, the noise around them fading away in their intimacy. 'I'd wanted a new challenge, although I hadn't expected to find it back at home. Once I started to think about the estate's resources and ways to use them, I pretty much knew I had decided to stay.'

Annie understood him instantly as she thought of what he had already achieved since coming home.

'How about you? Are your parents still living abroad?' He reached for his drink, curiosity in his expression.

She began to relax again, wondering if any shared detail between them had been forgotten. The waitress returned with their meals and they were silent until she had placed their plates on the table. Jon thanked her and after she'd left, Annie continued. 'Yes. They moved to an apartment in Malta when my dad retired. They were used to living in the sun and didn't want to come back to England.' She smiled wistfully, still trying to work out the best way to eat her hot dog, relatively plain and simple compared to Jon's, which was loaded with cheese and a smoky sauce. 'I don't see very much of them but Malta is lovely to go to for holidays.'

'Whom do you take after?' he asked curiously. 'Perhaps I shouldn't ask but you don't sound like either of them from what you told me earlier.'

'Don't worry, I'm not adopted.' They laughed together, and she knew he was still listening as he ate. 'I suppose I'm quite serious, like my dad. I'm told I look like my grandmother on Dad's side – my hair is a similar colour to hers. I never knew her. She died before I was born.'

'She must have been very beautiful.'

The intended compliment was impossible to ignore, and Annie swallowed, feeling as though she was standing on constantly shifting ground and couldn't be sure where to place her feet safely. 'Thank you,' she answered breezily, pretending she hadn't really understood his meaning. 'I believe my grand-father thought so.'

Jon clearly saw through her attempt to dodge the compli-ment and the wink he gave her was quick and flirty, the sensuous gaze gone. She was reminded of the first day at the cottage when he'd discovered her in the garden, feeling as though it was an age ago, even though barely two weeks had passed. The memory was enough to set her senses alight when she pictured his expression then, and now she couldn't tear her eyes from his, wondering how it was they seemed to understand one another, her curiosity still growing.

'May I ask you a personal question?' She wasn't surprised when he nodded. 'Have you ever been married?'

He shook his head, reaching for a napkin to wipe his mouth and replacing it on his nearly empty plate. 'No. I did propose to a girl at Cambridge, but she had more sense and turned me down – we were far too young. I guess I was just looking for some certainty. We were about to go travelling and I didn't want to lose her.' Jon's expression became thoughtful and she knew that what he would tell her next was more serious. 'I met somebody else while I was living in Kenya. She was from Ireland and we worked for the same mission. But eventually she wanted to get married and start a family and I didn't, not at that stage in my life anyway. Niamh was a couple of years older than me and felt it was time, for her.'

'Were you together for a long time?' Annie saw recollection in his eyes as his thoughts drifted into memories. She was finally making headway with her hot dog, trying not to let everything slide off it and land on her lap.

'Three years, on and off.'

The waitress was back, and Annie was glad to gather her thoughts for a moment as the drinks were replenished, his words a sharp reminder of the comment she'd overhead about his ex-girlfriend at Sarah's party. Jon didn't speak again until they were alone, his voice low, eyes holding hers.

'I've been a Christian since I was twenty-one, almost fifteen years now, and if I'm honest I knew I didn't want to be committed to a marriage for the rest of my life back then. But living in Thorndale and managing the estate has made me think of the future and I've realised I'd like those same things that Niamh did. Marriage, hopefully a family one day. I love living in the house but it's less of a home on my own. It was built to share.'

Dismay dropped through Annie's stomach with a sudden plunge that left her trembling and the rest of her meal on the plate. She looked away, watching the movements around the noisy little diner as the silence between them grew. They were in very different places with their thoughts about marriage and she fixed her eyes on a poster of *Dirty Dancing* on the wall behind his head, sure he would understand the reason for her unease as she tried to picture what a future between them might be, one that seemed unlikely to bring all he apparently wanted. The waitress returned to clear the table and offer dessert menus. Finally, Annie looked at him and he lightened the moment, waving the menu at her.

'Dessert?'

She shook her head, smiling to disguise the sadness. 'I couldn't. Have you seen the size of the ones on the table over there?'

'Maybe we should have a soda float at least, or a milkshake, seeing as I'm trying to give you a Yorkshire flavour of America.'

Annie caught the menu in his hand and took it from him. 'Well, in that case I'll have the banana peanut butter milkshake. Might as well go all out on the American flavours.'

'I'll have the same.'

The waitress returned and Annie ordered their shakes and they chatted above the music until their drinks arrived. Her eyes widened at the size of the glass topped with cream and ice cream. It was delicious if sweet, and she admitted defeat halfway down.

'I'm done. Gorgeous though.'

'Me too. I don't have a very sweet tooth.'

They ordered coffee to finish and conversation was easy and fun, the weight of everything they'd shared before lightened now. Eventually Jon caught the attention of the waitress and moments later the bill was settled.

'Jon, please,' Annie said determinedly, her hand going to her bag. But he was already standing up, and she felt tiny in her flat pumps as she slid out of the booth and stood next to him.

'Absolutely not.' He took her jacket, holding it out so she could shrug into it. She lifted her long curls out of the way, his hands lightly brushing her neck. 'We can argue about it if you like but you're my guest and I promise you I won't change my mind.'

The town was quieter when they stepped outside, the warmth of the day's sun diminished by the evening drawing in. The salty seaside smell drifted amongst that of the fish and chip shop nearby, still doing a roaring trade judging by the queue on the street. The town looked beautiful, the buildings clinging to the hillside opposite them lit by warm lamps, casting a glow onto the people strolling along the harbour and the fisherman getting ready to sail. Slowly they began the walk back to the car, chatting easily about things that were much simpler, though Annie's mind was still whirring with everything Jon had told her.

Soon they were speeding home through the darkened countryside and she knew their date had been almost as perfect as it was possible to be. Jon had been charming, funny, and interesting and she tried to sort through her muddled feelings. She liked him and was certain of the attraction between them. But what could it amount to, if he was hoping for a commitment that could lead to a family? And she was desperate not to offer her heart, only for it to be shattered once again. The spectre of the endometriosis and Iain's betrayal lingered, a small voice telling her that she wouldn't be enough on her own, if she couldn't offer him everything. Normally so decisive and level-headed, she was completely taken aback by how Jon made her feel whenever he looked at her, so different from anyone she had known before, even Iain. Everything seemed to be racing out of control, and she desperately wanted more time to cling to her defences and learn to trust again.

All too soon she recognised the signs popping up through the shadows and Thorndale appeared, slumbering through the night. Moments later they were outside her house and he turned off the ignition, the cottage in darkness and the uneven path darker still. Jon spoke first and his simple words heightened her apprehension, twisting her stomach into knots of nervousness as their ease with one another disappeared.

'Thank you for your company tonight. I had a really great time.'

She let out a breath, overwhelmed by the sudden urge to cry, hopelessly aware that the perfection of their beginning had brought with it their end. How much easier to dismiss him, had he not been everything she'd loved about tonight? Swallowing past the lump in her throat, she tried to keep her voice even as she replied. 'Me too. Thank you.' Not the right words, she knew, not enough to describe the wonderful evening they had just shared. 'I should go. Good night, Jon.'

'May I see you again?'

She knew his eyes were on her and caught her breath, squeezing her lids shut as the tears threatened to spill this time.

'Annie?'

Slowly, she shook her head. 'I can't.' Her voice was a tiny whisper through the quietness as she gave him the answer her common sense – and her still-mending heart – demanded. 'I'm really sorry, but I don't think it would be a good idea.' At first, she thought he hadn't heard her reply and then he sighed, a brief, disappointed exhalation she almost missed but understood instantly. He turned his head away and she put one hand on the door, about to leave, until he spoke again.

'Will you tell me why?' There was no discernible difference in his polite tone, and she couldn't see his eyes to read his expression.

She paused, wishing she could flee into the isolation of the cottage without answering, because to tell him everything would be to admit too much. She didn't want him to know how easily she could fall in love with him, and how afraid she felt of the emotional turmoil it would bring when it inevitably ended. Her thoughts brought sharply back the devastating end of her engagement just a few months ago and the news about Iain's baby that had followed, and it steeled her. She replied honestly, without revealing all.

'I'm just not ready to start dating again,' she said quietly. 'I'm sorry, Jon, I thought I might feel differently after tonight. It's too soon after everything that happened with Iain. I'm not really over all of that yet.'

'Annie, you can't spend the rest of your life hiding from anything that might hurt you,' Jon said gently. He turned to look at her and she folded her arms across her chest in stiff resistance. 'Please don't tell me you'll never allow yourself to fall in love again because you were hurt once before?'

It was far too close to the truth and she raised one shoulder in a silent shrug. 'Thank you for dinner,' she said with a brightness she didn't feel. 'I really am sorry.' She pushed at the door and stepped outside into the lane, clutching her jacket tightly. Jon leapt from the car and shoved the gate open, his hand touching her arm briefly as she passed him. He was behind her as she walked up the path and they didn't speak again until she'd opened the front door and switched on the hall light. She turned around, shaken by the regret in his blue eyes revealed by the glow from the cottage as he looked at her.

'Night, Annie.' He bent his head and brushed his mouth against her cheek, just once. She felt the fleeting roughness of his skin next to her own and a searing heat where his lips had touched her face as her breath caught. 'See you.'

And he was gone, roaring away in his car while she stood in the doorway still, allowing tears to slide from her eyes now that he couldn't see them. Coldness settled around her heart as she began to wonder what she had done in sending him away.

Chapter Thirteen

The following morning Annie was finding it difficult to believe that the date with Jon had come and gone already. The irrepressible high of anticipation had been replaced by gloom as she mooched around the cottage and tried to push thoughts of him from her mind.

Later on she cooked supper for Sam, and they had a lovely evening and, Annie at least, a couple of glasses of wine too many. She eventually told Sam about her date with Jon and how perfect it had been. When Sam asked her if she was going to see him again, Annie found that her reason why not sounded very feeble in the light of everything she'd shared with Jon and the attraction simmering between them. She ended up telling Sam about Iain and the baby. Sam sympathised but said something similar to Jon, about not allowing the past to permanently influence her future and reminding Annie that she didn't need to rush into anything. There was understanding in her new friend's face and Annie knew she was right, even if putting it into practice seemed almost impossible.

Ignoring the pile of work in the study, Annie had a lie-in on Saturday morning, allowing herself the luxury of tea and toast in her pyjamas in the garden. She'd discovered that she could sometimes get a signal on her phone if she stayed close to the kitchen window and she caught up with a few messages before the signal disappeared again. She nipped into town to re-stock on groceries and it was only as she was driving home that she suddenly remembered the cricket match this afternoon. She had made a half tipsy promise to go and watch it with Sam and groaned. Annie hated cricket but she'd promised Sam and didn't want to let her down, especially as Charlie was playing.

She dragged her shopping out of the car and was halfway down her garden path when she did a double take, looking around in surprise. The overgrown grass had been mown and she thought of Jon's offer to have Arthur cut it for her, thrilled he hadn't changed his mind after their date. It wouldn't have been at all like him to renege on his promise and sudden delight brought a smile to her face as she realised that she had a reason to speak with Jon again and thank him.

The weather was looking promising when Annie set off clutching a wide-brimmed hat, sunglasses and the few things she'd thrown into a bag to make a simple picnic. She arrived at the cricket ground and spotted Sam already sitting on a rug near the boundary to the left of the pavilion. Sam waved and Annie made her way across, saying hello to the people she knew as she squeezed through the hordes jostling for a good position.

'Hi,' Sam called, wriggling over to make room on the rug. 'Come and have a drink. It's so warm already.'

Annie sat down, spying Charlie emerging from the pavilion with a couple of other players, including Mark Howard, and Charlie made his way over.

'I can't stay.' He gave Annie a quick grin, and she sensed his impatience to start playing. 'We've lost the toss, we're fielding.'

'Where's Jon?' Sam asked.

Annie hoped the sudden rush of heat to her cheeks wasn't visible and she pushed her bag away, allowing her hair to fall over her face.

'Surely he should be here by now? I thought he'd be opening the batting with you?'

'He's not playing.' Charlie pulled a face, and Annie felt her heartbeat slow again. 'His finger's not fully healed from the whack he got in nets and he doesn't want to fracture it again.'

Annie's mind darted back to their date and Jon's hand holding hers, and she stifled a smile. His fingers had felt fine then. More than fine and there was that quiver again, whenever she thought of him.

'So not the groin strain then?'

Charlie grinned. 'No, I think that's better. It was only a mild tear he picked up on a rescue.'

'Isn't he even coming to watch? It's not like him to miss the match.' Sam still hadn't given up and Annie was all ears while pretending not to be.

'Should be, you know what he's like. He's got something on at Kilnbeck and then he's coming down.' Charlie turned to make his way back to the pavilion.

'Good luck,' Sam called as he strode away, and Annie saw him raise a hand in silent reply. Sam turned to Annie with a grin. 'Neil Dawson's sister's friend is going out with somebody who used to keep wicket for England a few years ago. Jon found out and drafted him into the team. We wouldn't normally use such underhand tactics, but Calstone have brought in a spinner who played for Middlesex so at least they're probably about even.'

'Aren't there rules about those kinds of things?' Annie raised her voice above the sudden cheering of the crowd as the rest of players appeared on the pitch with Charlie.

'Not exactly.' Sam reached for her sunglasses nearby and slipped them on. 'This match is only played once a year for charity. In 1880, when the estates at Thorndale and Calstone were divided up, the two heirs fell out over the same girl. She couldn't decide who to choose, so the boys agreed to play a game of cricket and she would marry the winning captain.'

'Like a duel with teams,' Annie said, intrigued by the story. She slipped her hat on to shield her eyes from the sun. 'But no pistols. Or bodies.'

'Precisely. The game became a tradition, until it died out during the First World War. Jon's grandfather reintroduced it when he bought the estate.'

'Who won?'

'The girl? Frederick Sykes from Calstone. Legend has it that he was really the one she wanted all along, and it must have been true because they were married for thirty-six years and had seven children. Rather her than me.'

People were still arriving, spreading rugs across the grass and encouraging excited children to go off and play in the furthest corners of the field, far away from flying balls. Sarah Holland caused a bit of a stir when she rolled up with a couple of glamorous weekend guests and the newly famous Jed March in tow.

'I wonder if he really is back with Sarah.' Sam was watching Jed, head bowed over his phone. 'At least then she might leave poor Jon alone.'

Annie winced as the unwanted thought of Sarah not leaving Jon alone popped into her head. 'I didn't realise Jon was into cricket,' she said idly.

Sam looked at her beadily. 'Didn't he tell you? He's very good. He had a trial for Yorkshire when he was at Cambridge and played for the village team until Kilnbeck opened and then he had to give up.' She retrieved a bottle of water from her bag and Annie watched drops fizzle onto the ground when Sam opened it. 'I used to think Charlie was competitive until I watched Jon. He gets really irate if he doesn't play well. I saw him chuck his bat into a tree once when he was given out on a dodgy decision, and he had to climb up and retrieve it when he'd cooled down.'

The two opening Calstone batsmen appeared and Annie sighed. Now the boring stuff would begin. She watched as Charlie positioned his players in the field, and then the bowler, who she saw was Mark, marked out his run-up. She looked around the ground, wondering if Kirstie was here to watch him, but couldn't see her. Mark thundered up to the batsman and hurled the ball straight at him to loud cheers. The batsman ducked just in time and the wicket keeper missed a catch, the ball hurtling away. There were two runs on the scoreboard before a portly middle-aged fielder managed to lob it back. The crowd hissed, and Annie laughed. Maybe it would be bearable after all.

But her interest in the game began to weaken as the Calstone total grew steadily and the Thorndale crowd became impatient. Things livened up as Sarah Holland made her way around the boundary, chatting to almost everyone and even picking up a baby, holding it well away from her designer dress. Then it was Annie and Sam's turn. Annie couldn't help sitting up a little straighter as Sarah approached them. She looked up, already at a disadvantage as she squinted into the sun.

'Hi, you two,' Sarah said breezily. To Annie's amazement, Sarah sat down beside them and removed her beautiful, wide-brimmed hat. Her eyes weren't quite as warm as her greeting when they met Annie's, but Annie was determined to be nice and she smiled back. 'Enjoying the game?'

'Not yet,' Sam muttered darkly, shuffling around to get a better look at the players. 'Oh good, Charlie's repositioned the field. Would you like a drink, Sarah?'

'No, thank you,' Sarah replied. Annie noticed Jed chatting to a couple of girls, hearing their laughter from across the field. 'I can't stay long. I just came to support Jon. I thought he was playing today,' she said casually. She clapped as more runs were notched on the scoreboard.

'That's not our team,' Sam pointed out with a grin and Annie laughed.

'Oops, sorry, it's so difficult to tell. Why don't they wear different colours, like footballers do? Anyway, you were telling me about Jon?'

'Was I?' Sam asked. 'Oh yes. He's injured, so he can't play. Groin strain, goodness knows how he did that. Or maybe it's because of the broken finger? So hard to keep up. Do you know, Annie? Did he mention it the other night?'

Annie felt her lips twitching as she tried not to laugh at Sam's impishness. 'No, sorry. Cricket never came up.' She rummaged in her bag for sun block and began to smooth it across her arms and shoulders.

'What a pity,' Sarah murmured. 'He'll be so disappointed not to play. I wonder why he didn't mention it when we met yesterday.'

'Maybe the strain happened overnight then,' Sam said slyly. 'Oh look, there's Megan with her friend from Brighton.' She waved to the older ladies and Annie felt Sarah's cool gaze upon her as she stood up.

'I never liked that particular lotion, Annie. I always found it seemed to disagree with my skin and I have to be so careful, given my career. But I'm sure it will suit you – you obviously freckle so easily.' Sarah was already walking away, but Annie was certain she must've heard Sam's scream of laughter and her own indignant snort.

'Why does she always try to make me feel about six years old with my hand in the biscuit tin,' Annie hissed to Sam, who was still falling about. 'Just when I thought she was going to be nice.'

'Rest assured, you clearly look gorgeous or she wouldn't bother. I'm sure it's not personal but she must have noticed that you and Jon are spending time together, and it seems she isn't ready to chuck in the towel just yet.'

Suddenly they were all startled by a savage yell from the bowler, and the entire Thorndale team erupted in a cheer when the umpire finally held up a finger, the opening batsman out. Crossly the batsman swiped his bat across the ground as he left the field and the Thorndale players gathered in a jubilant huddle.

After that, the rest of the Calstone batsmen didn't seem to be up to much, and when the game broke early for tea they were all out for one hundred and nineteen. Annie's face was freckling, despite the sun block and her hat. At least Sarah couldn't see her. Most people had disappeared to buy ice cream and she helped Sam spread out their picnic.

'Annie, can I be cheeky and ask you to help us?' Sam said sleepily. 'We have a meeting every other Tuesday for the local teenagers to get together and we always feed them. It's our last one before the summer break. What can we give eighteen teenagers that's simple to prepare? I think they've had enough pizza and fries to last a lifetime.'

Annie didn't get around to replying straight away. She was going to say yes, she would help, but that was before she spotted Jon heading for the pavilion. Despite her resolution not to see him, her heart soared at knowing he was nearby. He greeted people on the way but wasn't pausing to chat. She knew Sam's eyes were on her as she dragged her attention back to the question, embarrassed by how easily she had been distracted. She felt almost dizzy with the onslaught of mixed emotions and knew that the pulse in her neck was beating a little faster.

'What about a curry?' she suggested, fixing her eyes firmly on her friend. 'We could make two, with plenty of bread and rice and maybe an apple pie to finish.'

'Brilliant, I knew you'd have an inspired choice. Thank you so much, we can sort out the details later.'

They all stood to clap then as Neil Dawson reached his half-century. Neil held up his bat to acknowledge the cheers from the crowd, taking off his helmet to milk the applause as Charlie slapped him delightedly on the back. They only needed eighteen more runs to win but moments later Neil was bowled out, and he kicked at the ground angrily as he headed to the pavilion. She watched as Jon shook Neil's hand to congratulate his innings anyway, the game almost won. Not once had Jon looked in her direction.

The infamous ex-England wicket keeper came in next. He wasn't troubled very much by the bowlers, despite the once professional spinner, and soon he and Charlie had scored the winning runs. The rest of the Thorndale team, including Jon, rushed onto the pitch to celebrate with them and the crowd sportingly cheered both teams on a lap of honour.

Most of the crowd hung around for the presentation and Charlie accepted the trophy. Annie saw Jon go to each Calstone player and shake hands, trying to commiserate with their loss while celebrating Thorndale's win. But Sarah was still hovering and when she finally had Jon's attention, she kissed him on both cheeks, her hands resting briefly on his shoulders, congratulating him as though he'd been the one to win the match for Thorndale. Grumpily, Annie gathered her things as she said goodbye to Sam and turned for home.

–

Schoolwork took over the rest of the weekend and most of Monday, and Annie was glad to catch up so she would be free to cook on Tuesday. But to her horror, when Sam rang to say that Charlie would do the shopping for the meal, she informed Annie that they always met at Jon's house.

Dreading the possibility of seeing him later at his home, Annie was nonetheless ready to go by four thirty, wishing she had arranged to meet Sam at the vicarage instead. Clutching a sturdy cool bag filled with the drinks she'd offered to provide, she walked through the village to the big, open gates at the entrance to the Hall. The sweeping drive to the house, half hidden behind an avenue of soaring lime trees, seemed imposing and yet somehow inviting. Annie dithered in the lane and then began to walk decisively up the drive, hoping fervently that Jon wasn't at home.

Built of creamy sandstone, she couldn't help but stare at the beautiful Georgian house. Beneath a broad and tiled roof, six windows reached across the building on both floors, the entrance dominated by a wide front door underneath a portico of stone columns. Lush parkland crept higher as the ground rose behind the Hall, sheltered by huge trees separating it from the moor above, with cattle grazing in a field, dotted about like abandoned toys. She spun around as she heard a car, an unwelcome heat on her face as she recognised Jon's

Land Rover. Her shoulders sank and she dawdled near the front door as he leapt out and headed towards her.

'Hi,' she called brightly, trying to make her uncharacteristic arrival at his house seem completely normal. Other than the brief glimpse at the cricket match, it was the first time she had seen him since their date, and she was astonished afresh by his physical presence. She blurted out the first thought on her mind as she tried to pretend that everything between them had reverted to simplicity and not the intimacy they had shared. 'I'm er, waiting for Sam and Charlie, I'm supposed to be helping them with the meal. Sorry, I didn't realise, until today anyway, that it would be here.' She stopped abruptly, realising she was babbling and felt a little better when he gave her a brief smile.

'I know, Sam called me.' He stopped nearby, isolating a key from the set in his hand. 'I've come to let you in as our housekeeper isn't here today. They shouldn't be too long.'

'Oh.' Annie couldn't read his eyes, hidden by sunglasses, as he finally looked at her. He was still in work clothes, his scuffed boots covered in dried mud. Roughened stubble darkened his face, and tempting memories rushed into her mind as she recalled the touch of his lips against her cheek.

'Come in.'

He sounded brusque and her unease flared again as he unlocked the door and pushed it aside so she could enter first. They were in a large, almost square reception hall, its white walls divided by rectangular panels and partially covered by oil paintings, a door in each corner of the room and a fireplace was laid but unlit. Jon dumped his keys and phone on a circular table in the centre beside a vase of beautifully scented freesias and roses. He picked up some of the post, glancing at it idly as he pushed the sunglasses into his hair.

'So many doors,' she said finally, slowly turning around until she was facing him. He dropped the mail back onto the table and glanced at her. She was sure he would be glad to see the back of her and wished she'd never come. She had never dreamt that being in this house with him could feel so inappropriate.

'Those two don't lead anywhere and can't be opened.' He pointed to the doors either side of the fireplace. 'When the house was built in the eighteenth century, they were only included to make the room appear symmetrical, to balance the design. I'll take you through to the kitchen.'

She realised that he probably thought she was prying when all she'd wanted to do was break the silence growing between them. He took the heavy bag and she trailed miserably along a corridor after him, their feet tapping evenly on the stone. He thrust open a door and once again stood aside for her to enter.

The huge room was even bigger than she had been expecting, divided between a kitchen and a family room that looked well used. A scruffy table, big enough to seat twelve, bridged the gap between the two, half hidden beneath carrier bags of shopping. In the family room, a pair of sofas sat at right angles to a coffee table, littered with newspapers and a couple of half empty mugs near a laptop.

The pale grey, almost white walls were splattered with modern abstract pictures, a few family photographs stuck onto a board and a framed map of the farm next door. The last of the evening sunshine was trickling into the kitchen through the large windows overlooking a courtyard garden outside.

'Everything should be here or in the fridge.' Jon pointed to the table and Annie nodded as he dumped her bag alongside the pile. 'But look around, help yourself to anything you need. Most of the pans and stuff are in the cupboard next to the Aga.'

'Thank you.' She felt as though they had been here before, although when she had cooked at Kilnbeck, things between them had been different. The suggestion of a beginning then, an end not yet arrived. She began rummaging through the bags as he moved around behind her.

'See you later. We meet at seven, I'll be back by then.'

'Aren't you staying here?' she asked, astonished and a little alarmed at being in his house alone.

Jon shook his head with a smile that didn't lessen the detachment in his eyes. 'No. I've got to get back to Kilnbeck.'

She began to empty the first bag so he couldn't see her disappointment and heard him unlock the door to the garden and go outside. She was sorting through a pile of vegetables when he suddenly reappeared and she glanced at him in surprise.

'Thanks for helping. I know you'd probably rather not, but I appreciate it and Sam does as well.'

'I don't mind,' she started to say, but he had gone, banging the door behind him without waiting for her reply. Twenty-five minutes later, she had two big pans of onions gently softening on the Aga, and nearly jumped out of her skin when Charlie and Sam burst in through the door from the hall.

'Sorry we're late.' Sam was apologetic as she carefully lowered a large enamel jug of cream onto the table and dashed over to give Annie a hug. 'We planned to be here sooner and then Charlie was called away. Are you okay? It smells delicious.'

'Everything's fine,' Annie assured her. 'The chicken's ready to go in and the peppers just need chopping for the vegetarian curry.'

'I'll do that.' Charlie grabbed a knife and started hacking at courgettes and peppers, and Annie laughed as he hurled big chunks into her pan. They nattered as they worked, and Sam made coffee for all of them.

'You are staying, aren't you?' Sam asked sleepily from the depths of a sofa. 'We're watching a movie after we've eaten.'

'No. Once everything's ready I'll go.' She smiled helplessly when she heard Sam's voice floating across the room.

'We need you to stay,' Sam said firmly, and Annie glanced at Charlie when he laughed. 'I didn't ask you to help just to chuck you out when the cooking's done. Besides, you might enjoy it, and I'm sure Jon won't want you to disappear.'

Annie wondered if Sam was trying to persuade her to stay in order to throw her and Jon together again. She knew she was beaten and accepted defeat, knowing perfectly well that she did want to see Jon again before the evening was over.

The two curries were simmering gently by the time the door sprang open again and Jon walked back in. Annie felt her breath stutter in her throat when he caught her eye and she looked away hastily. He said hello to Sam and dropped onto a sofa to pull off his boots.

'I'm going to shower. I won't be long.' He left the room without giving Annie another glance.

It was too much. The thought of him soaking wet upstairs sent her wits spinning, and she hacked the peeled apples into small chunks as she tried to concentrate on what Charlie was telling her about the forthcoming agricultural show on Saturday, the one Robert had roped her into helping at.

Jon was back in less than fifteen minutes and she recognised the scent of his cologne immediately. It was the same one he had worn for their date, and she wondered crazily if his choice this evening had been deliberate. He hadn't shaved, his hair was still wet, and he was wearing worn jeans and an ice-blue shirt.

'What shall I do?' he asked briskly, looking from Charlie to Annie. He came and stood beside her, and she was certain he was only pretending to be interested in the food when she felt the brush of his arm against her shoulder.

'DVD,' Charlie said, glancing across to him. 'Where is it?'

'In the library. I'll go get it.'

She heard the smile in Jon's reply. Her face was flaming, and she was furious with herself for responding so foolishly to his simple gesture. The teenagers began to arrive a few minutes later, sidling into the kitchen in boisterous groups. They were laughing together, messaging constantly, their fingers and eyes seeming never to leave their phones. Annie tried to remember their names as Charlie introduced her, and one by one they nodded hi, helping themselves to the drinks Sam had already laid out. They settled around the table and sprawled across the sofas, making themselves at home as Jon reappeared.

Cara Dawson arrived with her gaggle of friends and Annie went over to say hello, noticing that, for all her indifference, Cara's eyes spun round the room as she searched for somebody. But Nathan wasn't there, and Annie wondered why not.

She tried to watch Jon surreptitiously as she tipped the curries into serving bowls. He wandered around, speaking to everybody, laughing, joking, listening as he topped up drinks and gathered everyone together. Soon afterwards, Nathan slipped in almost unnoticed and Annie immediately sensed that he had been waiting for everybody else to arrive first. When his eyes found hers briefly, she mouthed a hello to him. He nodded casually and looked away, sliding his hands into low-slung jeans pockets.

'We're just going to give thanks and then we'll eat. Charlie?' Jon looked across to Charlie and the group fell silent as Charlie spoke a blessing and Annie closed her eyes. When she opened them again, Jon was looking straight at her and she tore her gaze away, not wanting to understand whatever he was thinking.

'Okay, let's eat.' Somehow there seemed to be just enough seats for everybody and when they were all hungrily devouring their food, Annie filled a plate and propped herself against the table.

Jon stood up and pointed to his chair. 'You can sit here.'

She shook her head. 'I'm fine, really.'

'Annie, please, take my seat. I'm not sitting while you stand up.' He made his way over to the table, and that was enough to make her go and sit down, feeling several pairs of eyes on her. Most people had finished already and were helping themselves to seconds, Jon included. He caught her eye and she glared at him, letting him know she didn't appreciate being told what to do. His smile was so fleeting she almost thought she'd imagined it, turning to listen to Sam.

Once or twice she noticed some of the group talking with Nathan but each time he answered shortly and lapsed back into silence. Annie knew Jon was watching him, and she made sure to keep his plate loaded, trying to include him in the chatter. He sat as far away from Cara as possible, and Annie decided there really couldn't be anything between them. Once dessert was finished, Annie insisted on clearing up while everyone else headed into the television room. Nathan stayed behind, shaking his head when Jon came to talk with him, and looked at Annie.

'I'll give you a hand.' He stood up, carrying a pile of plates to the dishwasher. Surprised, Annie watched him as Jon paused in the doorway.

'I can manage,' she insisted to Nathan. 'You go and watch the film.'

'No thanks, seen it before.'

Jon disappeared, and even though she wished Nathan had gone to join the others to try and enjoy himself, she was glad of his help. She told him so as he dried all the dishes that had to be washed by hand.

He shrugged casually, giving her a quick glance. 'I'm used to it.'

'What do you mean?' She knew she sounded curious as she refilled the sink with hot soapy water for the next heap of washing up.

'I've got three younger brothers and my mum works full time as a nurse. I do the cooking when she's not at home.'

It was quite different from her own childhood, but she recognised in his voice the pang of disappointment he tried to disguise and she gave him a smile that told him she understood what it meant to grow up before your time. 'What do you like to cook?'

He glanced at her, surprised, as he considered the question. 'Curry. It's easy and my brothers like it.' He grinned, lighting up his face as the wariness in his eyes disappeared. 'But we still have a roast dinner on Sundays when Mum's home. She makes the best Yorkshire pudding.'

'Who's cooking for your brothers while you're away?' Annie asked, and the shutters came back down over his eyes as the smile faded.

'My cousin. She's a year older than me. Mum pays her to help.'

'Your family must miss you,' she said quietly, turning her head to look at him and he raised one shoulder in a silent shrug.

She reached out, touching his arm gently. 'Come on, let's go and watch what's left of the film. Do you know where to find the others?'

He nodded, and they left the kitchen. Annie followed him through the house to a darkened sitting room, a huge TV screen dominating one wall. Heads turned as they walked in and she squeezed into a space at the end of a sofa. Nathan settled nearby on the floor, wrapping his arms around his knees. She couldn't see Jon through the gloom, and she was glad as she tried to concentrate on the film.

When it was over, she and Sam returned to the kitchen to rifle through the cupboards and dole out biscuits, making endless cups of hot chocolate for the ones who hadn't remained behind in the television room. Nathan sat at the kitchen table and Annie was sure he saw everything, despite his casual indifference. Cara was nearby, and Annie sensed they were watching one another and determined not to betray it.

'I didn't realise this was such hard work.' Annie was filling yet more mugs as Sam piled biscuits onto plates, watching them disappear faster than she could unwrap them.

'It's worth it. And thank you again, for coming. You've made it so much easier for us and it's been lovely to have you part of it. Hasn't it, Jon?'

Annie hadn't noticed Jon returning, and she couldn't meet his eyes as he casually agreed with Sam. She looked up when a pretty blonde girl in a black top spoke to him. He had pulled out a chair from underneath the table and was holding a mug in one hand.

'Is it true you lived in Kenya, before here? My dad said he didn't know missionaries still existed. He's never met one before.'

Annie watched Jon as he thought about his answer and he grinned. 'I did, yes. I didn't have any specific plans then, I just wanted to go where God wanted me. I definitely didn't expect to stay for six years.'

'But why did you go?'

Jon smiled. 'Simple, really. When I was at university I met a girl who was already a Christian, and she asked me to go to Brazil with her during the summer holiday. I was madly in love with her, so I went.' Everybody laughed at that, and Annie was reminded of their date, when he had told her of the girl he had wanted to marry.

Jon leaned forward with his arms across his thighs in a gesture Annie already knew so well. 'That first mission changed my life. I saw what it meant to really live by faith, with the certainty of knowing who Jesus is and how that changes lives.'

There was a hushed silence in the room, and he smiled, softening his expression without diminishing the impact of his words. 'But it was months before I felt completely certain about my own faith and after I graduated, I worked in London until the right opportunity came along to re-train.'

He paused as a few more people crept in to listen. 'I know some of you are thinking about faith right now and I've been there. Not sure what to do, whether it's real. It's real for me and I can't tell you that choosing faith is an easy option because it isn't always, decisions sometimes get tougher. But Charlie, Sam or I am always here to talk through anything you want to know. Think about it. God bless you.'

For a moment there was silence around the room as Jon finished. Gradually people began to move, reaching for food and stretching sleepy limbs. Annie was glad to busy herself while she thought through what Jon had said, his words filling her mind. Nathan had quietly disappeared, and Annie saw Cara glancing around the room for him. Jon was at the door, saying goodbye to everybody and making sure they knew about the summer break and when they would all return. Sam made her way to Annie and squeezed her hand.

'Thank you, for everything. We're going home, shall we drop you off?'

Annie realised it was dark outside, and she was very tired. And she didn't want Jon to think she was outstaying her welcome, such as it was, so she accepted with a nod, hurrying to grab her things.

'Are you leaving?'

She looked up at Jon as she collected the cool bag. 'Yes. Charlie and Sam are going to give me a lift.'

'Let me take you.'

She blinked, wondering why he wanted to bother. 'No, thank you.' She realised she sounded curt and tried to explain. 'They're going now and it's out of your way. Good night.'

Chapter Fourteen

All week Annie tried to forget that she had promised to help at the agricultural show on Saturday. She didn't mind helping but felt certain she would bump into Jon at some point and the show was impossible to ignore as lorries staggered through the village, bearing trade stands, seating and sponsored marquees. On Thursday, when she'd hurriedly ventured to the post office for urgent supplies of dairy-free ice cream – she was expecting Kirstie for supper – she'd even seen a huge crane tottering along the high street. She'd tried not to laugh when Jerry Gordon had come tearing out of his house and shrieked angrily at the driver as a couple of his colourful hanging baskets were sent flying backwards, narrowly missing the vintage MG he'd just washed with loving care. She had seen Jon twice, once as he drove through the village and once with a group from Kilnbeck. Both times he had given her a polite wave and a quick, impersonal smile.

Robert had asked her to arrive at the show at eight thirty, and thoughts of seeing Jon later were tumbling through her mind as she twisted her hair into a plait. The weather was fair, and she dressed in cropped ivory linen trousers, a pale pink sleeveless top and flat gypsy sandals. She locked the cottage and set off, unable to resist bending to sniff a cluster of perennial sweet peas in the front garden, deciding to pick some later for the house.

Cars were already trickling through the village, directed to the Home Farm show entrance by officials sweltering in bright yellow jackets. Annie followed, briefly pausing to say hello to a couple of boys she recognised from the Hall on Tuesday evening, who had been drafted in to help with traffic duty and not looking too pleased about it. She ignored the Hall when she reached its gates and carried on until she was tripping up the roughly mown grass track towards the show in her unsuitable shoes. Strands of dried hay tickled her feet and scratched her ankles, and she began to regret her choice of footwear.

She hadn't been to the show for years but as she waved her volunteer's badge at the entrance, she was amazed by how much it had expanded since her last visit. Robert met her as promised at the committee's marquee and asked her to help on the WI cake stall as somebody had gone down overnight with a tummy bug. Annie hoped that the woman in question hadn't been eating her own baking.

'You're bound to be busy, lass,' he said cheerfully as she trailed beside him, already cross because she had been stung by a nettle and a blister was beginning to swell on her left heel. 'But you've got a good view of t'main arena.'

Robert introduced her to Elsie and Sheila, stalwarts of the local WI chapter, and who Annie guessed had a combined age of about a hundred and fifty. She tried to help them with the unpacking, but they shooed her away, telling her politely but firmly that they knew just how to do it properly. Her mouth watered as more and more amazing cakes and cookies were slowly revealed, and one by one volunteers and helpers sidled up to make their purchases before the stall opened properly.

'Don't put that out yet!' Sheila barked at Annie. She blinked in surprise, clutching a heavy chocolate cake, and feeling as though she'd been about to steal it. 'We've only got the two from Mavis, so we'd better save that one for later when there's not much left. Here, I'll take it.'

Annie muttered something under her breath as she obediently handed the cake over. She hovered at the front of the stall, writing names on bags to be collected later and kept hidden from the sun underneath a table at the back. There was a short lull as the gates were opened to the public and she glanced around idly. Gigantic shire horses were already lined up in the main arena, stamping their feet and shaking their short tails to keep away the barrage of flies. The grandstand was filling up as people rushed to grab a seat, shuffling between rows of plastic to find a better view. Show jumps were stacked on one side of the ring and a couple of horses objected to the sight of them, dragging their handlers around until they were hauled back into line. The commentator was hidden inside a little hut nearby, and Annie listened as he explained the events to follow later. Another show ring had been tacked onto the main arena, full of cows and their calves slowly trailing around after one another. One little chestnut calf managed to escape and she laughed as it scattered a pile of straw bales.

The children's play area was well away from the arenas, dominated by a bouncy castle wobbling nervously as it waited for the inevitable onslaught to come. The food court was handily close by, already doing a roaring trade in bacon rolls and hog roast, and she pulled a face when the unmistakable smell of fried doughnuts drifted towards her. Wherever she looked, sponsored trade stands were groaning underneath cars, agricultural machinery, trailers, and specialist farming equipment. Nearby the greyhound rescue and donkey sanctuary were attracting lots of visitors and Christmas cards and next year's calendars were already being stuffed briskly into carrier bags.

Then the torrent began. Barely had the WI stall opened properly than people made a beeline for it, unable to resist the home baking on offer. Soon Annie wished she'd worn a different top as the sun scorched down onto her shoulders through the factor thirty lotion. She didn't have to look at her feet to know that they were filthy and hot, and the flat sandals offered no support whatsoever to her already aching soles. Elsie handed her a cup of tea from time to time, and the two ladies talked non-stop, only pausing to add up with creaking fingers slowly writing everything down. Annie sighed as she wrapped another half dozen scones, hoping she wouldn't be stuck here all day. She hadn't seen anything of Jon, not sure if she were relieved or terribly disappointed.

She half listened to the conversation around her as she handed the scones over to her customer. Elsie was complaining loudly about the mobile library being reduced to one visit per month, and Annie caught her customer's eye as he paid. She noticed his brown eyes were exactly like milk choco-late beneath messy dark blonde hair. He was about her age, looking every inch a countryman in his checked shirt, dark yellow waistcoat and green cords splattered with something she didn't really like the look of. He seemed in no hurry to leave, despite the queue behind him and he bought another cake, winking at Annie as he walked away. Surprised, she watched him go, hoping he hadn't noticed her scarlet face and unruly curls escaping from her plait.

It was almost lunchtime, and she longed to sit down with a cool drink, but Elsie and Sheila seemed to be able to whisk more and more baking from the depths of their stall, as if by magic, and Annie could see no respite. She bent down to pick up yet another box of brownies, grumbling quietly to herself and yearning to go home for a bath. But a familiar voice interrupted her muttering, and she straightened up hastily, dropping the box on top of a cream sponge. Embarrassed, she fished it out but not before she heard Sheila's cluck of disapproval and mutter about the waste of a good cake. Annie thought crossly that it wouldn't be wasted at all; she'd ram it in somebody's face soon.

She looked up. Jon was standing in front of her and she wondered grumpily how he always seemed to catch her at her worst. Dark navigator sunglasses covered his eyes and it was impossible to see the expression behind them.

'How are you?' he asked politely. Her reply came out more sharply than she'd intended, feeling stupidly crushed by the courteous and yet indifferent inquiry.

'Fine, thanks. Busy.' She tried not to dither as she wiped jam and cream from the tablecloth, torn between hoping he would leave her alone and afraid that he actually might.

'I won't keep you long. Dad and Emma are here, and I'd like to introduce you to them.'

Startled, she shook her head and tried to tell him no, absolutely not now, not looking like this. But it was too late as he was already turning around, and she saw a couple making their way across to her. Her heart sank as she left the relative safety of the stall.

'Emma, Dad, I'd like to introduce you to Annie Armstrong, Molly's goddaughter,' Jon said as his father drew near in his electric wheelchair. Annie hovered uncertainly before Sir Vivian smiled at her, just like Jon. She gulped as she took his hand and he shook hers very firmly. 'Annie, this is my dad, Vivian, and my stepmother, Emma.'

Annie met Vivian's twinkling eyes, a darker blue than his son's, smiling at him as he released her fingers from his strong grip. Vivian seemed to have recovered from the bout of ill health Jon had spoken of and his face was tanned dark brown. His powerful chest and shoulders appeared even broader than Jon's and he wore a lightweight suit, the jacket slung around the handles of his chair.

'Pleased to meet you, Annie,' he said unhesitatingly. His voice wasn't as deep as his son's, but the local accent was more pronounced, and he looked at her with interest. 'It's good to have you back in the village. You won't remember me, I daresay, but Molly was a fine friend.'

Annie nodded, thinking of what Jon had told her of his father's friendship with Molly. 'It's lovely to meet you. I do remember Molly speaking of you. And thank you for the card you sent after Molly died.' Annie turned to Emma and held out her hand. Emma's expression was open and welcoming, and the natural sincerity in her eyes made Annie feel instantly comfortable as they briefly shook hands. Annie was horribly aware of her appearance, compared to Emma, who was impeccably dressed in a beautiful floral skirt and flattering cream blouse. Her flat shoes were certainly far better designed for agricultural shows than Annie's gypsy sandals, her ash-blonde hair tucked behind her ears with sunglasses perched on top of her head.

'I'm so glad to meet you at last,' Emma said, smiling warmly. 'I'm sorry we were away when you arrived. I hope you've settled in?'

Annie was all too aware of Jon's silent presence nearby, and she wondered anxiously what he had told his family about her. 'Yes, almost, thank you. The cottage needs more work than I'd realised but it's starting to feel like home. Have you had a good holiday?'

Emma absently pushed a loose strand of hair away from her eyes. 'Lovely, thank you. We've been on a cruise for the first time and Vivian's enjoyed it far more than he's prepared to admit. He's usually so active, and I thought on a ship he might eventually run out of things to interest him. He'd have to sit back and relax for a change.'

'Rubbish!' Vivian retorted, waving to somebody passing by, and he winked at Annie. 'I didn't get to do half the things I wanted.'

'Next time,' Emma said brightly. Annie saw the surprised expression on Vivian's face and heard Jon's short laugh. 'Don't worry, I'm already looking. I think some winter sun would be good for you.'

Annie's irritability level suddenly shot up at the unwelcome appearance, to her at least, of Sarah Holland, who managed to greet everyone except Annie with a kiss. She seemed to make a particular fuss of Vivian, bending down to peck him on both cheeks and even playfully straightening his tie.

Vivian looked a bit startled and he watched Jon curiously as Sarah turned to him, allowing her hands to linger on Jon's shoulders for just a little longer than was necessary. She managed a brief nod at Annie, whose heart sank, unable to find fault with Sarah's gorgeous summer dress and pretty suede handbag.

'Darling,' Sarah said to Jon, her hand somehow finding its way back to his arm. 'Thank you so much for sending Arthur round again. I really don't know what I would have done without him. You must let me thank you properly, perhaps over that lunch we spoke about? I simply must get rid of that wretched gardener if he ever turns up again.'

Jon nodded, his face impassive. 'You're welcome.' His gaze swung back to Annie, his eyes unwavering as he looked at her, and Sarah's hand fell away.

Annie felt disappointment welling up inside her when she realised that Jon had not singled her out by sending Arthur to her. She was absolutely determined that he shouldn't see how this made her feel, and yet she knew the look she gave him was easy to read in its regret.

'I should go.' Emma gave Annie a warm smile as she adjusted her sunglasses and then glanced at Vivian, who nodded. 'I promised to judge the Best-Behaved Pet competition and it will be starting any minute. There'll be a riot if the ferrets escape again and go after the rabbits. I hope you'll come to us for lunch soon, Annie. Goodbye Sarah.'

Annie said, mainly to irritate Sarah, that she'd really like to, and Vivian grinned at her.

'Don't be a stranger,' he said cheerfully. 'Come and see us. We won't bite. I'll tell you some stories about Molly.'

They said goodbye, and Annie made her way back to the business side of the stall. Sarah and Jon were still near enough for Annie to hear their conversation, feeling certain that Sarah had raised her voice on purpose. Annie supposed it was all that drama training, and she shoved an empty box back underneath the table, watching them surreptitiously.

'I wanted to ask your advice about hens,' Sarah said girlishly, smiling up at Jon and pressing on regardless. 'I've heard that they're very economical to keep and so useful for recycling kitchen waste. And all those yummy fresh eggs, for baking and breakfast. What do you think?'

Annie saw Jon look at Sarah in surprise. 'I don't know anything about them,' he said, starting to laugh. Sarah adjusted her hat, Annie thought grumpily to get a better view of him.

'I can't believe that.' Sarah sounded playful, seemingly unperturbed by his indifferent answer. 'You're a farmer, surely all farmers know about keeping livestock?'

'Not hens,' he said shortly, suddenly quite interested in the motorbikes hurtling around the arena. 'Elizabeth and Robert have chickens at home, you should speak to them.'

Annie knew it wasn't the answer Sarah wanted and she couldn't restrain the bright smile spreading across her face as she handed over the change from her latest sale. She wished they would both go away and leave her in peace. Jon turned to face her and she knew then that her wish was about to become a reality. Despite everything she had told herself, her heart sank.

'See you later,' he said abruptly, nodding to Sarah as he strode away.

'Don't forget that you're helping me to present the prizes in the WI cheese classes later,' Sarah called, darting after him. 'And the lettuce championship.'

Annie watched until she saw Sarah fall into step beside Jon and tuck her arm through his. She turned away, beginning to think that perhaps there was more to his relationship with Sarah than she'd realised, or he'd admitted. Within an hour, the stall was finally sold out, and she hung around to help pack up and ram everything back inside Elsie's little car. The two ladies seemed genuinely glad of her help and they pressed a chocolate cake into her hands. Annie noticed it was the one she had almost sold earlier, and thanked them gratefully, pleased to have her own little treat to take home. She left it with the pound stall next door and set off to walk around what was left of the show. People were beginning to drift home, and she saw that the donkeys had settled down for a bit of well-earned peace and quiet.

Almost by accident she found the falconry stand and recognised the man with the chocolate brown eyes she had seen earlier. He was bending to untie a large owl and she watched as it hopped onto his gloved arm. She backed up, intending to disappear before he saw her, but it was too late. His eyes met hers and he walked straight over, bringing the staring owl with him.

'You found us,' he said cheerfully. 'What have you done with Thelma and Louise?'

She grinned, trying not to look at the intimidating bird perched on his arm. 'We've sold out. I think they've gone home with Brad Pitt.'

He laughed then, and she couldn't help liking the way it lightened his weather-roughened face. The owl screeched, and he tapped it gently on the head. 'We're almost finished here.' He nodded at a younger boy as he untied a hawk and slid it back into its travelling cage. 'A few of us are going to the pub before we head back, do you fancy a drink?'

Annie was about to refuse and then a sudden voice in her head reminded her of Jon's remarks after their date, about hiding herself from the possibility of further hurt. If, as it seemed, there was no longer anything between them, then she supposed that now was a good a time as any to have a casual drink. 'Okay. I'll see you there, then.'

'I won't be long,' he called over his shoulder as he quickly slid the owl into a cage and dragged a leather satchel from his shoulder. 'I'm Greg.'

'Annie.' She walked away, already wondering what she had done by accepting the unexpected invitation. She collected her cake and made her way to the exit, smiling when she saw Jerry Gordon causing a commotion. He had waylaid the community policeman, who was off duty with his wife and son in tow. Jerry was complaining indignantly about the state of car parking in the village and demanding that the police clamp down on it as a matter of urgency.

Annie sidled past, offering silent sympathy to the young constable, who looked thoroughly fed up. When she reached the village, cars were snaking slowly along the high street, creeping away from the show and turning for home. She dawdled as she walked along, watching the activity around the green. A few noisy children were lobbing sticks into the river and running about excitedly, while weary parents lay sprawled on the grass, trying to ignore their offspring and catch some sun. The pub was quieter than she'd expected and she found a table outside and waited for Greg to appear.

She didn't have to wait long. He pulled up in a car with two other men around the same age and she wondered idly what had become of the birds and the young boy. As he was striding towards her with a grin, she suddenly realised how young he seemed. She tried to push comparisons with Jon to the back of her mind where they lingered, niggling her. Greg insisted on buying her another drink and disappeared inside while she fidgeted on her seat, already impatient to leave as she tried to make polite conversation with the others. Greg was soon back, and they chatted for half an hour before she could bear it no longer. Greg was nice but he wasn't Jon, and she had no wish to drag out something that would never happen.

'I should go,' Annie said finally, leaping to her feet suddenly to emphasise her point. 'Thanks for the drink. It was nice meeting you all.'

Greg stood up with her, and she was caught off guard when he reached for her hand and pressed a card into her palm. 'Here's my number,' he said casually, and she knew from his expression that they both understood she would never call. 'Just in case you change your mind.'

He released her hand and she closed her fingers around the card, nodding quickly. 'Bye.' Annie hadn't even finished her drink but she grabbed the cake and set off across the green, sidling past the people still hanging around. She slipped Greg's card into her pocket, her head as low as her spirits as she walked. She wondered what Jon was doing, if he had taken Sarah out, and admonished herself for caring.

She glanced up at the edge of the green and halted. Shock made her heart thump wildly as she saw Jon standing alone outside the post office, and she knew at once he had seen her with Greg. She was near enough to see the indifference in his expression as he watched her, his sunglasses pushed back onto his head. They were on opposite sides of the river and she began to walk towards him, her confidence wavering beneath his cool stare as she crossed the bridge.

'Are you walking my way?' she asked brightly, prepared for his refusal. She wanted to banish the coldness from his eyes and be friends again.

He seemed surprised, and although he nodded, his answer was short. 'Sure.'

The silence between them still hadn't been broken by the time they reached the Howards' farm. Annie twisted her fingers anxiously as she glanced up at him, knowing their time together was almost at an end as her cottage came into view. 'Jon, have I done something to offend you?'

She heard his short, wry laugh as he looked at her, chilled by that same aloofness in his eyes once more, her body tensing as she waited for his response.

'I just wish you'd been truthful with me, that's all,' he said abruptly. They reached the gate outside her house and she paused, astonished by his reply. They stared at one another until it seemed that he was going to turn around and leave. She reached out and grabbed his arm, not even aware that she had moved.

'What do you mean?' she asked hotly, angered by the implication that she had lied to him. 'I don't understand.'

He gazed down at her hand on his arm and she snatched it back, allowing him his freedom if he chose to walk away. But he didn't. He looked straight into her eyes and his voice was cold as he spoke.

'You told me you don't want to see me again because you aren't yet over your fiancé and don't want to begin dating again. Fair enough. And then I saw you just now with some guy from the show. I don't think you've been truthful, Annie. I think you meant you don't want to date me, and I would rather you'd said that in the beginning.'

She gasped, her mouth widening in surprise as she realised that he had been jealous when he had seen her with Greg. He turned and began to walk away and she was horrified he had not waited for her to reply. She raised her voice to make him hear.

'You're right. And I'm sorry.'

He halted at once, spinning around to stare at her, even though he made no move to approach. 'Right about what?' His question was sharp, matching the expression in the blue depths of his eyes.

'Dating you.' Her words were a whisper, her attraction to him tightening the tension between them whenever she saw him, making everything at once simpler and so much harder. 'I thought it would be best not to.'

'So are you going to see him again, that guy from the show?'

'Of course not.' Her voice fell still further, aware she was once again trying to resist what she wanted, what she felt for Jon already, and she was so tired of being torn and afraid of what she might not be able to give him. 'It was a casual drink, a chance to see how it felt to meet someone else. Someone who doesn't make me feel the way you do.'

'How do I make you feel, Annie?' Jon couldn't quite keep the impatience from his voice, lowered now as he watched her, his hands rammed into his pockets as he forced her to continue.

She took a breath, knowing that the time for pretence had passed and she could no longer feign indifference. 'Safe. Afraid. More than that.' The tears trailed down her face and she didn't care. She was already hurting, and she wanted him to hold her, scattering the fear and uncertainty, her voice falling to a whisper. 'It was nothing, with Greg. He could never hurt me.'

There was a second as Jon stared at her and then he strode towards her, no indecision, no question in his eyes when he took her in his arms, pulling her tightly to him so that he might more easily reach her lips with his own. She felt the warmth of his mouth on hers and melted against him, sliding her hands onto his shoulders as her knees crumpled beneath her. The chocolate cake slid to the ground as she felt the taut strength of his chest, and her fingers found their way into his dark hair as he lifted her, tightening his arms around her waist as he kissed her on and on.

When he finally set her down, still holding her against him, she felt an unwelcome coolness when he dragged his mouth away from hers until the heat of his lips blazed across her skin, softly kissing her face. He trailed one hand slowly up from her waist until it was resting on her neck, and she curved her body towards him as he coiled long strands of her hair between his fingers, the other hand in the small of her back, keeping her close. Eventually, he spoke, and her stomach disappeared when she heard the uneven roughness of his voice.

'I can't give you guarantees,' he muttered huskily, brushing his lips against her ear. The sensation took away the last of her ability to concentrate as she clung to him. She knew, with a sharp thrill, that the reality of his kiss was far more incredible than she had imagined night after night alone in the cottage. 'But I never want to hurt you, Annie. I think about you every moment.'

'So do I,' she admitted, tipping her head back to see his face. Her smile was tremulous as she finally accepted that the risk of her admission had been worth everything which had followed in these first, very new moments together. She understood the dark glow in his eyes as he lowered his mouth to kiss her again, pulling her against him, her hands exploring his shoulders. She had no idea how long they stood there, until the unwelcome bang of the farm gate nearby distracted them both, and he smiled as the kiss ended. She buried her head against his chest, breathing in the smell of him and when the walkers had gone, she looked up, her eyes brightening once more as she saw the elation in his expression.

'Shall I walk you home?' he asked, and she nodded at once, floating in wonder and desperate to prolong the sudden new intimacy between them. She wanted to laugh out loud at the dizzying sensation in her head and the unsteady limbs she no longer seemed able to control. He released her from his arms to capture her hand, holding it firmly inside his own as he pushed the garden gate open and Annie quickly scooped up the remains of the flattened cake and they laughed.

She turned to face him when they reached her front door, and he took both of her hands in his. Disappointment began to replace elation as she knew their time together was about to end. She was so tempted to invite him inside, and yet craved the opportunity to be alone and think about what had unexpectedly developed between them.

'I'm sorry I behaved badly,' he said ruefully, and she saw the regret in his eyes. 'I guess I was jealous, and I didn't react very well. Please will you forgive me?'

'You're already forgiven.' She knew her tone was flirtatious, but she couldn't help it; that was exactly how she felt. 'I loved the kissing and making up.'

He laughed and then his expression became serious again as they gazed at one another, and she knew everything in her mind was reflected in her eyes. Perhaps later she would regret revealing so much, but not now, beginning to shiver in the cool night air.

'I should go, you're getting cold,' he said reluctantly. He reached out and gently drew her against him as they stood beside her silent house. 'I have to go to the show dinner tonight. Would you like to come...?'

She stepped back before he could finish the question, reaching for her key to open the door. 'Not yet.' She smiled to lighten her refusal, trying to explain. 'I think it's too soon.'

'May I see you again?'

Annie hesitated, her answer already given in the kiss they had shared but she couldn't quite shake off all reason, even now. 'Jon, you know I wasn't looking for this, after everything that's happened.'

He reached for her hand again, stroking her fingers gently, his gesture reflecting the tenderness in his eyes. 'I know. But we don't have to rush into anything, Annie. Maybe just a few dates, nothing complicated, and we'll see how it goes? What do you think?'

She nodded, smiling, knowing that whatever caution she had tried to muster before tonight, she had flung it into the wind with her simple reply. He bent down, his answering smile against her lips as he kissed her briefly. Before she could reach up and touch him, he had already turned away and was walking quickly through the garden. He didn't look back and she waited until he was out of sight before closing the door, alone once more.

When she woke before sunlight the next day, elation had returned, banishing doubt somewhere far away, and she fell back into a dreamy sleep, full of half remembered glimpses of Jon. But with daybreak doubt slunk back, bringing fear with it, and chasing jubilation from her mind as though last night had been only a fantasy. Tantalising reminders of him and the expression in his eyes crept into her mind as she thought of him pulling her into his arms and kissing her on and on. She had no idea when she would see him again, but it would be soon, and knew that she couldn't wait.

Chapter Fifteen

By Wednesday Annie was struggling to keep a ridiculous smile from her face, very aware she was ignoring her schoolwork as well as everything else around the cottage. She had seen Jon every day since Saturday, albeit briefly, and each hurried glimpse of him left her longing for the next. He had turned up on Sunday evening and they'd sat outside, concealed from the rest of the world as they'd held hands and talked quietly until daylight had given way to darkness. He came on Monday, hardly staying a minute as his pager went off and he raced to respond, away long into the night to locate someone who had fallen, and it reminded her of the reason why he volunteered. They had hurriedly made plans for Tuesday evening, their first proper date since everything had altered. But on Tuesday morning, when she had bumped into him outside the village hall, she'd concealed her disappointment when he had asked if she minded changing their date to Wednesday because he'd forgotten he had arranged to take a small Kilnbeck group night hiking. He had kissed her quickly and left her wishing that it were already the following evening so that she might have him all to herself for a little while.

Annie was going to cook supper for Jon at the cottage and set out after breakfast to shop for their meal. In town she was distracted by an antiques shop and spent ages wandering around its funny little rooms until finally she paid for a beautiful old-fashioned settle covered in a green and white checked fabric. It would be perfect in her study and she darted into another shop to buy cushions to decorate it.

When she staggered back down the hill to the car park with carrier bags bumping against her legs, she was surprised to spot Nathan, huddled against a wall near the railway station and Annie wondered what he was doing there. He didn't see her, and she decided not to go over and say hello. Even from a distance he looked forlorn and aloof, and she guessed that perhaps he was on an errand for Jon and not too pleased about it.

When she returned home, she tidied the cottage and picked some flowers from the garden, stuffing sweet peas and pale blue cornflowers into a vase she'd found in the pantry. She stood them on the hearth, after she had laid the fire in case the evening became cool. She smiled to herself, remembering the night of the storm and how reassured she'd been by Jon's company and the memory was quickly followed by the exhilarating anticipation of seeing him. The rest of the day seemed to pass unbearably slowly, and she couldn't do much in the kitchen until he arrived.

She diced pancetta, covering it in foil and whisked egg yolks together with parmesan, leaving the bowl beside the pancetta in the fridge. The carbonara would be cooked at the last minute and the fresh linguine she'd bought that morning added to it. It seemed like years since she had last prepared a meal for two. Somehow it wasn't difficult to forget about Iain now, as thoughts of Jon's blue eyes danced in her mind all day. She made pastry and baked it in the Rayburn's hot oven while she began the maple and pecan nut filling. She hadn't asked him what he would like to eat but hoped he would be happy with her choices, and she had fresh strawberries from a local farm shop if he didn't like the dessert.

Annie didn't linger in the bath in case he was early, and at six thirty she was hovering between the kitchen and sitting room, listening for a knock at the door. She was dressed in a simple, off the shoulder white top and cropped jeans with a pair of blush-coloured leather flats. She poured herself a glass of white wine and sat near the fireplace, trying to relax and quell the trembling anticipation at the thought of seeing him.

By seven fifteen she was only halfway through her glass of wine and certain she heard his knock with every sound. She almost wished she'd chosen something more elaborate to cook; at least it would give her something to do. She sauntered upstairs and found her book but after a few minutes, when she had read the same page three times, she chucked the book to the floor and poured a second glass of wine. Still there was no sign of Jon, and the exhilaration of seeing him began to fade, slowly replaced by disappointment, then anger that he hadn't let her know he wasn't coming. By eight thirty she was afraid for him, praying it wasn't a rescue that had gone wrong somehow and he was unable to reach her. She checked her phone several times, hanging out of the bathroom window and standing on the doddering bench. Still nothing.

She took her nearly empty glass into the kitchen and began to cook to distract herself, throwing the ingredients together. She fried the pancetta and added the hot pasta to it, pouring in the egg and cheese after switching off the heat and then it was ready. She divided the food between two plates and shoved them into the warming oven. Annie cleared the kitchen while she waited for the pecan tart to bake, staring out of the window, and not really seeing anything as the evening became dark. She took the dessert from the oven and left it on top of the Rayburn and wearily switched off the light.

Peering into the night through the sitting room window, she tried to guess where he might be and what kind of emergency he had been called away to. Nothing stirred beyond the cottage and she turned away, sinking onto the sofa as she fought back tears of worry and frustration, shocked by the hurt spilling into her heart. But as she sat alone in the dark, she didn't really believe that he had done it on purpose. She stood up anxiously as fear took hold again, lurching horribly in her mind as she wondered if something terrible had happened to him.

It was almost nine when a sudden flash of light lit up the lane outside and the loud roar of an engine was swiftly silenced. Moments later he knocked sharply at the front door, and her instant rush of thankful relief was joined by concern for what had occurred to keep him from her as she switched a lamp on and stepped into the hall to meet him. When she opened the door, Jon looked distracted and Annie was taken aback once again by his height and aura of self-assurance, wondering how she was coming to feel so much for him so soon and trying desperately not to let it show.

'I'm really sorry,' he said immediately. He reached out to take her hands but she kept them out of reach, still trying to sort through the riot of emotions rushing to the fore. 'May I come in?'

She stood aside to let him pass and closed the door after him. He went straight to the fireplace, almost as though he was trying to warm himself and hadn't realised it wasn't lit. She saw how tired he looked, and the darkening stubble, jeans and plain T-shirt beneath an open windbreaker jacket told her he must have come straight from the estate or Kilnbeck rather than a search and rescue.

'Is everything okay?'

Jon looked at her and she saw the distraction and worry return to his eyes and he sighed. 'It's Nathan. He's gone missing and I've been searching for him. The police aren't treating it as urgent yet because they don't consider him to be at risk, and I can't call the team out as we've no idea of a location or any sightings.'

Annie felt her heart bump in shock, and the disappointment of their interrupted evening was lost in the new concern darting through her mind. 'But how? When did he disappear?'

'He was working at Brenda Chapman's cottage, next door to Megan. Megan nipped in to see Brenda while he was there. She doesn't usually bother to lock the door if she's not going far and, when she got back about twenty minutes later,

174

somebody had been in and taken her purse, some cash from her desk and her father's watch. She ran back to Brenda in panic to tell her and when they tried to find Nathan to ask if he'd seen anything, he was nowhere to be found. Haven't you heard?'

Annie looked at him in horror. 'No. I was out until after lunch and I didn't leave the house once I came back. Poor Megan. How is she?'

'Okay, trying to be brave but it's shaken her. Brenda's with her. She's going to stay over until Megan feels comfortable again. I suppose it was inevitable if she doesn't lock up, but it shouldn't be.'

'You don't think Nathan did it, do you?'

Jon shook his head grimly. 'No. But we don't know where he is, and that makes him prime suspect number one right now. I don't think he's ever stolen before and I know he feels he's let his mum down already. I just don't believe he'd cause more trouble for the sake of a few pounds. He's had his problems, but theft has never been one of them, even if he did know Megan had gone out. I want to find him before the police do so I can talk to him first.'

'Do you think he's all right?'

'I hope so. He's streetwise, that's for sure, but I'm more concerned about what he's thinking right now.'

'Thank you for coming to apologise. I should let you go.' She began to walk towards the front door and Jon crossed the room in two long strides, ducking beneath the beams as he caught her arm, whirling her around to face him.

'I wanted to be here, Annie,' he said quickly, pushing his free hand through already tousled hair. 'But I have responsibilities to the estate and to other people. I can't always get away. I called you twice and left a message both times.'

'You called me?' Astonished, Annie felt her hurt dissolve into relief followed by disappointment. 'I didn't get them. The signal's really unreliable and sometimes voicemails only come through hours later.'

Jon was still holding her arm and his hand slid down until his fingers were stroking hers. 'Is that what you thought? That I didn't bother to let you know or mind that I couldn't be here?'

She tipped her head forwards, unwilling to reveal quite how worried and then relieved she'd been as her hair covered her face. 'I'm so afraid of trusting you,' she whispered, distracted by his fingers trying to smooth away her fears as he listened. 'I don't want to sit at home night after night worrying if you're okay when you don't turn up and praying you're not upside down in a ditch or drowning in a flooded cave. Everybody always seems to leave me and I'm so tired of trying to keep up.'

'Hey.' His voice was gentler still as he stepped forward and drew her tightly into his arms. The relief of being so close to him was overwhelming and she rested her cheek against his chest, feeling the hard length of his body against her own. Her hands crept around him, searching for assurance. 'I don't want to leave you, Annie, or do anything to prevent you trusting me.' He lifted her chin with one finger, and she looked into his eyes, lost in the softness of his gaze. He pressed his lips against her forehead. 'I promise.'

She wound her hands into his dark hair and drew his mouth onto hers, hazily aware of the explosion of desire in his eyes. All her uncertainty was swept away in the scorching intensity of their kiss, her stomach spinning with longing for him as her legs began to tremble. The heat of his chest was imprinted against her breasts and she arched towards him, the thin top and his T-shirt barely a barrier between them. Finally, he drew away, raising his head to look into her eyes. She heard the rasp of his breathing as he lifted a finger to trail it down her neck and slowly across one bare shoulder. Her breath caught and his hands fell to grasp hers.

'I am sorry, about tonight,' Jon murmured into her hair. 'It wasn't how I wanted the evening to be.'

Annie tipped her head back to look at him, understanding he was telling her the truth. 'Don't,' she said in anguish, placing her palm against his cheek, feeling his roughness beneath her skin. 'Please don't. I'm sorry I was angry. I was worried about you.'

Jon nodded, shifting his head to look into the dark night beyond the window, and Annie tried to think how she could help, her thoughts following his to Nathan.

'Coffee? Or do you need to go now?'

Jon pulled his phone from a pocket and glanced at it, the distracted look returning as he ran a finger over the screen. 'Coffee would be great. If there's nothing new after that then I'm going to go back out, see if he's turned up at Arthur's yet.'

Annie headed into the kitchen, her glance going to the reminder of their meal on the table still set for two and a sudden thought struck her. She spun around, almost crashing into Jon in the doorway as he followed her. He caught her, his hands going to her shoulders as her eyes flew up to his. 'What is it?'

Annie rushed out her words, remembering her shopping trip earlier in the day. 'Nathan! I saw him, about lunchtime.'

'What? Where?'

'At the station, in town. I thought he was doing something for you.'

Jon's eyes widened as he listened and she grabbed his hand impatiently, the coffee forgotten. 'Come on, let's go and see if we can find out where he went.'

Minutes later they were in Jon's car, speeding through the darkened countryside and retracing her steps back into town.

'I didn't speak to him and now I wish I had.' Annie remembered how forlorn and alone Nathan had seemed. 'He looked so distant from everything around him, like he wasn't really there.' And now she knew why. She tried to think where he might've gone but it was hopeless. She had no idea.

Jon reached for her hand and squeezed it gently. 'You weren't to know.' One hand remained on the steering wheel as he kept his foot pressed on the accelerator. Annie glanced out of the window as the lanes flashed by, eventually widening into busier roads with street lights above them as they approached the town. But something else was troubling her, and she had to tell him.

'Jon,' she began, feeling the warmth of his fingers still resting on her thigh. 'When you arrived you must've thought I knew about Nathan and didn't care what had happened to him as long as my plans weren't spoiled.' She paused. 'I do care. I would have helped you look earlier if I'd known.'

He raised her hand to his mouth and kissed it briefly. She felt him smile against her fingers and knew that he understood. His phone rang and when he pulled over to answer it, she saw his expression change again and he sounded grim as he disconnected the call.

'Sorry, the speaker's broken. That was Neil Dawson.' Briefly he looked at her as they drove off again. 'His daughter's missing too. Cara hasn't come home and she's not replying to messages. She was supposed to be out with friends from college.'

'Do you think they're together?' she asked anxiously, thinking of how worried Neil and Angie must be.

He shrugged. 'Maybe. She might know where he's gone and could have followed him.'

The station was almost deserted when they arrived, and Jon caught her hand again as they rushed to check the timetable. So many trains had come and gone during the day, and it was impossible to guess which one Nathan might have taken. The ticket office was closed, and nobody seemed to be around to ask if he had been spotted again.

'I don't think he'd go home yet,' Jon said finally, and Annie heard the doubt in his voice. He turned to scan the platforms nearby. A couple of teenage boys were staring, and Jon nodded at them casually. They shrugged and looked away. 'Maybe he just jumped on the first train he saw, to go and get lost in a city. If he has it'll be almost impossible to find him if he doesn't want us to.' He sighed. 'And I suggested he gave up his phone which will make locating him even harder, so his so-called mates couldn't get in touch either. I'd better call his mother.'

The cool air smelt grimy and an old man, sitting on a bench clutching a scruffy holdall, began to cough. It sounded creepy in the half-lit station, and Annie sidled closer to Jon as he reached into his pocket for his phone. She was shivering in her thin top and he quickly shrugged out of his jacket and draped it around her shoulders. She glanced at the darkened coffee shop, its door covered by an ugly metal shutter, still shivering as she wondered where else they might look for Nathan. Far down the platform beyond the cover of the domed roof, she saw two shapes huddled on a bench. She took a step forward, hardly sure what she had seen and yet certain it was them.

'Jon,' she whispered urgently, grabbing his arm with one hand, and pointing. 'Look!'

His eyes followed her outstretched hand and then he rammed the phone back into his pocket. 'Come on.'

Their footsteps sounded horribly loud as they hurried to the bench, and with every stride Annie expected the figures to take flight. But they didn't. Nathan and Cara stood up and faced them warily. It was impossible to see Nathan's face, concealed beneath a dark hood, and to Annie he appeared more intimidating than he'd ever seemed before. Cara looked tiny and very young at his side, and Nathan slid a protective arm around her shoulders. Jon casually let go of Annie's hand and stepped forward to meet them.

'Are you both all right?' he asked quietly. 'We're all worried about you.'

Nathan's snarl of laughter was scornful, and Annie was taken aback by the anger and hurt in his eyes when he furiously yanked down the hood. 'Come and get me,' he said, holding his arms straight out in front of him. 'That's why you're here, isn't it? To make sure I take the blame and you can send me back.'

Jon remained still, his hands at his sides. 'I'm not sending you anywhere, Nathan. I want you back at Thorndale. Cara's parents are very worried, and your mum will be too when she finds out. If you're truthful with me, I will do everything I can to help you.'

'Do you think I did it? You have to be honest with me first.'

'No. I don't believe you stole from Megan.' Jon took a step forward. 'I'm not here to judge you, and I will support you as long as you come back and face the consequences of running away. I want you to stay.'

Nathan's face began to crumple as he stared at Jon, a shred of relief flaring in his eyes. He looked much younger than his years, looking more like a little boy again. 'It wasn't me. I'm not lying. I wouldn't do that to you.' His voice was almost a whisper and Annie heard the break in it. She rushed past Jon and put her arms around Nathan.

'Come home,' she said softly. He tensed and then his head fell onto her shoulders. She felt his soundless sobs as she held him, and he clung to her. He was so thin and slight, and she didn't let go of him until the tears had ended. She stepped back, and Cara took his hand and led him to Jon. When the young couple reached him, Annie saw Jon drape an arm across the boy's shoulders and, all together, they returned to the car. Cara sat in the back with Nathan, and Jon immediately rang Neil Dawson to let him know they had both been found safe and well. On the way back to Thorndale Jon asked Nathan what had happened that morning and he began to talk. He sounded very matter of fact, and Annie guessed he might have to repeat his story several times more.

'I was fixing the kitchen tap at Mrs Chapman's. I heard Megan say she was going out – she'd knocked on Mrs Chapman's door. Mrs Chapman came into the kitchen and told me that Megan had gone to The Courtyard to pick up an order.' He paused, and Annie glanced sideways at Jon, wondering what he was thinking. And then Nathan continued. 'Mrs Chapman said she was going upstairs to change the beds and I carried on working. About twenty minutes later Megan came rushing in, I could hear she was upset. I was still in the kitchen and I heard Megan tell Mrs Chapman that she'd been burgled.'

'And what did you do?' Jon asked quietly.

Nathan's voice fell. 'I panicked. I was sure they'd think it was me cos I knew Megan had gone out and everyone knows she doesn't always lock the door. I ran out the back and just kept on running. I jumped on the first bus I saw and when I got to town, I rang Cara to let her know I was going. That's why we were still at the station because I wouldn't get on a train until she'd promised to go home, and she wouldn't go unless I went with her. I'm really sorry, I didn't mean to cause trouble for you.'

'It's okay, Nathan. I believe you,' Jon assured him. 'Now we'll do everything we can to prove it wasn't you and help the police find out who did it.'

They were already back in the village, and Jon pulled up outside the post office. Almost immediately Neil and Angie rushed out as Cara climbed warily from the car. Angie dragged her into a tight hug as Jon spoke with Neil. Just once Neil glanced at the car, and Annie felt his cool gaze searching for Nathan. She shivered as Jon jumped inside and drove off. Moments later Annie saw the gates of the Hall rearing up through the darkness, and he drove up to the house, parking close to the front door. Nathan leapt out quickly and Jon turned to Annie, speaking quietly as he reached for her hand. 'Please will you stay with him until I get back? I won't be long. I'm just going to see the community officer, he lives in the village.'

Annie nodded at once and he gave her a weary smile as he handed her his keys. She was barely out of the car before he hurtled off again, spraying gravel around her feet. It took her a few attempts to unlock the big old door but eventually they were inside, and she fumbled around for a light switch until she found the right one.

'Let's get you something to eat,' she said briskly to Nathan and he nodded meekly. 'Come on, we can sit in the kitchen.'

In the kitchen she steered him to a sofa and he sank onto it, staring blankly into space. She rummaged in the fridge and made a big plate of sandwiches from a chicken and some salad she found inside. She handed him a plateful and then boiled the kettle as she stirred chocolate powder and a little milk into mugs. She added hot water, wishing she'd found a bottle of brandy to lace it with. Nathan looked frozen and she knew it wasn't just because he was cold.

'It'll always be like this, won't it?' he asked her as she passed him a steaming mug. 'Every time something happens people will just assume it's me because I'm different. I don't belong here.'

'I don't know,' she replied honestly, sitting down and meeting his questioning gaze. 'Not everybody will think like that and once they get to know you better, you will have proved the others wrong. You have nothing to hide.'

'I'm not really very hungry.' He put the plate back on to the coffee table. 'Sorry.'

They both looked up as the door opened and Jon appeared, alone. Annie saw hope flare in Nathan's eyes as Jon grinned. 'Good news.' He dropped onto the sofa beside Nathan. 'I've seen the community guy. He's confirmed that someone tried to use Megan's debit card at a petrol station after it was reported it stolen, so they're checking CCTV to identify who that person was. Megan might get the watch back eventually but, unfortunately, I don't suppose the insurance will cover the money because the house wasn't secured. Whoever did it probably saw Megan go out and took a chance to sneak in.'

Annie looked at Nathan. He was smiling tentatively, his long fingers trembling around the mug of hot chocolate.

'Nathan, it means we can prove you were somewhere else when the card was being used.' Nathan looked at Jon and Annie saw that he was surprised. 'Annie saw you today, at the station.'

Nathan looked at Annie and she nodded, giving him a warm smile. 'I was shopping in town and I thought you were on an errand for Jon, so I didn't come over,' she said. 'It was about one o'clock. And there will be CCTV too.'

For the first time Nathan smiled widely, and Annie saw the relief in his eyes. 'I don't know what to say,' he muttered, and he looked at Jon and then Annie. 'Thanks for, well, believing me. It means a lot.' He swung his gaze back to Jon. 'I won't let you down,' he said seriously. 'I swear I won't.'

Jon reached over to place his hand on Nathan's shoulder, squeezing it firmly. 'I know. But you still need to make a statement about what happened. I'll come with you in the morning. And I think you should speak to Cara's parents. Give them a chance, Nathan. You don't really know how they feel but be honest with them if you want to see Cara. I've asked them to do the same for you. Anyway, I don't know about you but I'm starving. I didn't have any supper.' He gave Annie a sideways glance and she laughed, enjoying the sudden tease in his eyes.

Between them Jon and Nathan demolished the plate of sandwiches, and Annie was about to make some more when Nathan yawned, his eyes half closing.

'Come on, I'll drive you back to Arthur's.' Jon stood up and Nathan climbed sleepily to his feet. He looked at Annie gratefully.

'Thanks.'

She nodded, smiling at him. 'See you soon. Good night.'

Annie cleared up while Jon was gone, and he was back in less than half an hour. She made coffee for them and he sat beside her on the sofa, sliding his arm around her shoulders and drawing her against him. 'Thank you,' he said tiredly, absently stroking her neck. 'Sorry about tonight.'

Suddenly she had a flash of insight as she looked into his life and saw the way it was. So far, she hadn't allowed herself to wonder too much about this whole other existence she knew almost nothing about. But now she was beginning to realise the responsibilities of his position, and the extent of his involvement in the business he had created and the community around them. She knew, with an unexpected surge of understanding, that it stemmed from his faith and evenings such as this would almost certainly happen again.

'It doesn't matter,' she said truthfully. She reached up, trailing her fingers gently along his face and he closed his eyes, half smiling. 'We can do it another time. I'm just glad we found them. Do you think he'll be all right?'

'He just needs a chance. It's not easy to be different in a small village like this but he'll manage. He's stronger than he realises. I know how much he wants to be here, and we'll keep on finding ways to make it work for him.' Jon paused, opening his eyes to look at her. 'Annie, I'm really glad you came with me.'

She didn't know what to say, so she simply nodded, wrenching her glance from his before he saw too much. 'I should take you home. It's very late.' Jon released her as he stood up. He rubbed his back absently and Annie was glad she'd resisted the impulse to leap up and do it for him.

Once they were outside her cottage, he left the car to walk her to the front door. She opened it despondently, wondering why she hated seeing him leave time after time. He took her hands and held them tightly in his own.

'Night.' He bent down and brushed the corner of her mouth with his lips. 'Thank you for coming with me. I'm sorry about supper.'

'Sure,' she said lightly, stepping away from him. He hesitated, and she wondered what he was about to say. She didn't blurt out the only thought in her mind and ask when she would see him again. He let go of her hands and she hovered in the dark hall.

'Night.' He turned and walked back to the car.

Stung by his indifference, she shut the door. Before she reached the kitchen, she heard the front door opening again and hurried back. Jon was standing in the sitting room and he looked apprehensive.

'Annie,' he said rapidly, and the grin he gave her was suddenly nervous. 'I know I'm supposed to be trying not to rush things, but may I see you again tomorrow?'

It was hopeless trying to prevent laughter lighting up her face, and she felt him smile against her lips when he crossed the room to kiss her again quickly.

'I'll call you. Hopefully this time you'll get it.'

Chapter Sixteen

Annie couldn't keep the smile from her face the next morning as she attacked the scruffy old herb border and dug out masses of self-seeded catmint cluttering up the garden. Jon was every-where, in her thoughts, in her heart and eventually she hurried inside to bath quickly, impatient to see him. Afterwards she set off into the village, wondering if they were the topic of every gossip after last night. But only Neil was in the shop, looking distracted, and when Annie had filled a basket with cheese, pâté, fresh rolls and tomatoes she went over to speak with him.

'How's Cara?' she asked quietly, placing the basket on the counter. 'Are you and Angie okay?'

Neil glanced around to make sure that there was no one else in the shop before he replied. 'Cara's fine.' He sighed. 'But she scared Angie witless. She never turns her phone off and we'd already heard Nathan was being blamed for the break-in when we couldn't get in touch with her.'

'You know he didn't do it?'

Neil nodded glumly. 'But every time I see him, I think he's going to bring nothing but trouble, and I can't bear the thought of him breaking her heart and just disappearing again.'

Annie nodded sympathetically. 'If it helps at all and I know it probably doesn't, I think underneath there's a nice kid who's just trying to work things out. And I know he cares about Cara. He wouldn't leave her by herself in the station.'

Neil sighed and Annie knew she hadn't really convinced him. 'Thanks. We've agreed to give him a chance if they stick to some rules, otherwise I suppose she'll just see him anyway. At least this way we might be able to keep an eye on them.'

They said goodbye and once she was outside, Annie's heart sank when she saw Sarah Holland emerging from her car. Annie was tempted to turn back until Sarah had disappeared. Annie had heard on the village grapevine that Sarah was supposedly away filming somewhere glamorous, or at least that was what she'd told the parish council when she had turned up at the last meeting. Sarah looked as elegant as ever and Annie summoned all her courage and carried on. She was almost past Sarah's house when she heard her calling. Reluctantly, Annie turned around.

'Hi, Sarah.' For once Annie didn't feel untidy, although the pleasure in her lavender ruffled top and skinny jeans was diminishing as Sarah coolly looked her up and down. Annie was wondering if she knew about her and Jon, the answer becoming obvious as Sarah spoke.

'How's Jon?' she asked cosily, tossing her beautiful hair beyond her shoulders. 'I hear you probably know better than most people.'

Annie bit her lip but not her tongue. 'He's fine. I'm just on my way to see him.' It was true but she had no idea if he would actually be there when she arrived. She smiled at Sarah, trying not to feel at all triumphant, and Sarah smiled back.

'Oh? How odd. When I saw him yesterday he mentioned he would probably be out all day today. Still you know what he's like, here one minute, gone the next. I do hope he hasn't forgotten you.'

'Well, there's always next time,' Annie called over her shoulder as she walked away. 'Bye.'

She marched through the village, replaying the conversation with Sarah in her mind as she headed up the drive to the Hall, the avenue of limes swaying high above. There was no sign of Jon's car at the house, and she began to think that Sarah may have been right. But then she remembered that his office was not in the house but in the Home Farm courtyard. She saw the lane leading away from the house and followed it, crossing a cattle grid. Stone buildings surged up on either side of the lane, surrounded by tall horse chestnut trees. A large farmhouse was half hidden behind more trees and she saw a garden over the wall, cluttered with children's toys and a couple of wire chicken runs scattered on the lawn. As she neared the yard some of the barn doors were open and she glanced inside at rows of little sheep pens, the scent of silage and livestock lingering in the air.

She walked through a high stone arch into a large square cobbled courtyard, spotting a long barn, its low windows revealing tables and chairs set into groups. An old stable block on the left looked as though it was still in use, while all the other buildings appeared to have been converted into office accommodation. On the right, beside an oak door, she saw 'Estate Office' engraved on a plaque attached to the wall and hesitated, then pushed the door open and stepped inside. The room was modern and bright, and several paintings hung on cream walls with a discreet automated visitor system open on an iPad nearby.

Three comfortable leather chairs were clustered around a circular table, piled with country home and farming magazines and a local newspaper. There was no one around, and Annie could hear the quiet bubbling of a nearby coffee machine. One of three doors was open, and she peered along the corridor, half hoping Jon would find her before she had to go looking. The carrier bag of lunch bumped against her legs as she hovered, and then she headed decisively down the corridor. Her feet sounded terribly loud on the wooden floor; nevertheless she heard the unmistakable sound of his voice and she gulped. She knocked on the door at the end of the corridor, and he immediately called to come in.

Jon's head was bent as he scribbled something on a pad, clutching his mobile to his ear while he talked. She stared at him wordlessly, absorbing the details as though she hadn't seen him for months instead of barely twelve hours. A white shirt, worn with a tie already loosened, made his brown hair seem even darker, and the casually rolled-up sleeves revealed his tanned arms. Thoughts of last night came rushing into her mind as she remembered clinging to him when they'd kissed, and she felt giddy. He looked up as he ended the call.

'What are you doing here?' he asked incredulously, dropping the phone onto the desk, and shoving his chair back swiftly. She knew the expression of surprised delight on his face was reflected in her eyes, and he gave her an enormous smile as he stood up.

'I've brought you lunch,' she said shyly, holding the bag up. He barely glanced at it as he quickly came around the desk, and it slid to the floor as he wound his arms around her waist, lifting her up against him and kissing her. She kissed him back, curling her fingers into his hair until he reluctantly set her down again.

'That's going to distract me for the rest of the day.' He was still smiling as he took her hand and led her towards the desk. 'But I'm not complaining. Do you want to sit down?'

He pointed to his seat and she sat, feeling tiny in his big leather chair. He propped himself on the edge of the desk, facing her, his thigh only inches away. She looked around the office, all too aware of him close by. Like the reception, the plain cream walls were hung with paintings by the same artist and a large, obviously old, yellowed map of the estate. Two tall bookcases, almost hiding the wall on the left of his desk, were filled with ancient ledgers and some newer books. An untidy pile of paperwork nestled on the desk between a flat computer screen and a cordless telephone standing in its base. The arched window overlooked the whole courtyard and there was a wonderful view of the farm and the land beyond.

'I wasn't sure you'd be here.' She glanced at the bag, still lying on the floor where she had left it. 'I've just brought some bread, cheese and tomatoes. But it's fine if you're busy. I imagine your housekeeper…' She tailed off, not sure what to say.

'She doesn't cook for me,' he replied, amused, one long leg dangling above the other. 'I've lived on my own for years, I can look after myself. She supervises all of the domestic side of the business and takes care of the house.'

'Oh.' Annie felt pleased, not sure why it mattered.

'So, thank you, whatever you've brought will be perfect.'

'As long as it's not cake,' she retorted, and he smiled again. 'How's Nathan?' She changed the subject, wanting to know how the young boy was after yesterday as Jon made room on his desk for the food. 'Has he seen the police yet?'

Jon pulled another chair closer to hers. 'Yep, we went first thing. He was a bit nervous, but it was fine. He's given a statement, so I don't think he'll be involved any more. Megan was waiting when we came out and she insisted on dragging him over to The Courtyard for breakfast.'

'How lovely!'

'I'm not too sure that's what Nathan thought. He was a bit startled but it was a really sweet gesture. She wanted to make sure the whole village knew he wasn't responsible.' Jon found plates and brought them over to his desk as Annie spread out their lunch.

'So what did he do?'

'He gave me a pleading look as she marched him away and promised to be back at work within the hour.'

'And was he?'

'No idea, I didn't check. I trust him.'

They chatted while they ate, and Jon brought them coffee from the machine in reception. All too soon they had finished, and she tried not to linger, not wanting to keep him from his work.

'Would you like to have a look around?' he asked casually, chucking some rubbish into a bin nearby.

'I'd love to.' Her eyes lit up and she was still smiling when he reached for her hand and they headed outside. They paused in the courtyard, side by side and he pointed to the Hall, just visible through the trees.

'The house is eighteenth century, although there was a farm here long before then. It belonged to a family from Northumberland and they used it as a second home until two heirs were killed in the Great War and the third son split the estate to pay debts. The house became a convalescence home during the war and my grandfather bought what was left of the estate in 1955.'

He gestured to the building behind them. 'There are two flats above the offices. Our housekeeper lives in one and Emma's mum in the other. The other offices, next door to ours, are leased to an IT consultancy, a web designer and a skiing holiday company, all local businesses.'

He was still holding her hand as they wandered over to the stable block. The building felt cool inside and Annie was surprised to see that two of the big stalls were clearly in use, even though the occupants were nowhere in sight. 'You have horses?'

'Yes, but not for riding. We have a pair of working Dales ponies. The estate has around eight hundred acres of forestry and a few years ago our head forester brought in a horse-logger on contract. Horses cause less environmental damage and they're much more manoeuvrable. After a couple of years, we persuaded the contractor to stay and now we have two earning their keep.'

They left the courtyard and as they neared the farmhouse, they could hear children running into the garden. Dogs barked excitedly, and they laughed when they heard a chicken squawk in alarm. 'Our farm manager must be back,' Jon said, looking across to the house. 'His father was the gamekeeper before him – those are his chickens. The most valuable moorland was sold off years ago, so we don't have a traditional gamekeeper now.'

'So, no shooting?'

'Only clays. Dad introduced a shoot a few years ago and we run it just for corporate days. He still looks after it.'

'Are you sure I'm not keeping you from something?' she asked as they left the courtyard, walking slowly towards the Hall. Her hand was tucked tightly inside his and she didn't really care if she was distracting him; she just wanted to be with him, and the knowledge amazed her. Jon paused to glance at her, and the smiling answer in his eyes was all she needed to know.

'Yes, everything.' He pulled her to him, placing his lips briefly against her temple. 'And all of it can wait. Come on.'

Thrilled, she followed him through an archway smothered in climbing roses and into a lovely walled garden filled with vegetable and herb beds bordered by neat box hedging. A beautiful wide border framed three sides of the wall, dividing the garden in half. They walked beneath an arbour almost hidden by sweet peas and honeysuckle, and she saw a wrought-iron gate ahead tucked into the wall and offering a glimpse of the formal garden beyond. They walked side by side to the kitchen door, his hand on the small of her back.

He led her through the house, not pausing again until they had passed through the reception hall and then he held a door open for her. She couldn't prevent the smile that lit up her face as they entered an exquisite drawing room. Its pale green walls were divided into panels, larger than those in the hall, and hung with pictures more suited to their size and she glanced at the paintings with pleasure. Two full-length bay windows, French doors between them, overlooked a terrace leading to the garden. Sunlight poured in through the two windows on the south side of the room, where the parkland sloped down to the lake. Original wooden shutters and heavy, pale terracotta curtains surrounded each window.

Only the ceiling and cornice below it boasted beautiful plasterwork similar to that in the hall, and a striking chandelier hung in the centre. Matching floral patterned chairs were clustered around occasional tables, each covered with a lamp, books and family photographs, and Annie tried not to stare at the pictures. Two small sofas, identical to the chairs, stood against the wall opposite a chimney breast, while two, more modern, striped sofas in pale green and white huddled around the fireplace, their cushions scattered in disarray beneath tall standard lamps staring down solemnly. The wooden floor was almost hidden beneath a floral carpet, its edges not quite reaching the walls.

She spun around to look again at the painting of a young couple above the fireplace. The man was in uniform, his stare straight ahead, while the woman gazed up at him adoringly. Annie had to look again before she realised that they were holding hands.

'Are they your grandparents?'

'Yes. The picture was a wedding gift, painted just after they were married. How can you tell?'

It was a good excuse to glance at him and compare, and after a few seconds he laughed, bending down to kiss her quickly.

Annie smiled, batting his hand away from her face. 'Family likeness. But you're darker than your grandfather and I'd say you're taller. You have his eyes.'

They stared at the portrait together as Annie imagined what life would have been like for Jon's grandparents in this place, so many years ago. 'Why did your grandfather choose to live in Thorndale?' She glanced sideways at Jon. 'Was he born here?'

Jon shook his head with a grin. 'He was a romantic, or so my more pragmatic grandmother liked to tell me. Pretty unusual for a Leeds city boy. He'd always lived in town, and he had a dream of buying a farm and living off the land. His father's business was in steel and my grandfather trained to become a barrister. He fell in love with the estate when it came up for sale and gave up the law to buy it.'

'Definitely a romantic,' Annie said dryly, even though she couldn't help liking the story.

'Yep. He rescued the estate before it was completely broken up, and by restoring it he helped to bring some of the life back to the village, even when farming was still in a depression. He only ever employed local people, and he knew he had a lot to learn before he could expect to see real progress. I never met him. He died on holiday, six years before I was born.'

'I'm sorry.' She reached for Jon's hand and wound his fingers between her own. She was beginning to understand how much his family had inspired him and what he was continuing to achieve in the place his grandfather had chosen.

'Thanks. I guess I inherited his desire to farm and he always said, right up until he died, that he still had lots to learn. I feel that way too. I don't really use this room when I'm here alone, we keep it for when we have guests. There's a smaller sitting room and I use the library as a study. I'm in there or the kitchen most of the time when I'm in the house.'

Annie jumped as Jon's pager beeped, and he scrolled through the message with one hand while reaching for his phone with the other, replying at once. He looked up and she was already smiling as she read the regret in his eyes.

'Sorry,' he said ruefully. 'We had a standby earlier, but this is a new one. Teenage boy trapped in rocks and it's a full team callout. Gotta run.'

'Absolutely.' Annie followed him as they swiftly returned to the hall. 'I really ought to be doing some work anyway.'

At the front door Jon kissed her briefly, pressing a set of keys into her hand and lifting his head to look at her questioningly, his voice low. 'You could work here if you like, make use of the Wi-Fi. I'm sorry I can't say when I'll be back and I don't mean to sound as though I'm assuming you can just hang around for me, but could we continue this later?'

'Can't, sorry, I'm meeting Kirstie.' Annie shook her head with a grin. 'Go on, go.'

He laughed as Annie returned the keys, quickly locking up and sprinting to his car and then he was gone, leaving her watching on the drive. She began the walk back home, anticipating a couple of hours of work before she'd go out again.

Chapter Seventeen

'I usually try not to take much notice of gossip but you and Jon Beresford seeing one another is proving hard to ignore. I bet the village is captivated – they've been wanting to marry him off for ages.'

Annie groaned, hiding her face in her hands from Kirstie's all too inquisitive gaze as Kirstie smirked, nudging her gently.

'Is it true, then? Anything you'd like to share?'

They were in town, edging through a growing crowd as they made their way to the main square to find their seats for a live music set, part of the two-week Arts Festival that had grown over the years to encompass theatre, poetry, music, comedy, books and art. Annie had never been before and she loved the atmosphere, somewhat similar to but much smaller than her beloved Edinburgh festival. Kirstie knew a couple of the musicians taking part and had managed to secure tickets at the last minute.

'No,' she told Kirstie firmly but a big smile on her face belied the tiny word. She laughed, warmth stealing through her as she thought of seeing Jon earlier and their hurried parting. She hoped the rescue had gone well and wondered if he was home yet. 'It's seriously early days.'

'Or just serious? That's a very silly grin you've got plastered on your face, Ms Armstrong.'

They were squeezing between other people to take their seats on the third row. The band was already tuning up and Annie had tried to feign interest in the flyers constantly being stuffed into their hands as they'd wandered around, grabbing coffee to take away.

Kirstie nudged her again, and Annie knew she wasn't going to take no for an answer, raising her voice over the noise of the band. 'Not serious, no. I've only known him for a few weeks. Neither of us are looking to be committed to anything else, so it's just a few casual dates and we'll see how it goes.' Annie's gaze was troubled then as she looked at Kirstie. 'Meeting someone like Jon was the last thing I expected, to be honest. After everything with Iain, I really wasn't looking for anyone and then, well, he was just there.' She paused, a glow lighting her eyes. 'And he's lovely. I do like him.'

'What's not to like?' Kirstie told her with a grin. 'He's hot, Annie, I'll give you that. But be careful, okay?'

Alarmed, Annie's eyes flew to Kirstie's, the flyers dropping to the floor and the coffee cup in her hand tilted, spilling some on the cobbles beneath her feet. 'What do you mean?'

Kirstie was waving at someone on the stage in front of them and her smile was sympathetic when she returned her gaze to Annie's. 'I'm sorry, that sounded pretty interfering and judgemental. It's just after everything you've been through, I'd hate for you to get hurt again.'

'But what do you know about him? Come on, Kirst, you can't not say now.'

Kirstie sighed. 'I haven't been around the whole time he's been back, Annie, but I heard a rumour about an ex-girlfriend, someone he was serious about and that maybe she's still on the scene. I'm sorry, I don't know the details and it was none of my business anyway. Most people like him, Annie. It's hard not to. But he's not easy to get close to, however friendly he seems.'

Annie's stomach lurched into a spiral of anxiety at Kirstie's words, reminding her again of the comments she'd overhead at Sarah's party. She tried to bring her mind back to what she knew for herself of Jon and drive away the doubts clouding her thoughts. 'You're not serious! That doesn't mean anything. We've no idea of the circumstances or context. I know he keeps his personal life private and that's fair enough, given that people seem to like making it their business to speculate about him.'

'Hey, sorry, okay?' Kirstie reached across to squeeze Annie's hand. 'I'm sorry. Truly. Just, you know, look after *you*.'

Annie nodded, trying not to feel chilled by Kirstie's warning. Whatever had gone before in his life, Annie had seen and understood the intensity in his eyes, knowing it was reflected in her own whenever she and Jon looked at one another. She couldn't measure what she'd learned of him against a man who had a reputation for being difficult to capture. 'I will,' she said quietly. 'I appreciate your concern, really I do. But I feel as though I know him already, Kirstie, however unlikely that seems.'

Kirstie nodded sympathetically as the band were introduced and Annie fell silent as music followed and the crowd roared encouragement. Annie sensed Kirstie looking at her from time to time and she smiled, not wanting anything to spoil their renewed friendship, understanding that her friend's warning was born out of care.

The musicians were very good, and when it was over Annie wished she had enjoyed it more, but Kirstie's words had planted in her mind a seed of doubt she wanted to forget. They managed to find a table in a busy little Italian trattoria for supper and Jon wasn't mentioned again. When they eventually parted, they shared a hug. Annie was inside her car, about to start the engine when her phone beeped and she opened WhatsApp, smiling the moment she saw Jon's name, despite Kirstie's concern.

> If you fancy abandoning your car outside the barn again on Saturday, you might get it washed this time. You coming?

He'd attached a copy of the poster for the family fun day at the fell rescue headquarters and Annie glanced through it, already knowing the events that were planned.

> I am. Making cake. Not for you. :) Might bring the car though. If you promise not to tow it away

Elizabeth had asked if she would help at the bake off and Annie had been happy to agree. She grinned as she saw the laughing emojis following her reply.

> If I promise to wash it personally and not tow it away, do we have a date?

> At a car wash? Wow. That's a first.

Annie added an emoji crying with laughter.

> I won't be washing cars all day. There'll be time later if you're free?

> Let's see, shall we?

He followed her reply with two more emojis, one fingers crossed, one blowing a kiss. The second was a first for them and Annie replayed their messages in her mind as she returned home, still smiling.

Despite what Jon had said Annie didn't take her car into the village first thing on Saturday. She knew there would be little room to park and she walked down in good time to help set up, carrying a tin of red velvet cupcakes for her bake off entry. There was a marquee propped across half the green, and the other half was scattered with chairs and a few wooden picnic tables, the barbeques far away from the cakes. A cone system for directing traffic in and out of the car wash was set up on the track outside the fell rescue's headquarters and two all-terrain vehicles were parked outdoors, ready to show visitors what went into a rescue and how highly trained and dedicated the volunteer team was.

A huge, clear tank, a red seat suspended above it, stood at the far end of the green, slowly filling with water, attached to a yellow plastic screen with a red target in the centre. She found Elizabeth in the marquee, safely stashed the cupcakes ready for later and was soon busy helping to hang colourful bunting and set out entries. Elizabeth told her they'd managed to secure the services of an award-winning local artisan baker to judge the competition, and lots more people were spilling into the marquee, keen to purchase their cakes in advance of the sale later.

Annie saw the baker arrive, and he was immediately swept away by the small committee of organisers. Everyone else was chased out of the marquee so judging could commence, and she was happy to escape the warmth inside, strolling casually through the growing crowd to the fell rescue. Lots of people were milling around the entrance, children clambering inside the Land Rovers and trying on helmets that were too large, as visitors enthused over the range of specialist equipment and watched a film running on a loop on the whiteboard inside the barn, of the work of the association through the years. The car wash was also proving popular and she glanced sideways, spotting Jon, who was busy with two other members washing a very dirty four-by-four. He seemed to sense her looking and glanced up, catching her eye and she couldn't resist going over. He was wearing a red fell rescue T-shirt and shorts, and she reached up to wipe away a blob of soap from his face, warm and roughened by stubble.

'Thanks.' He grinned, catching her fingers for a second, quickly swiping a blob of the same soap on the end of her nose with the sponge in his other hand.

'Hey,' she protested, laughing. 'Don't start a fight.'

'Why not,' he teased, smoothing the soap away with a gentle thumb that left her wanting more of his touch. 'I'm the one with the buckets and sponge. You're the one at a disadvantage.'

His eyes slid down, taking in her denim shorts and green top and her pulse soared at the intimacy she read in his eyes. Another sponge sailed through the air, hitting him on the shoulder and leaving a soaking patch on his T-shirt. They both looked over, laughing, to see who had thrown it.

'Get back to work,' one of the other volunteers shouted across with a grin. 'There's a queue here and we haven't got time to stand around watching you pair flirting.'

'Where's your car?'

Annie stepped back, not wanting to hold him up or be soaked. 'At home. Thought it might be in the way.'

She heard Jon's laugh at that, and she was still smiling as she crossed the green. The queue for the tea rooms snaked beyond the front door and the ice cream hut was absolutely packed, the weather for once obliging with warm sunshine. Children were splashing in the river and chefs from the pub were busy barbecuing, and yet more people were waiting their turn for food. Annie felt a thrill of real happiness and pleasure stealing through her as she strolled around, waving to Charlie when she saw him rushing down the high street. Sarah Holland emerged from her house, looking as stunning as ever in a floral mini skirt with ankle boots and a sleeveless cream top, and Annie scowled, her pleasure in her own outfit diminishing. Jed March was with her and it wasn't long before they were accosted by people wanting selfies, both appearing happy to linger and smile for the cameras.

Once the judging was over Annie was supposed to take her turn inside the marquee for the cake sale. She saw that the sign keeping people out of the marquee had gone and she made her way across, pushing aside thoughts of Sarah. Inside she was thrilled to have won a third prize and stuck the certificate in her handbag, dropping her bag on the floor beside her table. Someone had thoughtfully provided a fold-away camping chair, but Annie was quite happy on her feet, chatting to people in between tea served in giant stainless-steel pots as she wrapped up endless slices of cake. Emma and Sir Vivian were making their way around the marquee and they came over for a chat before going off to meet some friends. Annie saw Sam and waved. Sam wandered over, her bump larger than ever as she lowered herself carefully into the camping chair.

'Do you mind,' she asked Annie, looking up with a cheerful smile. She had changed her hair since Annie had last seen her and it was now blonde with red highlights running through the tips, her trademark Doc Martens ever present. 'Hope I don't break it.'

'You're not that big, Sam! Loving your hair, that colour really suits you.'

'Thanks.' Sam was failing to hide her amusement as she gave Annie a sideways glance, and Annie became suspicious.

'What's so funny?'

Sam was stroking her bump but still looking at Annie with a merry expression. 'Some woman's just offered Jon fifty pounds to wash her car topless,' she said gleefully. 'Sarah heard and offered to double it.'

Annie's gasp of surprise lengthened into a shout of laughter as her gaze became incredulous. 'What did he say?'

'He very charmingly told them it wouldn't be a good idea at a family fun day as they couldn't expect all the volunteers to do the same. Don't think Sarah was impressed though. I think she thought he actually might do it, as it's for charity.'

'I'd pay,' Annie said dreamily, hearing Sam's scream of laughter.

'For you, Annie, he'd no doubt do it for free. And probably wouldn't stop at just the top, either, if you asked him.'

'Sam! Stop it, before someone overhears!'

'Have you heard that Sarah's thinking of volunteering with the fell rescue?' Sam asked her idly, reaching for a bottle of water in her bag and looking sideways at Annie as she took a drink.

'No. Do you think she's serious?'

'Dunno. Can't see how she'd be able to make the time. Apparently, she's up for a part in a Netflix series which would mean weeks away so what's the point in applying? She's been hanging around on a Monday night, helping to sort equipment and stuff during training.'

Annie saw Jon making his way across the marquee to them and her heart leaped, her concentration suddenly gone.

'Hey, you two.' He was smiling, damp from washing cars, his gaze going to Sam before returning to Annie, effortlessly holding her still with just a glance. 'May I have your car keys please?'

'What! Why?'

'I promised to wash it, remember?' His voice had lowered, leaving Annie longing to be alone with him as his smile lengthened into a grin, emphasising the lines around his blue eyes. She heard Sam's muffled shriek beside her and turned her laughing gaze to look at her friend, trying to be stern and failing utterly.

'Sorry, Jon, run that by me again.' Sam was wiping her eyes now and Annie's mind was filled with images she had no intention of sharing. 'You're going to wash Annie's car for her?'

Puzzled, he looked from Sam back to Annie. 'I said I would. What's so funny?'

'Are you doing it here, or, you know, in private, at home?'

'Here, of course. We'll be packing up soon.'

'Fully dressed?'

There was curiosity in his expression before he realised what Sam meant and he laughed. 'You heard about that then?' he asked Annie, shaking his head. His glance suddenly became lazy, his eyes narrowing as he stared at her. 'Maybe some other time.'

He stuck out his hand and Annie reached into her bag, removing her keys and dropping them onto his waiting palm, and he smiled at her as he turned away. Her stall was mostly sold out now and she returned to the green after helping to quickly tidy up. Jon was back in less than fifteen minutes, crammed behind the steering wheel in her little Mini, and she knew half the village was watching as he parked it and the team set to washing it, Jon included.

Once it was done, he drove it back to her cottage and when he returned he joined her on the green in the huddle that had lined up to watch the first of the volunteers sitting nervously above the tank of freezing cold water. Children were chosen to sling the first balls at the target and the worried occupant started to relax as the first few shots missed, even summoning up a casual wave for the crowd. A middle-aged man stepped up and the first ball landed on target, triggering the lever which tilted the seat, dumping the volunteer straight into the cold water. He shook himself as he emerged and after a couple more dunkings, was offered a towel and a change of volunteer. He stepped aside and the pattern was repeated with a woman Annie recognised as another volunteer from the fell rescue.

She saw one of the organisers waving at Jon and he bent down to speak into her ear. 'My turn. Are you free after this?'

There was nothing to say other than yes, thoughts of anything else disappearing in the desire to spend more time with him and Annie saw him smile.

'I won't be too long, then we can go if you're ready.'

She nodded, watching as he strode across to the tank and swung himself onto the seat. She couldn't resist; she dashed forward, paid the money and took aim, aware of the growing crowd behind her. Playing netball at school had improved her hand to eye coordination no end and her first shot landed dead centre, catapulting Jon straight into the tank. The crowd roared and she laughed, hanging around to see him stand up and shake his head. He lifted his hands to wipe the water from his face, running them through his hair and slicking it backwards. Annie swallowed as she saw the soaking T-shirt clinging to his chest, outlining the width of his shoulders, and then he was laughing, his eyes searching for her. She refused her other two shots and a little boy was helped to land the target too, dunking Jon again. After another ten minutes he was relieved of duty and climbed out, dripping water onto the grass around him. Annie watched, her breath stilling, as he strode straight over, a grin still on his face.

His arms went around her the moment he reached her, lifting her, and transferring his wetness onto her clothes. She squealed, trying to wriggle away but he wasn't to be dissuaded as he bent his head to kiss her quickly. If there had been any doubts about the nature of their relationship, he'd banished them with that gesture and Annie sensed that the crowd was seeing everything while trying to pretend otherwise.

'You didn't tell me you were such a good shot,' he murmured into her ear, his breath tickling her ear. 'I wasn't expecting that.'

'There's lots you don't know about me,' she whispered, tilting her head back as he set her down.

'I'm planning to find out.' He slipped an arm around her waist, tugging her against his side. 'Shall we go?'

She nodded, copying his gesture as they walked away, arms wrapped around one another, soaking wet. When they returned to his house everybody else had left for the day and they were alone. Annie helped Jon cook a simple supper and they ate in the kitchen after she laughingly refused to eat in the formal dining room. It was almost midnight when he walked her home and what had begun as an afternoon together had turned into the remainder of the day. She knew he was as reluctant as she was to say goodbye. Before he left, he invited her to be his guest at a party in a couple of weeks and she accepted at once.

Chapter Eighteen

Annie found out later the party was a silver wedding celebration for a couple with whom Jon had worked during his time in Kenya, and she was filled with doubts as she wondered how she would feel amongst some of his oldest friends and colleagues. It meant they would be away overnight, and she knew they had been invited to stay with Carrie and Owen at their home in Chester, where the party would be held.

Meanwhile, Sam's blood pressure had gone up and she had been ordered to rest, so in between preparing for school and seeing Jon as often as possible, Annie was endeavouring to fill Sam's freezer and do some pre-baby shopping for her new friend. But she was fed up of shepherd's pie and ratatouille, and when Jon dropped in at the cottage one afternoon, she was baking hot and wishing she'd never started cooking chicken cacciatore, a recipe she'd picked up in Italy. Stirring the huge pot on the Rayburn, she jumped when he suddenly appeared, sliding his arms around her waist and kissing her neck quickly.

'Aagh,' she squealed, starting to laugh as she spun around to face him. 'Don't, not unless you want to scrape this off the floor.'

She had got into the habit of leaving her front door unlocked whenever she was around so he could let himself in. Once or twice, when she'd insisted she really must work, he had turned up anyway with his laptop and mobile and worked in the kitchen. She had shut herself away in the study and tried not to think of him nearby. Sometimes she couldn't resist going to him and would peer over his shoulder, discovering that he liked to share his work with her. He talked about his plans for the estate and Kilnbeck, how he was in the process of setting up a scholarship to sponsor two students through agricultural college. He wanted to offer one place to a student from the village and he was about to offer the second place to Nathan. Annie had been thrilled by his plans, realising how much she had misunderstood him when they'd first met, imagining him breezing through life with his easy grin and friendly approach. The serious side of him was becoming familiar to her and she knew now that he was a person who cared for people and depended on his faith.

They'd spent a lazy afternoon at Fountains Abbey, supposedly gathering information for her school project, and had ended up picnicking besides the ruins before staying on to watch an outdoor screening of *Dirty Dancing*, which Jon had never seen and Annie had insisted he must. He hadn't loved it as much as she did, but it had been a really fun evening and they'd teased one another about the dancing afterwards. He'd come with her to visit the woodland memorial ground where Molly was buried, and Annie had smiled through her sadness at the surrounding view of the Dales that Molly had so loved. They'd laughed together at the sheep busily grazing in the meadow, knowing how much Molly would have loved the idea of the animals improving the soil and increasing biodiversity on the land.

'Are you ready for tomorrow?' he asked casually, one hip perched on the kitchen table as he watched her.

Nodding absently, she poured half a bottle of Chianti into the dish and thought about what tomorrow might bring. She was so looking forward to spending time with him, and yet nerves clashed with anticipation as she tried to imagine what to expect once they were away from the village. She had bought another new dress and was almost packed and having finally completed her timetables and the Fountains Abbey project, felt she could take a weekend off and not think about school for once. Her parents were coming over for a visit soon and she was so looking forward to introducing them to Jon. But there was the party to get through first.

'They will like you.' He took the spoon, placing his hands on her shoulders to gently turn her around. She smiled nervously, and he drew her towards him, cupping her face with one hand.

'What have you told your friends about us?' She could feel the warmth of his fingers against her cheek, tipping her head back to look at him properly. She didn't want her question to seem like a roundabout way of forcing him into an admission neither of them was ready to hear, and yet she wanted to know a little more. These past few days with him seemed to stretch back years, even though they only really amounted to moments. She knew he had rearranged his schedule wherever possible to spend more time with her, and once she had joined him out hiking with a Kilnbeck group. Along with Mark, Kirstie had roped them into a volunteer day with the National Park and afterwards they'd had a takeaway, the four of them together squeezed into Kirstie's little cottage. Emma and Vivian had invited them to lunch twice and they'd discovered a lovely little tapas bar in town that was already becoming a favourite, and she knew, even as she wanted to pretend otherwise, that they were the talk of the village.

'That you're beautiful, kind, clever, fun, independent and a teacher. Oh, and sexy. Have I missed anything?'

Startled and flattered, she gently swatted him to cover her surprise. She wondered if he had avoided giving her a direct answer on purpose. 'You've forgotten I'm also a few years younger than you.'

He grinned as he smoothed a strand of hair away from her face and tucked it behind her ear. 'Don't worry, nobody will notice.'

'Thanks a lot.' She wriggled away, reaching for a wet cloth to throw at him. He ducked as it sailed over his head and they laughed.

When the food was ready, he walked with her to the vicarage. Each villager they met eyed them curiously as they shared greetings without pausing to chat. Sam was thrilled to see them, and Annie headed into the kitchen to leave the casserole on top of the Aga. Charlie arrived soon afterwards and invited them to stay for supper. He grinned when Sam pointed out that Annie had made it.

'I can't.' Jon sounded reluctant as he leant across to Annie and kissed her briefly, squeezing her hand as he stood up. 'I'm off to see the National Park about planning and then there's a meeting at Kilnbeck at seven.' He grinned at Sam. 'Make sure you do as you're told, for a change.' He turned his gaze to Annie, and she smiled as she saw the warmth in his eyes. 'See you tomorrow, about two?'

She nodded, following him to the front door so she would have another chance to kiss him goodbye. She reached up, touching his face gently with her hand. He kissed her fingers quickly and then he was gone, waving before he disappeared. She knew she was glowing when she returned to the sitting room and felt Sam's eyes upon her.

'It suits you,' Sam said knowingly, and Annie looked at her in surprise.

'What does?'

'Being in love.'

Startled, Annie felt even more colour rush into her cheeks, holding up her hands to deny Sam's remark. 'It's not like that,' she protested, suddenly afraid she was expressing even more than she dared to admit to herself. 'It's just a few dates.'

'Hmm. That's what Jon says too, and yet he's strutting around like a dog with two—'

'Sam!' Annie interrupted her before she could finish the sentence, and they laughed. But later, alone in the cottage again, she thought about Sam's comments. Was that what people were thinking? Were she and Jon being too open too soon? She wasn't sure, resolving to be more guarded when they were together. She hardly dared contemplating the future – it only seemed to exist until their next date – and she had no idea what would happen once the summer was over, and the school term arrived to claim her. The little voice in her mind, that reminded her he wouldn't commit, that he wouldn't choose a long-term relationship unless he believed he could envisage marriage and a family, liked to niggle her and cast doubt on what the future might hold for them.

Jon was on time when he arrived to collect her the following day, despite her concern that a crisis would spring up to hold them back. He teased her about the size of her suitcase as he carried it to the car, and she felt edgy and suddenly uncertain about the wisdom of going away with him. But it was too late. As she locked her front door, she knew for certain that everything between them would be different once they returned. She saw him cast an appraising glance over her skinny jeans and lacy top and felt the warmth of his hand on her back as she stepped into the Land Rover. He passed her an address and as she programmed the satnav for him, he told her about the family she was soon to meet.

'I met Carrie when she came out to Kenya as part of a team advising people on basic business principles to help them begin projects that earned money. She'd taken a career break from her job as an accountant and she was with us for about eight weeks. When she came back on her second trip, Owen and their two boys were with her. Eventually the boys had to go back to school and Owen stayed on to help design and build new schools. Now the boys are old enough to be left at home, she and Owen spend about four months of the year in Kenya since he sold his business.'

Annie looked at him curiously. 'So you've kept in touch?'

Jon nodded, sliding his hand onto her thigh as they drove along, and she covered it with her fingers, her resolve fading now they were out of sight of the village. 'They're good friends, as well as being very gifted and dedicated missionaries.

We still meet up from time to time but it's more difficult now. I'm sure you'll like them.'

'I'm sure I will.' She tried to imagine what they would look like, probably pale and earnest, with sandals. But she'd been wrong before, smiling to herself as she remembered her surprise when he had told her that he too had once been a missionary. 'Will there be many people at the party?'

She saw him hesitate, as though he was going to say something and then changed his mind. 'Not sure. I think it's supposed to be just for family and close friends.'

Once they reached the motorway the level of traffic took Annie by surprise, realising she hadn't spent much time away from Thorndale, or Jon for that matter, in the last few weeks, and already her life in Edinburgh seemed like a distant memory. Jon knew exactly where to go, confounding the satnav from time to time, and soon they were pulling up outside a lovely Victorian townhouse. 'This is it.'

Annie felt her nerves spinning as she surreptitiously tried to touch up her lip-gloss. The road was already crammed with cars, and Jon squeezed the Land Rover into a small space on the street nearby. She wanted to turn and flee, wishing she had never agreed to come to the party. But he was already waiting to take her hand as she left the car, and then they were at the open front door.

'Anyone home,' he shouted. Annie was glad he was still holding her hand and she clutched his tightly. Somebody shouted, 'Come in,' and she followed him inside, their feet tapping on the wooden floor beneath them.

'We're in here,' the voice called from the back of the house. They walked along a corridor, beside a staircase and then emerged in a bright and sunny kitchen with a large orangery leading into the garden. The kitchen was a hive of activity and lots of people threw them smiling glances as they bustled about without pausing. A woman emerged from the melee with a shout of glee, and Jon let go of Annie's hand to lift her into a hug and swing her around. Annie had a chance to look at her properly once Jon had set her down and saw that Carrie wasn't in the least pale and bespectacled. He turned to Annie, drawing her against him as he made the introductions.

'This is my good friend Carrie Graham. Carrie, I'd like you to meet my girlfriend, Annie.'

Annie's eyes flew up to his in surprise. This was the first time either of them had acknowledged the extent of their relationship to anybody else, and she was elated. The smile Carrie gave her was affectionate, even as she looked at Annie curiously. She was plump and curvy, with stylishly cut brunette hair feathered into sharp lines falling around her face. As it was a silver wedding celebration Annie had expected her to be older, but she saw that Carrie couldn't be much more than forty-five. She was beautiful but not in a conventional way. It came from within, from her bright and friendly eyes and warm gestures. She hadn't bothered with make-up and her face looked fresh, despite the fine lines around her eyes and mouth. Carrie threw her arms around Annie too, hugging her quickly.

'I'm so pleased to meet you at last,' she said, giving Jon a playful smile as she drew back. 'We've heard so much about you already. We couldn't wait to see you in the flesh.'

'Oh.' Startled, Annie looked from Carrie to Jon and he grinned easily as he shrugged, his arm back around Annie's waist.

'Oh, there's Owen,' Carrie said hurriedly, spinning around as a tall, thin man appeared in the orangery, waving him over. 'He's having problems with the lights outside so we might all be in the dark later. Owen, come and meet Annie.'

Owen was a little older than Carrie, perhaps around fifty, but his grin was just as warm as he shook Annie's hand and hugged Jon briefly. 'Come and help me,' he said to Jon, holding up a screwdriver. 'I seem to remember you used to be able to turn your hand to most things.'

'Not yet,' Carrie protested. 'Let me take them to their room and then you can borrow him. Have you seen Alex yet? He promised he'd be back by now. Our youngest son's learning to be a chef,' Carrie explained as she led them upstairs. 'He's supposed to be putting all that training to good use and helping with the party.'

She opened the door onto a lovely room, with a wide four-poster bed and a glorious view of the city walls from the window. Jon disappeared to get their cases and Carrie hovered, pointing out different landmarks until he returned.

'Come down when you're ready.' Carrie was at the door, about to excuse herself. She looked at Jon. 'If the lights go off, you'll know that Owen's blown the fuses. You'll probably both be roped into doing something.'

'I don't mind,' Annie assured her. She glanced at Jon, sitting on the bed and then looked away as a multitude of thoughts raced through her mind.

'You'll regret that,' Carrie said, laughing. 'But thank you.' She closed the door and they were alone.

'Come here.' Jon held out a hand and Annie inched towards him until she was standing between his thighs and he caught her, his hands on her waist. 'Have I told you how beautiful you are and how much you distract me?'

She smiled slowly, lost in his eyes as he pulled her down onto his lap and began to kiss her. His hands crept beneath her top to explore her back, tracing tiny patterns on her skin with his fingertips. She slid her hands onto his chest, hearing his muttered groan when she undid a button at the top of his shirt and her fingers slipped inside to caress him.

She dragged her mouth from his until her lips were against his ear. 'Do you realise this is the first time we've been alone in a bedroom?' It was impossible not be aware of the effect she was having on him, and he lowered his mouth to nibble her neck.

'You know I do.' One hand cupped her face and he raised his head to gaze at her, his blue eyes darkened with something she understood, and his smile was wry. 'But I don't think we can stay in here indefinitely. Come on, let's go and see what we can do.' He tipped her gently from his lap and they left the room.

Downstairs organised chaos reigned, and even more people had arrived and were helping to prepare mountains of food and set a table underneath a makeshift gazebo in the garden, which was already straining at its ropes. Alex, the missing son, had turned up with two friends and his girlfriend in tow and they were all busy talking noisily while peeling seafood for the huge paella he had promised to cook. Jon threw Annie an apologetic glance over his shoulder as he disappeared into the depths of the garage with Owen and a set of tools. Carrie poured Annie a drink and Annie volunteered to scrub the mussels lurking in the sink.

'Do you mind?' Carrie picked up a grey cat from the kitchen worktop and hurled it gently into the garden. 'Out, Smokey, I've told you before. Sorry, I know it's a rotten job but thank you.'

Annie set to work, pausing every couple of minutes as Carrie introduced her to more people and she tried to remember their names. But it was impossible: it seemed as though the whole street was trying to cram into the narrow townhouse, and Annie gave up as she finally scraped the last of the mussels clean and tipped them into a pan. It was almost an hour before she saw Jon again and by then she was past caring, half giddy on champagne and laughter. Carrie was welcoming and funny as she tried to keep the party going while applying make-up in the kitchen. Annie was scrawling place cards, which she was certain would never be needed, as people wandered around catching up with long lost friends, and her writing became worse with every card. Eventually she gave up and chucked them into a pile of post on a coffee table in the sitting room and wandered back into the kitchen. Her heart leapt crazily when she saw Jon squeezing through the crowd towards her.

'Sorry I was so long. Are you all right?'

'Absolutely fine. I've been having a lovely time. Did you fix the lights?'

Jon grinned. 'I think so. I'm going to change, see you soon.' He bent down, and she felt his lips against her cheek and then he was gone.

Carrie appeared, still clutching her lipstick and when she spotted Jon, she dashed from the room after him. 'Jon, wait! There's something I wanted to ask you. It'll only take a minute.'

Annie realised she was still wearing her jeans and lacy top and carted the pan of mussels across to Alex, who was already wilting over a huge drum as he stirred the ingredients. He rolled his eyes glumly as he thanked her, reaching for a drink with his free hand. Still people were arriving, and Carrie was looking increasingly aghast as she wondered frantically where she was going to put them all. Annie made her way back into the house and headed upstairs to the bedroom and opened the door, still smiling.

She dragged her case onto the bed and opened it, wishing she'd bothered to unpack earlier as she lifted her dress out and examined it before she hung it up. She took out a negligee that she'd decided to bring at the last minute and the pale gold chiffon rustled as she shook it gently. The door to the bathroom suddenly opened and Jon appeared, rubbing his hands with a towel. Surprise made her stop dead and her lips parted as her eyes absorbed every detail. Bare-chested, the breadth of his shoulders perfectly emphasised the implied strength of his body and the muscles she saw outlined. Dark chest hairs tapered from his chest down to his flat stomach and she closed her mouth hurriedly, realising she was practically gaping.

'Sorry,' she stuttered, smiling distractedly and quickly stuffing the negligee back into the case, wondering if he'd noticed it. 'I didn't know you were still in here.'

He reached for a shirt and started buttoning it up, and instantly she remembered kissing him on the bed earlier. She knew he was thinking of it too as he gazed at her, slowly fastening each mother-of-pearl button with long fingers. The classic, ivory Oxford shirt looked perfect with charcoal chinos and Annie couldn't control a tremble in her fingers as she fiddled with a shoebox.

'I'm done.' He dropped a quick kiss on the top of her head as he crossed the room to the door. 'I'll wait while you change. Sexy nightdress.'

He disappeared and she quickly re-did her make-up, brushing the sides of her hair back and catching them with clips, using a curling iron to create a high wave and pinning it back from her face. She changed hurriedly into ivory satin underwear and slipped a cream and gold dress on. The strapless corset clung to her figure, the skirt falling just above her knees and flaring out beyond her waist. She tied the narrow black belt and stepped into high-heeled pale gold sandals. A quick squirt of her Burberry perfume and she was ready. She opened the bedroom door and Jon was waiting, spinning around to gaze at her for a long moment.

'You look amazing.' His hands slid onto her waist, drawing her against him. 'Why don't we forget the party and just disappear?'

Stunned, she looked up at him. 'Are you serious? We can't!'

'Sort of. You don't know what I was thinking while you were in there getting changed.' He sighed, giving her a rueful grin. 'I know, I know, we have to go.' She took his hand and they returned downstairs, back to the din of the party already in full swing.

Chapter Nineteen

A DJ had managed to cram himself into a corner of the gazebo and was already belting out Pharrell Williams when Annie and Jon edged into the garden. Steam was rising from the paella, and Annie felt her stomach rumble hungrily as she smelled the food. A few children, already set loose amongst the guests by relieved parents, were sliding on their knees across the miniscule dance floor as a couple in their seventies enthusiastically brushed up their dance moves, despite seemingly arthritic joints.

'I had no idea we knew so many people,' Carrie shrieked as she passed by, clutching a rose bush, obviously a present, and using it as a shield to drive her way through the crowd. She was barefoot, still wearing the same crumpled linen trousers and top. 'I'm sure I haven't seen half of them before.'

Annie heard Jon laugh, but all she was aware of was her hand tightly inside his and being with him. The noise, the people, the food, all blended into their surroundings and she was conscious of only him. A bubble of happiness exploded inside her and she reached up to murmur into his ear, her high heels making it easier. 'Before this night is over, I want to dance with you.' She knew her comment had little to do with dancing, and everything to do with being in his arms and feeling his body against hers.

He grinned, squeezing her hand, gazing at one another. 'Sure. But I should warn you, I have about one and a half left feet. I'm no Patrick Swayze.'

'I don't care. I'd rather have you.'

The food was ready, and they drifted into the queue. Jon introduced her to a couple of people he knew vaguely, and she said hello politely, her hand still tucked inside his. When their plates were full, they sat down to eat on a low garden wall. Annie felt the spiky brush of plants against her back and as soon as Jon had dumped his half empty plate on the patio, he draped an arm across her bare shoulders. She abandoned her meal as she felt the warmth of his fingers, her appetite for food obliterated by his touch as she leant into him. They laughed as the lights around the gazebo suddenly went out and then lurched back into life a few seconds later, flickering tentatively. Carrie and Owen appeared on the dance floor, and the DJ turned the music down as Owen slipped his arm around Carrie's shoulders, intending to pay tribute to his wife on their anniversary. Owen fiddled with the microphone and the DJ reached across to help him.

'Ah, that's better. Anyway, we just want to thank you all for coming this evening, especially if you've travelled some distance. And huge thanks to all who've helped put the party together and provided food. God bless you and yours and enjoy the rest of the party. Don't wander off because you're in for a treat. A few people have been persuaded to reprise *Stars in Their Eyes* just for this evening and you really don't want to miss it.'

He waved as he handed the microphone back to the DJ, the music roaring back into life, and Annie's eyes filled with tears. So many moments crammed into a marriage over the years and it reminded her of everything that had changed for her so unexpectedly. Owen and Carrie disappeared into the house and she heard Jon laugh. She looked across to the DJ, stifling a laugh as a guest tottered towards the dance floor draped in a dark wig and sunglasses.

'Right then,' the DJ roared as he turned down the music again. 'Let's hear it for Brian, who tonight, ladies and gentlemen, will be Roy Orbison!'

Guests clapped as the guest took to the makeshift stage and grabbed the microphone. She and Jon tried not to laugh as he warbled his way through *Pretty Woman*, and the best Annie could say for him was that he wasn't too bad. A teenage cousin came next and floored them all with a wonderful rendition of Will Young's *All Time Love* and the guests fell silent as he finished, then clapped and cheered him until, embarrassed, he shot back into the house with a group of friends. Carrie and Owen reappeared, dressed in flares and sandals, reducing everyone to laughter as they dragged a couple of garden chairs onto the dance floor and launched into the Carpenters. They were surprisingly brilliant, with good voices and plenty of crowd appeal as they danced along.

'I won't be long,' Jon murmured casually to Annie as Carrie and Owen, enthused by their guests' response, agreed to an encore of *Top of the World*. 'Don't go away.'

She nodded, realising just how much she was enjoying herself even without Jon beside her, and after a few minutes she wondered where he had gone. She saw him then, and stared in astonishment as he strolled past her onto the tiny stage. He'd put on a blazer and undone a couple more buttons on his shirt but that was it, and her heart began to race as he smilingly took the microphone. He seemed completely relaxed, and Annie was struck all over again by his height and presence, hardly daring to move as he began to sing.

She'd never heard him perform like this before and knew at once his rich baritone voice was perfect for Elvis Presley's *Can't Help Falling in Love*. He was singing it to her, she was sure of it. He glanced at her frequently, until some of the guests were turning to look too, and she squirmed under their scrutiny. It was an introduction, not an impersonation, and as he charmed his way through the song, she knew he was leaving people in no doubt it was intended for her. He blew her a kiss when he finished and handed the mike back to loud cheers. She was scarlet and hot, her heart racing as she waited for him to re-join her, completely captivated by his sexy and intimate performance.

A woman stepped in front of Jon while he was on his way back to Annie. She was tall, with stylishly cropped dark hair, reaching out a hand to Jon and halting him. He grinned, brushing his lips against her cheek as they hugged. Annie watched them, stepping back into the shadows, not wanting Jon to notice her staring. They chatted together, an easy and familiar intimacy in their body language and Annie sidled away, glad of the din of someone on the stage belting out Neil Diamond's *Sweet Caroline* and trying to subdue a horrible feeling of jealousy rising inside her. Somebody she had met earlier claimed her attention in the orangery as she found another drink, and she was happy to listen, trying not to look for Jon over every shoulder. He reappeared a few minutes later as Annie was still listening to her new companion, and a tremor stole through her body as he bent his head to kiss her cheek.

'Sorry I was so long,' he told her casually as he took her hand. 'Bumped into an old friend.' He nodded at the woman standing near Annie, and as she opened her mouth to speak again, Jon tugged Annie away. 'Sorry,' he called over his shoulder. 'Annie promised to dance with me. I've been practising especially.'

'You haven't!' Annie watched as Jon shrugged out of his blazer and draped it over a nearby chair.

'No, I haven't, sorry. But it was the first thing that came into my mind so I could be alone with you again. What did you think of the song?'

She heard the casual note in his voice and could only be honest, looking up at him with eyes lost in something she couldn't yet voice. 'I loved it. I thought you were wonderful.'

She knew he was pleased with her compliment, and he squeezed her hand as they stepped onto the tiny dance floor, which suddenly felt much smaller with Jon on it. He drew her into his arms, slipping one hand onto the small of her back and resting the other on her neck, wrapping her long hair around his fingers. Her arms slid up his chest to his shoulders and she closed her eyes, breathing in the scent of his cologne. The music had slowed, and they danced unhurriedly, Annie utterly lost in the delight of being so close to him, trembling when he brushed his lips briefly against her hair.

She tried not to dream that the song could have been written for them, but it was so easy to pretend it might have been as they danced on. She heard the words again and again, as she imagined a lifetime of smiles and the seasons changing as they passed the years together. Every note seemed to close the distance between them until their bodies were touching, and his arms tightened to draw her closer still. The moment was abruptly lost as he stood on her foot and she yelped, feeling the weight of his size twelves on her toes.

'Oww!' They dissolved into laughter as they separated, and he helped her onto a nearby chair.

'I told you I was no good.' Jon bent down, still smiling, and gently lifted her foot. 'I'm so sorry. Are you okay?'

'I'm fine.' She closed her eyes as he took off her shoe and began to massage her foot gently. But then his hand rose higher to caress her calf as his eyes found hers and he smiled. Carrie rushed across to check on Annie, still wearing her flares, and insisted on dragging her into the house to find some frozen peas.

'It'll swell up if you don't,' she said firmly, taking Annie's arm and leading her away. She looked back at Jon and tried to glare. 'I saw what happened! You and those great big feet, Jon! Come on, Annie.'

Annie threw Jon a helpless glance and he laughed again as he shrugged his shoulders. 'I'll wait for you outside,' he called, sinking into her chair. Once in the kitchen Carrie fussed around, half pushing Annie onto a little sofa so she could lift her foot up properly and rummaged in the freezer for a bag of peas. A moment later, somebody dashed inside to claim Carrie for another song and Annie was marooned with her toes wrapped in a tea towel filled with a bag of organic peas. After a few minutes, she was thinking she'd probably left the ice on for long enough when the tall woman Jon had spoken with earlier entered the kitchen. Their eyes met, and she gave Annie a friendly smile as she made her way across the room.

'What have you done?' she asked sympathetically, helping herself to a glass of wine from a nearby bottle.

Annie felt tiny stuck in the depths of the sofa, and shuffled awkwardly. 'Oh, it's nothing,' she said uncomfortably, moving the bag of peas around before her toes went completely numb from the cold. 'Somebody stood on my foot dancing.'

The woman's eyes rolled in conspiratorial amusement. 'I saw you dancing with Jon. He was never much good at it. You must be Annie.'

Surprised, Annie realised the woman knew exactly who she was and who was responsible for her unexpected predicament. She didn't know quite what to say so she settled for a silent nod while she gathered her thoughts. The comment implied a certain intimacy between the woman and Jon, and she remembered the hug earlier, the easy way they'd greeted one another. They both looked across as Owen appeared at the kitchen door, clutching empty plates.

'Niamh,' he called delightedly, rushing across to dump the plates in the sink and wrap his arms around her. 'Carrie told me you were here, but it's almost impossible to identify anyone in this crush. I'm so pleased you could make it.' He paused for a second, a sombre tone replacing the quick pleasure. 'We were so sorry to hear about you and Kieran. How are you doing?'

Annie felt the colour draining from her face as it dawned on her who this stylish and elegant woman was. Niamh's Irish accent was faint, but it was there, and Annie was horrified by the realisation as Niamh confirmed she had come alone to the party. Feeling dazed, Annie seemed to be entirely surrounded

223

by Jon's past, including the woman with whom he had had his most serious relationship. She barely heard Niamh's reply to Owen and then he was gone, dashing outside to greet somebody else, and they were alone once more. Annie felt Niamh's eyes upon her, and she pushed the frozen bag from her foot and stood up, meeting Niamh's gaze, curious and strangely warm. Annie smiled blandly, questions leaping into her mind as she tried to quell the jealousy prickling on her skin.

'How did you and Jon meet?' Niamh asked politely, sipping her red wine, propped casually against the kitchen table.

'Oh, I moved to Thorndale at the beginning of the summer and we kept bumping into one another around the village.' Annie heard the truth of her answer, trying to measure it against how much she was coming to feel for him already and thoughts of what their future might or might not be.

'It's such a lovely place, isn't it?' Niamh's gaze drifted through the window to the noise and lights outside in the garden. 'Although I've only been a few times. And so tiny, it must be almost impossible to avoid each other in such a small place.' She looked back at Annie. 'So you haven't been together long then?'

Days, Annie wanted to shout out. *Just days, you couldn't even call it weeks. It's nothing compared to three years in Kenya; you're way ahead of me.* The sudden rush of insecurity, of doubt at herself being there with Jon at all when so much between them was unknown and after everything that had gone before with Iain, had Annie dashing out a fraught reply, more to convince herself than anyone else.

'No, not very. But it's more serious than I expected, although we're not really telling anybody yet. We wanted to keep everything quiet until after the party.'

Niamh's eyes widened, and she smiled as she placed her glass next to the sink, which was already overflowing with dirty plates. 'Congratulations.' She took Annie by surprise, crossing the kitchen to kiss her quickly on both cheeks. 'It's about time Jon settled down. I think we were all beginning to despair that he'd never find the person he'd want to marry and give him a family, so I wish you both all the best. Please, will you excuse me? I'm leaving early, and I ought to go and find my hosts and thank them. Lovely meeting you, Annie.'

Annie stared after her in horror, frozen to the spot where she stood and still without her shoes. She bent down and put them back on, her blood pressure beginning to rise in panic as she thought of Niamh's misunderstanding of her meaning. She had only meant to imply she and Jon were together but to go after Niamh now would be to make a fuss and shout out the truth in front of everybody. Annie hovered uncertainly for a few moments before she followed, hoping to find Jon, and put right her mistake before somebody else did.

Surprisingly, he was still waiting where she had left him, and her heart sank when he saw her and stood up, smiling as he watched her approach. She was vaguely aware of the DJ trying to teach merry groups of people to strip the willow as she moved towards him. He reached for her hand as an unfamiliar tension took possession of her body, dreading telling him what had happened.

'I just met Niamh in the kitchen,' Annie blurted out. She saw acceptance, and perhaps even relief, on his face. His secret was out in the open and she was suddenly struck by a thought as she looked at him. 'Did you know she was coming tonight?'

He hesitated. 'Not for certain. I thought she was in Belfast and wasn't really expecting to make it.'

Shocked, Annie stared at him, the realisation that he and Niamh must still be in touch dawning. The thought astounded her. She had always believed, without knowing anything different, that Niamh belonged in Kenya, in the distant, dry days long past. But evidently, she was wrong, and reminders of Iain flew to the surface, snatching away her simple belief and confidence in Jon along with the hand that she freed from his. 'Do you still see her?'

Jon met her look calmly, but she saw the way his eyes darkened as she questioned him. 'Occasionally. She's been to Kilnbeck a few times, through her job. We email from time to time. Annie, she's married now.'

Owen's words from before fell into her mind as she thought of him offering words of sympathy to Niamh for something that was obviously upsetting. Annie's heart bounced in worry as it dawned on her what that must mean in light of Jon's reply, and her question was a frightened whisper. 'Are you sure about that?' She knew he had never lied, but he clearly hadn't wanted to tell her about Niamh being here this evening, and she couldn't fathom his reason.

'Look, everything between Niamh and me was a long time ago.'

Why would that matter now when it hadn't before? Annie felt chilled by the realisation as the past seemed to be lengthening once again into her future. 'Did she know you were bringing me with you tonight?' Annie's voice was steady, but her fingers were trembling and suddenly his answer was especially important.

He nodded. But it wasn't enough, and she rushed on impatiently. All the questions they had managed to avoid about next month, or even next week, were dragged to the surface and she dreaded the thought that everything she'd sought in moving to Thorndale could now hinge on his reply. She'd risked her heart and her new life for him, frightened now that everything they had already shared was going to shatter her all over again.

'What did you tell her?'

He sighed, and Annie swiped at a strand of hair falling over her eyes as she waited for his response.

'Just that I was bringing someone with me.'

'Someone? Not girlfriend?'

He nodded again, and the bubble of happiness she'd known earlier fizzled away like flat lemonade, certain now she had imagined everything she thought she had seen in his eyes. Knowing that Niamh would be here and seemingly single once again, he had effectively reduced Annie, in Niamh's eyes, to little more than a plus one he'd brought along for company and misjudgement of how she imagined he felt about her didn't even come close. Tears were already filling Annie's eyes as she stumbled away from him, her remarks to Niamh seeming pathetically ridiculous now, rather than anything that could resemble the truth. He grabbed her arm and pulled her to a sudden halt.

'Annie, listen to me,' Jon muttered, drawing her back towards him. 'It's what we agreed at the start. Not to rush anything, casual dates. I thought it was what you wanted.'

When their bodies met she stiffened in resistance, when once she would have melted. The music was still thundering in the background and people were brushing past them as they tottered past. Annie couldn't believe they were having this discussion in the middle of a party, and she was in no mood to continue as she arched away from him.

'You're quite right.' She had to raise her voice above the din surrounding them and did her best to conceal the aching hurt threatening to crush her. 'It's exactly what we agreed.'

But it wasn't what she felt. Whatever words they had used, the simplicity of their agreement had long been dispelled by everything they had shared. His thoughtfulness towards her, all he offered of his life and work and always, always, the way they made each other feel whenever they touched or shared a glance.

She desperately hadn't wanted to be here, to be falling for someone who could so easily break her heart, and it was clear now she was the only one at risk. There was a long moment as they stared at one another, until Annie pulled herself free, and through her tears she saw Carrie making her way over to them. Something about her smiling expression immediately set Annie on tenterhooks as Carrie threw her arms around Jon, shrieking in his ear. And then she turned to Annie.

'Congratulations,' she yelled, flinging her arms around Annie as well. Annie wriggled away, horribly certain that her discussion with Niamh was about to be found out. 'Goodness knows why you wanted to keep your engagement quiet, but we're so pleased for you both. It's marvellous news and we're all delighted. I'd better go – Uncle Campbell's been at his hipflask and he's fallen asleep with his feet in next door's pond. I really ought to go and fish him out. Keep us in touch about the wedding, won't you?'

Jon reached out to Carrie to stop her, but she had already hurried away, and he looked at Annie, confusion furrowing his brow. 'What was that all about? Why does she think we're engaged?'

Annie swallowed nervously. She had to own up now before things got even more out of hand, and she knew the answer he sought was written all over her face.

'What's happened?' Jon asked grimly, and she shrank away from him and the suddenly cold expression in his eyes. 'What have you done?'

'I'm sorry,' she gabbled, stepping back until her heels touched the edge of a border and she could retreat no further. 'I said something to Niamh that she must have misunderstood.'

'Go on.'

'She asked me how long we'd been together, and I said it was more serious than I expected.'

'And?'

'That we weren't sharing it with anyone until after the party.' It was out, she had confessed her mistake. 'Jon, I'm so sorry. I was going to tell you at once. I meant our relationship, nothing more, but she must have taken it to mean something else. I had no idea she would tell Carrie.' But a part of her had wanted to believe an engagement was possible, that she might finally have been the one, and she was chilled by the ice in his eyes as he glared at her.

'Why would you say something so thoughtless?' He looked dumbfounded, hands hanging limply at his side. 'It's a ridiculous idea, letting people think we're engaged. We've only been seeing one another for a few weeks. We haven't even talked about the future, what we want...'

'Thanks a lot.' She snatched in a sharp breath, horrified by her mistake and stung by his appalled reaction, knowing exactly what he meant by the 'future' he wanted. A future with children, one they both knew she might not be able to give him. She pursed her lips against a bitter laugh and furiously blinked back the tears. 'You're right. It is a ridiculous idea. I apologise.'

A few seconds passed as they stared at one another, trying to fathom what to say next and how to make everything right once more, until Annie turned and stumbled away from him. He didn't try and stop her as she crept through the house to their room, thankful that most people were still outside, and no one could see her tears. She knew she had allowed an irrational jealousy to influence her behaviour, and she was ashamed of it now and her impetuous remarks to Niamh. Feeling suddenly insecure in the relationship, she'd reacted unwisely to something she felt threatened by, and now she sank onto the bed, sitting alone in the dark as she thought about the evening. A clatter on the landing brought her to her feet. The door was thrust open and Jon appeared. He looked at her briefly and his tone was brisk.

'I think we should go home, don't you?' he announced calmly. 'I'll get my stuff.' He strode across the room and began throwing his belongings into the small case. 'Carrie'll understand.'

Annie was relieved she wouldn't have to face everybody in the morning, and yet she knew she ought to have a say in the decision to flee back to Thorndale, to make a stand of some sort. But she didn't. 'What have you told them?'

As he picked up his bag, he paused to look at her. 'Just the truth. Can you be ready in ten minutes?'

229

So that was it. She nodded desolately and once he'd closed the door behind him, she packed quickly, crumpling the little negligee into a heap at the bottom of her case. She'd been wrong, so very wrong, about him and now the price would have to be paid. Jon returned to carry her case, and every shred of unhappiness was reflected in her eyes as she left the room and made her way downstairs. Carrie was waiting for them, and the look she gave Annie was sympathetic. She stepped forward to hug her.

'We so enjoyed meeting you,' Carrie said softly. Annie wondered what reason Jon had used that was so important they had to change their plans in the middle of the night. 'I'm sure we'll see you again soon. Thank you for helping earlier.'

'It was a lovely party, thank you,' Annie said quietly. 'Please will you say goodbye to Owen and the boys for me?' She hesitated. 'Is Niamh still here? I thought perhaps I should say goodbye to her.'

'She's already left, got an early flight in the morning.' It was Jon who replied. So they had already talked, and Annie was too late.

Carrie squeezed her hand and turned to Jon. He drew her wearily into his embrace, kissing her quickly. 'Thank you. Sorry to leave now.'

'Hope it goes well next week. Niamh's thrilled you're going to be there.' Carrie touched Jon's arm with a quick hand as he let her go. 'I know she really appreciates your friendship and support, especially as she and Kieran have separated. None of us saw that one coming.'

Annie felt the hurt and dismay rushing through her body at Carrie's words, and dragged in a silent gasp as she thought of Jon's ex-girlfriend, single again and waiting for him wherever it was he was going. Jon waved distractedly, and then they were outside in the cool night air, climbing into the darkened car. She waited until he had driven away from the house.

'Are you going away?' She felt his eyes upon her when he replied.

'Yes. I'm going to Belfast for a few days.' He paused. 'Niamh works for a Christian charity and she asked me a couple of weeks ago if I would speak about Kilnbeck and how we connect with the local community. Somebody dropped out and she thought of me.'

Annie's hands were clasped tightly in her lap. 'Oh.' She was cold without a jacket despite the comfort of the car, but she knew turning up the heat wouldn't be enough to warm her. She stared out of the window into the darkness, determined not to let him see foolish tears filling her eyes again. She realised he obviously hadn't thought his going away important enough to share with her, and couldn't believe she'd allowed herself to risk her heart once more, feeling it slowly breaking as she imagined the days ahead without him. There seemed to be nothing else to say as he drove them back to Thorndale, and when he pulled up outside her cottage, he impulsively covered her hand with his.

'Annie, we need to talk about what happened.'

She tugged her fingers from his, already pushing the car door open. 'I'm sorry for what I said and the impression it gave. But I think we both know how you really feel, and I just can't keep on hoping for the best and picking myself up time after time. It seems neither of us can give the other what we truly want.'

She climbed outside and Jon followed, taking her luggage from the boot, and opening the gate. She reached out and pulled her case from him. 'I can manage.'

'Annie, please, wait. At least let's…'

She shook her head, giving him a look over her shoulder that was bereft as she stumbled, shivering, up the path, lugging the case behind her.

She heard the engine roar as he gunned the car down the lane, feeling as though he had driven away with her heart. As she let herself in, the cottage was completely silent. She knew her little home was utterly unable to heal her this time, that she would find no comfort in its familiarity and seclusion. She settled on the sofa, staring into the cold fireplace as she went over the evening in her mind. As the tears came again, she resolved it would be for the last time, so she cried, certain her foolish comment had only hastened what was clearly the inevitable end of their relationship.

Chapter Twenty

When Annie woke in the morning, Jon was the first thought on her mind as ever, but pleasure quickly turned into despair as events at the party leapt into focus. The rest of the day faded into nothingness as she gathered up the leftovers of the life she had begun to lead when she came to Thorndale before she and Jon had become involved. It hardly seemed real, being reduced once again to this broken state as she thought of him and how he had received the news of her blunder.

On Sunday she considered not going to church at all, but her growing faith and the realization they couldn't avoid one another for long sent her to the service. But when she walked in there was no sign of him, and she had no idea if he had stayed away on purpose to avoid her. Afterwards Charlie sought her out, telling her casually that Jon had been called away to a rescue. She thanked Charlie but didn't linger, hurrying home to finish preparing the lunch that she'd arranged a few days ago with Elizabeth and Robert. Annie's mind was miles away as they ate, and when Elizabeth was leaving, once Robert was safely out of earshot, she took Annie's hand in hers and squeezed it.

'Are you all right?' Elizabeth asked gently. 'You seem a bit distracted.'

Annie looked at her brightly. She knew that it wouldn't be long before the break-up was the talk of the village, but she couldn't acknowledge it out loud, not just yet. 'I'm okay, honestly.' She shrugged. 'Just a bit tired. I'll pop down for a chat one afternoon.'

Elizabeth leant forward to hug her quickly, her gaze sympathetic. 'Lunch was lovely, thank you. You know where we are if you need anything.'

Annie thanked her gratefully, waving as Elizabeth caught up with Robert and they disappeared. Annie shut the door. It was as though she had stepped back six weeks in time and had to begin all over again. All she needed to do was drag the furniture outside and she would be right back at square one. Only this time, she knew it was much worse than before. Kirstie, tied up on a working holiday weekend, had texted her with a 'how was the party' message and Annie had eventually replied with a sad face. A couple of hours later Kirstie called, and Annie picked up the phone and headed outside before she lost the signal.

'What happened?' Direct as ever, Kirstie got straight to the point. 'Sorry if it sounds crazy in the background, we're in the pub and there's live music. I couldn't get a signal till now. Are you all right?'

Annie shook her head and became tearful again, despite her resolve last night. 'I will be,' she said, sniffing. Quickly she ran through the events at the party and heard Kirstie sigh. 'Don't say it, Kirst. I already know. You did warn me.'

'Oh Annie, that's the last thing I was thinking. I'm so sorry. Why don't you go and see him? It sounds like he wanted to talk.'

'Maybe. I'm just not sure it will make any difference to how we see the future, and I'd really rather not carry on dating him if it's going to be over soon anyway.'

'I'm not so sure, hon. Despite what I said about Jon, you two did seem very close the other day. Sleep on it and see how you feel in the morning.' Kirstie paused. 'Only you can decide if you're prepared to take a risk on him, Annie.'

They said good night and Annie eventually crawled into bed around eleven. *Oh God*, she prayed inwardly, *if you're listening, please tell me what to do*. And then, as though a voice had shouted instructions in her ear, the answer became clear and she knew what she was going to do. Kirstie was right. Annie would go to him, explain, make him understand, no longer prepared to give up everything they'd shared without knowing the truth of how he felt.

Decision made, it was ages before she fell asleep with thoughts of Jon racing through her mind, but when she woke up the next morning she felt wide awake and energised and was ready to go by eight, hoping to catch him before he started working. She leapt into the car, unwilling to waste time walking and raced through the village and straight to the Hall.

She had no idea where she might find him and left her car on the drive as she quickly made her way around to the offices. The courtyard was quiet for a Monday morning, and she opened the door to the reception area, looking up hopefully as she heard footsteps. But it was Emma, not Jon, who was approaching, and Emma's eyes lit up as she hurried forward to greet Annie.

'Annie, how lovely to see you.'

'Oh hi, Emma,' Annie said awkwardly, shuffling from foot to foot. 'Sorry to bother you. I was just trying to catch up with Jon. Do you know where I might find him?'

She saw Emma hesitate, and knew immediately that bad news was to follow. 'I'm sorry,' Emma replied uncomfortably, her smile fading until it became a tiny frown. 'Didn't he tell you?'

'Tell me what?' Annie forced the words out, her voice a frightened murmur as she thought of him hurt somewhere, or beyond her reach for hours on a long and difficult rescue.

'He decided to catch an earlier flight and left for Ireland last night.'

Shocked, Annie's spirits plummeted to her feet, hardly able to believe that he had really left her without saying goodbye. He had made no promises, and the realisation that he'd hurried to Niamh earlier than planned left her feeling winded. Every-thing seemed suddenly very clear in the light of the choice he had made. She felt dizzy, the recollection of having been here before trying to snatch away her composure as she made an unsteady turn for the door.

'Are you all right?'

Annie halted as she felt Emma's hand on her arm, and the glance she threw the older woman was swift. 'Yes, thank you. I'm surprised, that's all.'

'Ring him.' Emma spoke almost pleadingly, the urgency of her words reflected in the fingers tightening on Annie's arm. 'I promise I won't interfere but whatever it is, I really think you should ring him.'

'I'll think about it.' Annie knew she would probably do little else as Emma's hand slipped away and they said goodbye. She returned to her car, her mind spinning with thoughts of the future and whether she could remain in Thorndale, feeling as she did. Jon's life was rooted here now whereas hers had only just begun to flourish, so much of it bound up in him.

Annie had the perfect excuse to call him, or at least text, a couple of hours later when Arthur Middleton turned up with a trailer of neatly chopped logs ready for autumn. She insisted on helping him cart them around the back of the cottage, and when they'd finished stacking them, she made him a cup of tea. She enjoyed listening to him talking about the estate, but part of her knew that she wanted to prolong any kind of contact with Jon, however pointless. When Arthur was about to leave, he looked at her knowingly and told her if she needed anything at all, she was to come straight to him. Almost tearfully she thanked him, and he gently informed her he was following the instructions Jon had given him before he left. He smiled as he explained he wasn't really supposed to tell her that.

On Tuesday morning Annie was feeling more lost and uncertain than ever, and after a bath, she decided to go and see how Sam was, hoping it wasn't too early. As she walked through the village, she saw Cara, sharing a drink on the green with Nathan. She waved to them when Nathan caught her eye and he gave her a quick grin, and she thought how lovely it was to see them together. The vicarage was dozing in warm sunlight when she arrived, and she knocked gently in case Sam was resting. Moments later her doubts were dismissed when Sam opened the door.

'Hey, you.' Sam's face lit up, one hand resting casually on her bump as she stepped aside. 'Come in. How are you?'

'I'm fine,' Annie said blithely, not at all sure how much Sam knew about her and Jon. 'You look so much better, Sam. I'm really glad. I wasn't sure you would be up and about.'

Annie saw Sam smile over her shoulder as she followed her through the house. 'Come into the sitting room. It's cooler in there,' Sam said. 'I'm lots better, thank you. The rest seems to be working. My blood pressure's gone down, and the midwife is happier now. And I really want to thank you for everything you've done for me. Charlie was dreading having to go shopping for breast pumps and maternity bras.'

Annie grinned as she tried to imagine Charlie scuttling around a supermarket choosing disposable maternity knickers. 'My pleasure, I was just glad to help out.' They settled into comfortable chairs and Annie saw the direct look in Sam's eyes as she shrank back into her seat. Annie knew what that questioning gaze meant and she spoke first. 'Where is he?'

'Over at the hospital in town. He's been called away to see someone taken ill unexpectedly, but thankfully it's not serious. Would you like tea or a coffee?'

'No, thanks.' Annie curled her legs underneath her, trying not to fidget as she avoided Sam watching her steadily and searching for the right moment to speak.

'Annie, you're not really fine, are you?' Sam asked gently. 'You can tell me to mind my own business if you prefer but I'll listen if you'd like to talk. Is it Jon?'

Annie nodded sadly and gave Sam a grateful smile that quickly faded. She glanced out at the shady garden, wondering where to begin, sighing quietly. 'The evening away didn't go very well. I finally realised I was letting myself imagine that he was more serious about me than he actually is. And I said something which got out of hand and gave a few people the wrong impression. He wasn't pleased.'

'The engagement?'

'Yes.' So, Jon had told Sam and Charlie too, and Annie began to think that perhaps he'd already informed the whole village just in case the news had spread and people were ready to offer misplaced congratulations. A wave of horror shot over her as she wondered if Sir Vivian and Emma knew, too.

'Annie, nobody else knows, don't worry. Jon came to see us on Sunday before he left.' Sam paused. 'Are you certain of what you feel for him?'

Annie smiled, trying to hide the trace of bitterness and regret as their eyes met, and nodded slowly. 'I love him, Sam. I didn't mean to, but I do.'

'Oh, Annie, love. I knew it.' Sam climbed off the sofa to wrap her arms around Annie, her eyes strangely warm as Annie hugged her back. They let go as she sniffed, and Sam retreated to her seat to make herself comfortable again.

'But I don't think he wants to be committed to anything else.' Annie's voice was a whisper now, her gaze somewhere else. 'I might not be able to have children, and I can't cling on like before, knowing that he does eventually. I knew the moment I met him this could happen, and I don't want to have to pretend it means nothing to me. It's better to be apart.'

'Have you asked Jon how he feels?'

Surprised, Annie glanced up to meet Sam's look again. 'No. I think I know, and I really don't want to make him say it. It would never work between us anyway, we lead such different lives. He has the estate and Kilnbeck to run, he's busy with the fell rescue, and eventually he's going to be a baronet. I'm just a schoolteacher. How would I ever keep up or be able to support him?'

Sam laughed quietly, reaching out to squeeze Annie's hand. 'You already are. You do it without even knowing. Annie, I've never seen Jon like this before. He's so happy and content since he met you. He's always been warm and friendly, but this is so much more, believe me. And you must realise having a title is meaningless to him and he'll never use it. It couldn't be less relevant to everything he considers important.'

Annie tried to suppress a sudden gleam of hope beginning to flicker, until another jolt of realisation arrived to remind her, and her reply was flat. 'But he's made everything quite clear. He left without even saying goodbye and went to Niamh.'

'Annie, I'm going to tell you something that you ought to have heard from Jon.'

Annie's eyes widened in surprise, realising she was holding her breath as Sam began to speak again. 'He was going to ask you to go with him to Ireland. That's why he didn't tell you he was going away: he kept putting it off because he was afraid that you'd refuse. And after everything that happened at the party, he knew you wouldn't go.'

'But what about Niamh?' Annie's voice was a whisper, not yet able to quell the fear of a repeat of the breakup with Iain. 'She's single again. He's in Belfast with her.'

'She's his friend, Annie. That's it. And he might be with her in the most basic sense of the word right now, but they'll never be together again.'

'How do you know?'

'Because he told us and made it very clear it was only you he wanted there with him, whatever else you're thinking. The question is, what are you going to do about it?'

Annie felt the colour drain from her face as she listened and leapt to her feet hurriedly. 'I have to go,' she blurted out, glancing wildly around the room as though she could catch the first plane to soar past the window, and Sam laughed. 'Do you know where he is?'

'He's at the Hilton,' Sam said, and Annie dashed across to hug her tightly before hurrying to the door. 'Don't come back without him.'

Annie sprinted home through the village, her mind racing even faster than her legs as she ignored the bemused looks from the people she passed on the way. She had to fling herself into the hedge when Robert Howard roared past in his tractor, only spotting her at the very last moment. Packing a case was easy but trying to find the next available flight to Belfast without the internet wasn't, and she was almost screaming when she finally managed to secure a seat on a plane leaving Leeds at two thirty that afternoon.

When she landed in Belfast, she found a taxi and, as the car headed into the city, she suddenly began to feel nervous as she considered the wisdom of her decision to seek Jon out. What if she was wrong? What if Sam was wrong and Jon was horrified Annie had turned up when he was all set for a reconciliation with Niamh? But Annie knew that if she accomplished nothing else, she was determined to tell him how she felt, and the knowledge that somehow she was meant to be here reassured her. She twisted her hands in her lap, praying that the journey would soon be over and she would find him.

In the hotel foyer she realized she didn't even have a room and booked one quickly, hurrying upstairs to change. She'd barely thought about what to wear when she'd packed and pulled on a pair of jeans and a pretty lilac top. She left her hair loose, letting it tumble down her shoulders, and swiped lipgloss across her mouth, fighting the memories of kissing Jon as she stuffed the tube into her bag. She hurriedly made her way back downstairs and the helpful man at the desk pointed her in the direction of the conference suite. She followed his instructions and soon found herself in a small dining room already prepared for coffee and biscuits. Annie gripped the door of the meeting room nervously and took a deep breath.

She could hear faint voices, and she hoped to sneak quietly inside and then try and work out where Jon might be.

But then her courage evaporated, and she turned and fled away, her pulse roaring in her ears as she hurried back to reception. She hovered uncertainly, watching people come and go with simple confidence as they went about their business. She strode into the bar and ordered coffee. Perhaps if she just sat here and was patient, maybe he would eventually appear, and she could speak with him alone.

Annie noticed a few people glancing at her curiously and she tried to concentrate on a newspaper, finally pushing it away when she'd read the same page at least four times. After finishing her coffee and with still no sign of Jon, she stood up decisively. *You're being ridiculous,* she told herself crossly. *Just go and find him.* She made her way back to the meeting room and opened the door cautiously.

At least thirty heads turned around to look when she stepped in and she paled underneath her wretched freckles. She looked over the group to the speaker and felt the colour in her face come rushing back. It was Jon. He was here. He was in the middle of a presentation, waving a mouse at a laptop nearby as a big screen behind him projected his points to the delegates. Annie had almost forgotten how tall and dark he was, and her stomach whirled into a spin. Their eyes met and he paused, suddenly looking flustered and stumbling through his next comment. She glanced around wildly for an empty seat, realising in dismay there were none to be had. One or two people were standing at the back of the room, and she sidled across to join them as Jon recovered his composure and continued.

Somebody on the back row stood up and Annie saw, with horror, that it was Niamh, looking elegant and perfectly composed in a trouser suit and heels. Appalled, Annie wondered if she were coming over to throw her out of the conference but instead Niamh took Annie's arm and whispered, 'Take my seat.'

Surprised, Annie stared at her as she crept past. 'Thank you,' she muttered. She sat down gratefully, the drama over. All the attention had reverted to Jon, and Annie waited nervously for him to finish.

After his presentation, Niamh made her way to the front and thanked Jon, explaining that refreshments were being served next door and everyone should return in ten minutes for the final session of the day. People began murmuring as they left their seats and wandered outside. Annie watched as Jon dropped the mouse onto a desk, and their eyes met again as he walked towards her. She stood up, feeling her knees begin to tremble and she clutched her hands together. This was her moment. Instead, as he neared her, all her carefully rehearsed words took flight and she blurted out the first thought in her mind.

'I think someone sent me here on purpose,' she said shakily as she looked into his blue eyes. 'I don't think I would've made it on my own.' Jon was just inches away and she saw the surprise in his expression soften into warmth, giving her a sudden confidence.

He took a step nearer, reaching out a hand as though he was going to touch her. 'Annie, I...'

'Don't,' she said hurriedly, pressing herself against the chair. She was uncomfortably aware the escape for coffee had ceased and some people were hovering while they pretended not to listen. 'Please don't, Jon. I have something to tell you and if I don't say it very soon I most likely never will. I know it's probably not enough.' Annie spoke the words hastily, her eyes never wavering from his. 'I'm so in love with you, I'll do anything. I want to share your life and support everything you do. I can't help it, I'm sorry. But it's true. I love you.'

She fell silent, his eyes widening in amazement as they stared at one another. A smile was hovering on his lips and she snatched her gaze from his, turning to make her escape. 'I should go.'

At once his hand was on her arm, swinging her back to face him. 'I don't ever want to be apart from you again,' he said roughly, pulling her against him and trapping her in his arms as he muttered into her ear. 'Annie, I only ever tried to seem casual because I was afraid that if you knew how I really felt, you'd change your mind and decide it was happening much too fast. I'd planned to wait until the end of the summer to tell you because I guessed we wouldn't be together if you didn't feel something for me. I hoped by then you'd be ready to hear it.'

She knew he was speaking the truth. It was there whenever he looked at her, with playful and yet serious eyes, saying so much more with his expression than he had ever put into words. It was the one thing he couldn't disguise, and she knew now he had never tried.

'I've been in love with you since that first day at the cottage when I found you in the garden, and I seem to have spent the whole summer trying not to blurt it out and frighten you away.'

She felt him smile and pulled back to look at him incredulously as she realised what he was telling her. 'But I don't know if...' She paused, her voice falling to a whisper. 'If I'm enough, just me. What if I can't...'

Jon's hands went to her face, cupping her cheeks gently as he tilted her head back. 'Whatever blessings we do or don't have in our future, Annie, you'll always be enough, I promise. So much more than enough and I want the life we can have together, even if it's only ever just us.'

He lifted her chin with one finger, the heat of his adoring promise imprinted on her lips as he kissed her. And then, still holding her hands tightly, he stepped backwards, and her astonishment was complete when he bent down on one knee.

'It's not really the right place,' he said with his familiar grin, and then he looked serious once more. 'But it has to be now. I love you, Annie Armstrong, I know I always will. I want to share our lives together and for you to be my wife. So will you marry me?'

Annie nodded immediately as tears filled her eyes, thrilled by his admission. 'Yes,' she whispered. 'Of course I will.'

His smile returned as he leapt to his feet, lifting her up, and she wound her arms around him as they laughed together. He kissed her again and as she kissed him back, she knew with all certainty that she belonged with him. She became aware of applause nearby and he set her down gently, his arm around her waist to keep her at his side.

Niamh made her way over to them, already smiling. 'Let me be the first to congratulate you both properly,' she said, kissing Jon quickly on the cheek. 'I've ordered champagne. I think we may as well finish for today. I don't think anyone will have any questions after this.'

She turned to look at Annie, who blushed as she remembered the chaos of the party a few days ago.

'It was obvious at Carrie's party how Jon feels about you, Annie,' Niamh said, taking Annie's free hand and squeezing it quickly. 'He told me before I left that he was in love with you.'

Annie's eyes widened in surprise as she turned to look at Jon and he grinned, touching his lips to her temple as he spoke. 'I did say I'd told everyone the truth, even though I didn't intend for anyone else to know before you,' he murmured dryly. 'Carrie was the first to guess how serious I was when she knew I was bringing you with me, and when she congratulated us, my plan to eventually propose had been very publicly pre-empted. I was worried it would scare you away.'

Annie's answer was to touch his face gently with her hand, telling him with her eyes and her simple gesture that she knew she was home now, and her heart was his. He turned his head to kiss her palm, understanding everything she meant by it. One by one people made their way over to offer congratulations and the meeting was abandoned as the champagne arrived and glasses were handed around and quickly filled.

Annie and Jon drifted away to a corner on their own and he looked at her with a grin, slipping his signet ring off and sliding it onto her ring finger. 'This will have to do, until we get home.' He paused. 'Annie, darling, if you want it, I'd very much like to give you my grandmother's engagement ring.'

Her smile was delighted as she looked at him. 'I'd love that.' She glanced down at her hand. The oversized ring looked a little strange on her finger, but it felt so right, and she couldn't ever remember feeling so certain about anything before. Thorndale had been the means of giving them both so much, but Annie knew it was more than that. She felt they had been blessed, and knew her life had taken a quite different turn, and that theirs together was only just beginning.

Acknowledgements

So many people have encouraged me in my writing and this book would probably only exist in a ring binder without the support they've given me, and I'd like to thank them all.

The best step I took on my writing journey was to join the outstanding organisation that is the Romantic Novelists Association. Thank you to all who work so hard to enable the association to offer all it does, especially for new writers finding their way and the welcome that is offered to all. The New Writers Scheme is an amazing opportunity and I was thrilled to be a part of it.

Thank you to Susan Yearwood and Emily Bedford for believing in my writing and giving me this first professional opportunity. It has been a pleasure to work with you both and find ways to keep on improving.

I'd like to highlight the fantastic work of the Upper Wharfedale Fell Rescue Association and their amazing skills and dedication in coming to the aid of those around them. I very much appreciated the help they gave me and any mistakes in procedures are my own.

To my first brilliant beta readers, Joanna, Nicky, Jen and Becca, thank you, sorry about the size of the file! My fabulous mum and dad, Irene and Barry, respectively publicist extraordinaire and chef of all things delicious, and my lovely sister Deb, thank you for all your love and support over the years, as well as that very first typewriter. My mother-in-law, Irene, who constantly cheers me on and reads everything first, thank you for your prayers and always believing in me. Now you can download me on your Kindle!

The late Pat Howard and Mary Eccles were sisters, avid readers and the first people ever to read my writing. I didn't meet them until later but their encouragement and words to me, via text messages at the time, made me believe I might actually be a writer, something I'd dreamt of since I was little. I wish that they, too, were able to download this book and I hope they knew what a difference they made when I was starting out.

To my husband Stewart, my real-life romantic inspiration, and our wonderful son Fin, having your love and support means everything to me and you are my world, no matter how often I'm dreaming up another one. For all the times I disappear to write for a bit and come back hours later to find a meal made and the chores done, thank you. For the technical support, thoughtful gifts and always stepping in when I'm immersed in other people's lives, thank you. I love you both very much.